Love Drunk

MARINA SKYE

Love Drunk — Backcountry Series Book 2
by Marina Skye

CHAPTER 1

Suds in the Bucket

The air had already gone from crisp and clear to violently oppressive; unusual for early April. Typically, it's not until May that the humidity reaches rainforest levels and forces everyone to stay inside or risk drowning on their way to the mailbox. Spring came early, apparently summer was going to arrive early too. What would be a way to be productive yet still cool off? Marina put on her swimsuit—a black bikini—pulled her hair up into a ponytail, and fetched a bucket from the garage, condensation already gathering on her skin and giving her that summertime glisten. She stretched the hose out from the garden to the edge of the driveway where she parked the car in the grass, filled the bucket, and added soap. She sprayed her car down then dipped the giant microfiber sponge into the suds. She had scrubbed down one side and was scrubbing the hood when Sawyer pulled in.

He rolled the passenger window down as his tires slowly rolled through the mud and cat-call whistled at her. She laughed and waved. He parked the truck by the barn and walked back to her, looking at her as though he were mentally commending her tan lines.

"Hey, baby. Wanna wash mine too?" He swaggered up to her, his jeans and white t-shirt fitting just right.

She took his cowboy hat off him and said, "You don't wanna get that hat wet and your truck isn't even dirty."

He gave her a smooch and said, "I can run it through some mud real quick." He took his hat back, drawing a laugh from her as she slapped his chest.

"You're a dirty boy, Sawyer."

"I think you should give me a sponge bath then." He grabbed her by the waist and bit his bottom lip.

"Hard to do with your clothes on," she teased, sliding her hands under his t-shirt.

"We can fix that." He peeled his shirt off and dropped it right there in the mud at the edge of the grass.

She picked the hose up and sprayed him.

"Wait! My hat!" He ran his hat up to the porch and tossed it up by the door then ran back to her. She started spraying at him the moment his hat was in the clear, but he ran at her and scooped her up, earning him a screech of glee as he sat her up on the hood before settling his hips between her legs. She dropped the hose to the ground in the scramble. His wet, wavy hair fell forward, hanging in his face, and he reached down for the sponge in the bucket and ran it up her leg, leaving a trail of suds that ran down and off her toes. They had their sudsy hands all over each other as their mouths danced a seductive tango of desire. He pulled the string on the back of her bikini top but she caught it before it fell off just as a horn honked from the dirt road. Sawyer flipped his hair out of his face as he turned his head to see Chris's truck pulling into the driveway.

"Is that Chris?" Marina asked, quickly retying her bikini.

"Ahh shit! Yeah. I forgot they were coming over today. We're gonna start on the music room."

"Oh, nice!" She slid off the hood as Jake, Trev, and Chris all got out of the truck. Jake whistled and raised his brows as he lifted his sunglasses.

"You're whistlin' at Sawyer, aren't you?" Marina bantered.

Sawyer laughed and swatted at her rear. "Nah, he's whistlin' at you, baby. You're smokin' hot."

"Maybe I was whistlin' at both of you. Y'all out here all sudsy with each other. It's cute." Jake laughed.

"Yeah, yeah. I'll go get changed so we can start buildin' shit." Sawyer headed for the house and the rest of the guys tipped their hats to Marina before following suit.

"You want help first, darlin'?" he hollered back from the porch.

"Nah, you go on ahead and build shit." She laughed then continued scrubbing down her car while Sawyer changed into dry clothes.

"It would be more fun to watch Marina scrubbing her car from the window." Jake peeked at her through the blinds.

"I could look at that view all day but then I wouldn't be getting anything done," Sawyer agreed.

"I'm guessing the permit came through?" Chris asked as he checked out the foundation of the addition.

"Sure did. I got a head start."

The guys built a wall frame and put it up, then the next. Two of them would lift the wall while the other two would stabilize and secure it. They worked quickly and efficiently.

"I'm pretty damn excited about this music room," Jake said as he helped Chris hold the wall in place while Sawyer and Trev screwed everything together.

"So is the plan to use this room to practice or store your music stuff in?" Trev asked, holding a screw between his teeth.

"Practice. Well, both I guess. The walls will be soundproofed and I'm gonna do my best to maximize the acoustics in here, too."

"Sweet," Chris shouted over the loud screw gun.

Sawyer laid the tool on the floor and stretched. "Any of you guys ever done drywall?"

They all looked at each other and shook their heads no.

"Well, shit. Looks like I'm on my own for that part."

"Nah, we'll help," Trev offered.

"We'll figure it out," Chris agreed.

"I appreciate it." Sawyer shrugged.

"Pizza and beer on you and I'm in too." Jake laughed.

"Deal!" Sawyer gladly accepted.

CHAPTER 2

In This Together

Marina took a break from all the noise and walked out to the mailbox, enjoying the few minutes of deadening quiet while she drank her coffee, complete with drywall dust floating on the surface. She flipped through the envelopes as her flip-flops flapped against the soles of her feet. Two were addressed to her; one for her car payment and the other a credit card bill that she had been chipping away at for two years. She opened the envelope for her card first and the balance was zero. Her flip-flops fell silent as she came to a halt, confused. She looked through the payment activity. It had been paid off, but how? She opened the other envelope and it was the title to her car, so her car had been paid off too. She still owed a few thousand as of a couple of weeks ago when she made the last payment. This made no sense. She didn't open any of the envelopes addressed to Sawyer. She never did. She reached the porch and sat on the top step, dropping the rest of the mail by her feet, and both of her hands wrapped around her cup.

It was a foggy, misty morning. The cotton field across the road was hazy and blurry as she stared out into the distance. She thought about the last payments she had made...she had put the statements in a folder...but she left them in Sawyer's office...Oh, he didn't! Did he? He had to have. Sawyer stepped out the front door, covered in drywall dust head to toe, his black tank top and jeans powdered white. He tousled his hair and tried to brush himself off before stepping closer to her. He hiked the thighs of his jeans up and sat on the top step next to her.

"Taking a break?" she asked.

"Yeah. I needed fresh air." He coughed, a plume of dust rising around his entire body with the motion.

She put her arm on his thigh and was quiet for a minute, looking out over the field before asking, "Were you going to tell me about these?"

"Well, I figured you'd notice when these came."

"Please tell me you didn't, Sawyer."

"I told you I'd never lie to you, so…" He folded his hands in front of him, his elbows on his knees.

"Why'd you do it? You didn't need—"

He interrupted with a gentle hand on her back. "Baby. It's okay, I got you."

"This was my responsibility. It's my baggage that I had before we got together. It's not fair to—"

"Nope. You're my responsibility. I'll always take care of you."

"Sawyer. That's very noble of you but I'm an adult and we're not married yet."

"That doesn't matter, Marina. I don't need you worrying that pretty little mind of yours about stuff like this. I feel relieved knowing I can do that for you. Taking your stress away is my job. In fact…" He sorted through the unopened envelopes addressed to him and opened one. He pulled out a card and handed it to her.

"What's this?" she asked.

"Your new debit card." He continued flipping through his mail.

"This isn't my bank."

"I know. It's mine. I added you to the account."

"To *your* bank account? Why?"

"Because, baby. It's *our* account. I'll get you an updated card when your name changes."

"You don't need to do this. I don't want you to feel like I'm using you."

"What? Oh, no. No. I don't feel that way at all. We're about to be married. It's my job to take care of my wife. We're in this together. Keep your other account, do what you want with it. This account is for *our* bills, groceries, barn stuff, gas, going out, whatever."

"I need to pitch in so I'll just deposit into this account instead of mine then."

"No, ma'am." He smiled then kissed her forehead. "You're stubborn, ya know that?"

"I know I am. Thank you." She shook her head, knowing she wasn't going to win this debate.

"That's coming up soon. We should check out the auction." He held up a flier for the local 4H fair that was in the mix of his mail. "I better get back to the grind. How's the drywall dust taste in your coffee?" he asked.

She about spit out her gulp. "You noticed, huh?"

"I can't believe you're drinkin' that." He laughed as he stood.

"Yeah, me neither." She swirled her cup. "Can I do anything to help you in there?"

"Oh, I'm sure I can come up with something you can do, but I don't want you to feel obligated."

"We're in this together, remember?" She stood and took his hand. He smiled and nodded as they went back inside.

"I'll make a new pot of coffee for ya," he said, shutting the door behind them.

CHAPTER 3

Relay

M arina was dusting the house with the windows open, enjoying the late-spring breeze on a less humid day while Sawyer was at work. The construction had stirred up quite a mess. She was dusting Sawyer's desk in the office, which wasn't too messy, but she moved a short stack of papers and noticed the document on top was a print-out of the charities he donates to. There were several, including animal rescues and veterans' charities, but also a children's cancer charity. What a big, generous heart he has. There was a date noted next to one of the charities and it wasn't far out. She wondered why he hadn't mentioned it, but assumed he still would. She continued cleaning for a while: sweeping, mopping, and wiping down surfaces that drywall dust had settled on.

Sawyer came home from work right as she had settled in to start dinner. His boots came off at the door and his hat hung on the hook.

"Darlin'! Where ya at?" he hollered.

She came into the living room. "Hey, babe. How was your day?"

"Not bad. How was yours?" He swooped her up into his arms.

"Better now that you're home." Her lips mashed with his.

"Mmmm, I missed you. You have plans next Saturday?"

"I don't."

"So, there's a charity event I attend every year. Not sure how you feel about running a relay but it's for a good cause."

"Yeah, sure! I'd be up for that. What's the charity?"

"It's a children's cancer charity. It's bittersweet, really. It's great to see the kids that are healthy out there living, but it's hard to see those still struggling. So, it's up to you if you wanna go. Of course, I'd love for you to."

"I'd love to, Sawyer. I think it's wonderful you make time to do such things."

His smile widened. "Then it's a date!"

The week flew by quickly. The drywall was almost finished in the music room, Marina had picked up a bar shift, and Sawyer was swamped with work at the office. Once the weekend finally came, they were ready for quality time outdoors. The line to receive running numbers at the relay entrance was long. Sawyer and Marina stretched and hydrated. It was a hot and muggy morning. There were food vendors, a donation booth, and a local barbershop had set up a tent where barbers volunteered their services for the cause. They took hair donations to send off and make wigs for cancer patients.

"They didn't have that booth before this year. That's really cool." He raked his hair back from his face with his fingers.

"It is! It's getting attention already."

"You look so adorable in your shorts and tank." He crouched down to securely tie his sneakers and looked up at her before standing and adjusting his sunglasses on his face. He put on and straightened his backward ball cap.

"Well, thank you. You look hot in your shorts and tank too." She flirted as she pulled her hair back into a ponytail.

"Looks like we're about to start. You ready?"

"Absolutely." She nodded.

"Think you can keep up?"

"Would you really leave me in the dust?" she asked playfully.

He laughed. "Not a chance, baby. If you get tired you can hop on my back."

"Only if I get tired?" She sent a sly smirk his way.

He stepped closer to her and looked around before squeezing her rear and giving her a quick smooch. He could always make her giggle.

The relay began and they ran side-by-side, enjoying the easy gait and one another's company. There was a young boy, maybe eight or nine years old, who was having a hard time keeping up with the crowd. He had slowed to a walk up ahead of them, his hands on his thin thighs, leaning forward. They slowed when they caught up to him.

"Hey, kiddo. You okay?" Sawyer put his hand on the young boy's shoulder.

"Yes, sir. Just tired and trying to catch my breath."

"Have you drank water?" Marina asked, concerned.

"Yes ma'am." He paused to take a deep breath. "I've been sick so I'm just weak."

"There's quite a ways yet to go." Sawyer lifted his sunglasses, looking up the road at the long line of joggers.

"Yeah. I'll get there eventually." The boy stood up straight.

"No offense, but should you be out here running in the heat?" Marina asked.

"Well, I'm pretty stubborn. I really want to try."

"I'll tell ya what. How about you take a break and hop on my back? Just till you're ready to continue on your own. Or we can just walk with ya," Sawyer offered, his hands on his hips.

"Really?"

"Yeah, absolutely."

"I don't wanna drag you down slower though."

"Me? Nah! Adding a little weight to my back gives me a challenge. It's a better workout."

"Okay. Sure, thanks, sir."

"No problem, little dude." Sawyer knelt down on a knee to let the boy climb on. They walked for a while at a good steady pace, chatting.

The boy said his name was Luke and he was diagnosed with Leukemia several months prior. Luke said his mom was waiting at the finish line for him because he wanted to run it by himself. He didn't expect to run out of energy so quickly when he had felt so good at the beginning of the relay.

"There's no shame in needing a little help. I'll let you down a ways before that finish line so you can still finish on your own."

"Thanks, sir."

"Call me Sawyer, and this is Marina."

"Well, I'm sure glad y'all are here today and stopped to check on me."

"Aww. You're sweet." Marina smiled at him.

"Mom said we have to visit the barber tent at the end. I don't want to."

"Why do you have to?" Marina shielded the sun from her eyes as she looked up at him.

"Well, because my hair is falling out pretty good these days. She said I should buzz it before I get bald spots."

"I think you might just look cool with a buzz." Marina smiled, although her heart was breaking for the poor boy.

"Ya know? I've actually been thinking about a trim myself." Sawyer looked at Marina with raised brows.

She swallowed the hard lump in her throat and nodded.

"Really? You have cool wavy hair though!" Luke removed Sawyer's hat and tousled his hair, making Sawyer laugh.

"Thanks, dude. It's getting that time of year when it's too hot and muggy for so much hair though. It's always in my face." As if to prove a point, he swiped it off his forehead and shot her a wink. "Well, I see the flags coming up soon. You want down?"

"Yeah. I think I got this."

"I have confidence that you do." Sawyer smiled.

Luke flopped Sawyer's hat back onto Sawyer's head as Sawyer crouched to let him down.

"We'll hang with you in case you need anything," Marina added. They all three jogged to the finish line together.

Luke's mom cheered and clapped with tears in her eyes. She gave him a big hug and told him she was proud of him. Sawyer and Marina were nearby getting water and Luke waved to them. They returned the wave and nodded. Luke and his mom walked over to the barber tent and Luke sat in a folding chair, waiting his turn, his head hung down. He swiped tears from his face. Sawyer looked at Marina, who looked at him with saddened admiration.

"You know I have to do this, right?" he whispered. She smiled and nodded before he took her by the hand as they walked over to the tent. Marina squeezed Sawyer's arm before he sat in the chair next to Luke.

"You wanna go first or do you want me to?" Sawyer asked, his elbows on his knees.

"Huh?" Luke was confused.

"I figure if I can cut my hair, it might give you the courage to cut yours."

"You were being serious?" Luke asked.

"Absolutely. I mean, I love my hair, honestly, but this is for a good cause and if it makes you feel better about buzzing yours, well, that's a bonus."

"It's like double giving." Luke's spirit seemed to lift.

"Exactly. I'll go first." Sawyer stood and went to sit on the stool when the barber was ready for him.

"Are you nervous?" Luke asked, sitting on the edge of his seat.

"Oh, heck yeah! I haven't had short hair since middle school. This is gonna feel weird. You're still buzzing yours too, right? I can't have ya chickening out after he cuts mine now."

"No, sir. I won't chicken out, I promise."

"You ready to cut these purdy waves off?" The barber switched on the clippers.

Sawyer clenched his eyes shut and nodded yes. Marina took a picture with her phone, figuring Sawyer might like to have a picture with himself and Luke during this important event. She was about in tears, not just because she would miss that wavy long hair of his, but because he was willing to sacrifice something he cherished for a complete stranger. This man had a heart of gold. Luke's mom told Marina it was kind of Sawyer to do what he did and she appreciated him as Sawyer's wavy hair fell to the ground. He was nervous to see how it turned out.

"I can't believe you just did that." Marina reached out for his hands when he stood up and brushed himself off.

"Me neither," he whispered. He took a handheld mirror from the barber, looking at his new hairdo. The barber left a few inches on the top and buzzed the sides pretty short with a fade.

"You look so different!" Marina was saddened yet excited about his new look.

"Good or bad?" he asked quietly from the side of his mouth.

"It's hot!"

"Yeah? It's all right." He checked it out in the little mirror.

"I like it...a lot." She bit her lip.

"I think I'm brave enough now, Sawyer." Luke hopped up onto the stool and closed his eyes.

"You got this, kiddo," Sawyer encouraged.

Luke gave a thumbs up and his mom thanked Sawyer with a hug.

"Hey, Sawyer? You think I could call you sometime if I'm not feeling brave?"

"Absolutely. Anytime."

Luke handed Sawyer his phone to put his number in, then Sawyer used Luke's phone to take a selfie of the two of them together with their new hairstyles. Luke's got buzzed off similar to Sawyer's, except shorter on the top.

"If you ever feel like horseback riding, you give me a call. I've got the perfect calm trail rider."

"Wow! Really?"

"Yeah, anytime."

"Thanks!"

Sawyer smiled and fist-bumped him before giving him a gentle hug; Sawyer's eyes going a little misty.

On the drive home, Marina couldn't help but stare over at him often.

He noticed and asked, "What? You hate it?" He ran his fingers through his much shorter hair, clearly second guessing his decision.

"No! Actually, I love it. You could pull off any hairstyle, and what you did for Luke today..." She paused, tears about choking her. "Sawyer, I couldn't be more proud of you."

"Aww..." He took hold of her hand, "I can't imagine having a child going through that. The heartbreak and worry his mom must feel...I can't imagine being that young and having everything to live for, yet not knowing if you'll get to experience any of it. That kid pulled my heartstrings today. I had a hard time keeping it together."

Marina wiped a tear that began to drip from the corner of his eye, then wiped away one of her own.

CHAPTER 4

Getting Used to It

S awyer was buttoning his jeans when Marina woke. She stared at him, wearing only a smile and the silk sheet tucked under her arm. This new haircut of his was sultry. She bit on her fingernail while wishing he would crawl back into bed with her. Not wanting to interrupt him, for she loved to just watch him dress, she remained quiet. He peered back at her and smiled as he pulled his shirt down, covering his strong back. With bare feet, he walked to her side of the bed and bent down, gently kissing her forehead.

"Good morning, my love. Did I wake you?"

"Good morning, and no you didn't. I might have been staring at you while you were dressing though."

"Oh yeah?" He sat in bed next to her.

"Yeah." She cuddled up to him as he wrapped an arm around behind her neck.

"Why's that?"

"Because you're incredibly sexy and this new hairstyle is working for you."

"Is it? I'm still getting used to it." He ran his fingers through the few inches of hair on top of his head. He did that often since it felt so different than the jaw-length hair he'd worn for so many years.

"I'm loving it." She ran her fingers through it too. It was much shorter than what she was used to, long strands no longer tangled in her hand.

"Think I should keep it this way or grow it back out?"

"Keep it, for now at least. It looks darker being shorter but it looks great on you. Makes your jawline more distinct too."

"Hmmm. I think you're incredibly sexy too, by the way; you'd look even better without that sheet." He flipped it back, exposing her bare body next to him. He slid himself down a little to lie next to her at eye level, then flopped the sheet back over them both. He softly caressed her skin with his fingertips, down her arm, her side, down her leg. She wrapped her leg up around his outer thigh as they looked at each other with worship in their eyes.

"You know, our eyes made love long before our bodies did," he said in a low, sexy voice.

"I do believe you're right about that."

Their foreheads pressed against each other and he slowly brushed her hair off her shoulder.

"I've always loved the way you look at me, even before we were a couple." She ran her thumb down his chin.

"You knew I wanted you, didn't you?" He didn't break eye contact.

"Yeah. I really wanted you too. From that first moment we met."

"You played hard to get for a while, but sparks flew that day." He smiled with just one side of his mouth.

"They did. I'm so thankful that we were both there that day. Neither of us would have normally been there. What are the chances?"

"Me too. It was fate, Marina. We were supposed to meet, we were supposed to become friends, grow close, and let sparks fly again out on that tree stump. Sparks will always fly between us, baby. Always." His fingers ran through her hair.

"I hope that never changes. No matter what." Her eyelashes batted and tickled his cheek.

"It won't. It won't."

CHAPTER 5
Whiskey

S awyer started the coffee in the barn and found a note from
Marina sitting on the counter. She must have left it out
there the night before. It read "Happy birthday, my
cowboy." He smiled and poured his coffee then carried on with
chores. Marina came out to help about halfway through. He shut
off the hose spigot as she wrapped her arms around him from
behind. He turned around, pulled her close, and kissed her.

"Happy birthday," she said softly.

"Aww thanks, baby."

"I need to run an errand when we finish chores."

"Okay. I can finish chores if—"

"Nope. I'll help." She smiled as she interrupted, then went
into the feed room for hay and oats.

They turned the horses out then she left while he groomed
knots out of tails. She wasn't gone that long, but he had finished
grooming them by the time she returned and was putting the
brush away as she stepped into the barn. He felt a tickle on his
pant leg and looked down. Cute, fluffy ears perked up and a
speckled face looked up at him sideways.

"I see you've met your birthday present," Marina said from
her position in the doorway.

"Seriously?" Sawyer asked excitedly as he crouched down to pet the pup.

"He's all yours."

"He's adorable! Thank you so much, darlin'!" He looked up at her for a moment wearing a big smile.

"You're welcome. You need to pick a name; he hasn't been named yet."

"I'll think on it today." He stood up, holding the rambunctious pup and offering his chin as sacrifice to appease the puppy tongue. "This is so sweet of you, Marina."

"I hoped you'd be happy. I worried it might be too soon after Huck."

"I think it's great. I love him already." He gave her a kiss overtop of the pup, who was reaching for his face once again.

"What do you wanna do today?" she asked, her hand upon her hip.

"Well...play with this little fella and maybe go riding with you. Bar tonight? It *is* Friday."

"Sounds perfect. What are we going to do with him though while we're gone? I did buy a crate just in case."

"Nah, we'll take him with us. I took Huck a few times. Everyone will love him. He'll be fine."

"What if he makes a mess? He's supposed to be house-trained already but you never know."

"I'll take him out a few times. Does he have a leash by chance?"

"Sure does."

"Perfect."

They walked back to the house, the pup on their heels. Sawyer washed his hands in the kitchen sink as the pup ran after a ball Marina rolled across the floor in the dining room. The liquor cabinet shook when the pup slid into it, knocking over a decanter of whiskey. Golden liquid ran down the cabinet door and onto the pup's paw.

"Oh, crap!" Marina ran for a dish towel and Sawyer laughed as he rushed over and put the whiskey upright. The pup was licking the booze from his paws and the floor so Sawyer slid him away from the puddle.

"Whiskey!"

"I know, I'll clean it up, sorry." Marina came over with the dish towel and knelt down, mopping the floor with it.

"No, I meant his name. It's Whiskey."

"Oh." Marina giggled. "That's a perfect fit. It might get confusing at the bar though."

"True..." He laughed as he took the towel from her and finished cleaning. They sat together on the floor, playing with Whiskey, then crated him before heading out for a ride. They agreed not to take the chance of him running off.

Legend stood, waiting patiently with Marina already mounted, just outside the barn as Sawyer cinched Foxtrot's saddle strap. Legend shook an obnoxious fly from his ears and literally chomped at the bit.

"Wanna ride up the road?" he asked as he saddled up.

"Sure." She spun Legend around.

"We need to get you galloping soon. Dixie will be energetic so you'll want to be prepared."

"True. Maybe I should practice on Legend in the field when we get back."

"Sounds like a plan."

The horses walked side by side, hooves clunking the red dirt. Tails swooshed and leather saddles creaked with pressure as they chatted along the way.

As they turned back up the drive, Sawyer asked, "You ready?"

"I guess so." Marina squeezed her thighs tighter and clicked for Legend to follow Foxtrot into a trot. She put more weight into the stirrups, raising her rear barely above the saddle. They transitioned into a gallop as they reached the field.

"You're doing great," Sawyer cheered her on as they galloped next to each other. Marina felt as though she looked like a rookie.

In a way, she was, but she kept a good posture as her hair bounced on her back.

"It's kinda like the beat to music. Remember one, two, one, two with your butt in and out of the saddle. Let those thighs do the work," he directed.

"I'd rather watch your thighs work." She looked over at him as he laughed. He looked as though he was floating through the air, he rode with such grace.

"Wanna go full run?" he asked. A quick raise of his brow signaled that he wanted to. She hesitated, debating before nodding yes. She was nervous at first but got the hang of it quickly. The horses stopped at the pond for a quick drink before running back across the field to the barn, their nostrils large and manes and tails flying behind them. Marina and Legend trailed Sawyer and Foxtrot by a couple of yards. She was proud of herself for keeping up with him. Sawyer dismounted before Foxtrot was fully stopped and helped Marina down. The horses were led to their stalls and the tack hung up.

With Marina and Sawyer loaded up in the truck, Whiskey and the guitar in tow, they watched the sun sink beyond the tree line across the red clay road and cotton field. The breeze carried her hair behind her as the windows rolled down and the truck tires kicked up red clouds of dust, hands held as one on the center console the whole short drive to Backcountry. Her diamond refracted light in shades of rainbow and there was a twinkle in her eyes before the stars were even hung as the sunset's colors beamed off the windshield, exhaling the day.

Upon entering the bar, Whiskey ran around greeting everyone. His nub tail twitched back and forth as his nose touched everyone. He was loving the attention he was receiving from all the patrons. While Whiskey was making new friends, Bob called Sawyer and Marina up to the bar. He playfully chewed them out for not having come into the bar in weeks and with an icy shake of the metal shaker cup and a pour of blue liquid into a clear glass, Bob set a new mixed drink on the bar. He added a purple umbrella and mermaid tail stir straw. He set a bright-red drink on the counter and lit it on fire.

"These drinks here are called the Marina and Sawyer. They're quite the pair. They're also a congratulations on your engagement and will be added to the bar menu. Happy Birthday too, cowboy."

"Wow, Bob, thanks!" Marina swirled the straw around in the glass. "What's in it?"

"It's a blue raspberry vodka lemonade."

"Perfect!" She took a sip.

"Thanks. And mine?" Sawyer asked as he quickly blew the flame out.

"That's one hundred proof Hot Damn Cinnamon Schnapps."

"And hot, just like you," Marina added, nudging Sawyer's arm with her elbow.

He chuckled and said, "I doubt Bob would have added that in the drink description."

The rest of the band entered together and grabbed beers from Bob before heading up to the stage.

"Tip that drink on back and get that guitar out," Chris hollered as he began setting up his drum set. Sawyer tipped his hat at him then chugged his drink. The glass clunked onto the bar and Sawyer made his way to the stage. He grabbed his guitar out of the case and flopped the lid shut, a pick held between his teeth until he arranged himself on the stool. It only took the guys a few minutes to set up and tune before he gave Trev a nod and placed his hat on an empty microphone stand nearby. Jake pulled up a stool near Sawyer's and strapped his guitar around over his shoulder.

They started their set with *Yours* by Russell Dickerson as he looked at his fiancé with adoration. Everyone in the bar could feel the love radiating through the room. Marina couldn't help but smile at him throughout the whole song. His voice was similar to Russell Dickerson's, smooth, strong, and sexy. When the song ended, Sawyer stood up and pushed the stool back with his foot. With his hand on the microphone, he made an announcement, easily grabbing the room's attention.

"As all of you know, Miss Marina and I have been a match made in Heaven for a while now, but we've made it official since we saw y'all last. We're engaged!" Everyone cheered as the biggest smile stretched across his face. "She actually said yes to my crazy cowboy ass. Can ya believe it?" He laughed. "I'm excited to spend the rest of my life with that woman by my side. Marina, baby, I love you." He pointed to her and winked. She blew him a kiss and hollered, "I love you too!"

"We've prepped a fun song for y'all tonight. By the way, I proposed to Marina in the hay loft so she's gonna laugh at this song." The band played *Hillbillies* by Hot Apple Pie and even broke out other instruments for it. The whole place was up and dancing and Whiskey ran around excitedly, dodging shuffling feet. They went on to play a few more numbers including *The Way I Talk* by Morgan Wallen but mid-way through the song, a man stood from a back corner table and approached Marina. Sawyer focused on the song until it looked as though Marina was uncomfortable talking to the man. He recognized the man as Derrick, Marina's ex. He practically dropped his guitar as he set it on the stage and jumped off. The music slowly died out as the band realized what was happening. Jake propped his guitar against a stool, muttering "Aww shit, here we go again." He jumped off the stage, ready to be Sawyer's backup as Sawyer marched over to Derrick. Derrick turned to Sawyer just as Sawyer pulled a fist back. That strong, hard fist connected with Derrick's jaw, knocking Derrick back into the next table. Marina stood and grabbed Sawyer's arm.

"Boy, you don't learn, do you?" Sawyer yelled, his brows furrowed.

"Sawyer, please. It's okay." Marina tried to calm him.

Exiting the kitchen wielding nothing but a dish towel, Gladys yelled, "Dammit, Sawyer!"

"I told her she's making a mistake marrying you. She belongs with me." Derrick smirked, rubbing his jaw.

"The hell she does! She belongs where she wants to be. She wants to be with someone who respects her and cherishes her. You were warned to stay away. Thought you would've taken me seriously after I broke your nose the first time." Sawyer was in Derrick's face.

"Maybe I don't like seeing her with another man. I knew you had your claws in her the whole time. Boss my ass."

"Too bad! I showed her how she *should* be treated by a man. She's not yours anymore. You blew your chance and I'm glad you did."

"Sawyer, you have nothing to worry about. Come on, he's not worth it." Marina tried to pull him away.

"You're right, he's not." Sawyer looked Derrick directly in the eyes.

"I should press charges," Derrick said, straightening his shirt.

"I'm surprised you didn't the first go-round," Sawyer said with a smug look on his face, his arm around Marina.

"You're a caveman." Derrick shook his head.

Sawyer laughed, "Better to be protective than a piece of shit she needs protected from."

Derrick stepped toward Sawyer, who didn't budge, but Jake stepped between them.

"I wouldn't, dude. Sawyer will cut loose. You'll be hurtin'." Jake put a hand up and Derrick walked into it.

"I said what I needed to say anyways." Derrick headed for the door and Bob told him to not come back.

"Do we need to get a restraining order out on him?" Sawyer asked Marina, bear hugging her.

"I don't think he'll be back this time."

"He won't if he knows what's good for him," Jake added. "Not to piss you off or anything, buddy, but you've kinda gotta work on that new-found anger thing."

"Yeah, I should. I can't help it."

"At least it only seems to happen when dudes mess with your lady though," Bob chimed in.

"Truth." Sawyer looked down at her as he remained against her.

"I'm glad you think I'm worth protecting, babe, but I'll miss you too much if you're in the slammer." She held him tight.

"I won't let that happen. I'll try to simmer down a bit."

"A bit?" Jake raised his brows. Sawyer glared at him but not in an angry way, then chuckled.

"I kinda like the caveman version of you," Marina purred, running her hands up his chest.

"Maybe he can come back out to play later," Sawyer whispered close to her ear then gave it a playful nibble and tugged at her hair. She giggled and tapped his arm.

"We can't afford a lawsuit either, cowboy." Gladys swatted Sawyer with the towel she always had slung over her shoulder.

"Can barely afford to keep afloat," Bob muttered lowly. Gladys scowled at him.

Sawyer pretended not to hear and replied, "I wouldn't let that happen to y'all." He turned and ushered Marina over to a nearby table by putting a hand on her lower back. He pulled out a chair for her then sat when she did and leaned in toward her.

"Did you hear Bob? He said they can barely keep afloat," he spoke quietly.

"I thought that's what he said. Must be the bar isn't doing well?"

"I'll be finding out."

"You might have to find a new place to play and myself a new place to work. I would feel horrible for them, they love this place."

"This place is their life. Friday nights wouldn't be the same without it."

"What are you going to do?" Marina asked, concerned.

"I'll find out if they're strugglin' first. Then we'll come up with a plan if we need to."

"How are you going to ask?" she whispered.

"I don't know. In a way that won't embarrass them, I reckon. Maybe I'll mention upgrading a few things or fixing up some stuff myself and see what they say."

"Good thinking. That might work. Think they'll be honest with you though?"

Sawyer shrugged and sat back, folding his arms. "Well, they know I play here and you work here. I imagine they'd wanna keep us in the loop. We're about to find out."

Bob brought a second round of the Marina and Sawyer drinks over to them. Sawyer cleared his throat and asked, "So, Bob...I was thinkin'...maybe we should paint a wall or two in here, brighten the joint up a bit. Maybe replace some of this lighting." Sawyer looked around the room.

"Well, that would be ideal but it's not in the cards right now."

"What if I did it?"

"I could help," Marina offered.

"Well, that's sweet of y'all to offer the labor and I'd take ya up on it but I'd still have to buy the materials. Gladys says we can't and whatever she says, goes. She's the boss. I just do what I'm told. You should know that by now." He laughed and returned to the bar.

"Well shit." Sawyer raised a brow at Marina.

"That doesn't sound good." Marina rested her chin on her hand with her elbow on the table. They were both quiet for a moment before Sawyer leaned in again and said, "Hey, I have an idea."

"What is it?" She leaned forward.

"I could buy the bar."

"What?"

"Yeah. What if I bought the bar and they pay rent each month, which would be way less than what they pay now? Like, barely any rent. It could still be their business; I just own the property and building. They'd never have to worry about a shitty landlord or maintaining the place or losing the business altogether. They would order the booze and food and such just like they do now. Maybe they would be able to hire another person to help out too. I already take care of the place; maintenance and landscaping whenever I can. They live upstairs. If they lost the bar, they'd be literally losing their home too. They're hard workers and great people. I just hate to see them struggle."

"Me too. Not to stick my nose where it doesn't belong, but are you able to do that financially? That kind of investment?"

"Baby, your nose can wander wherever it wants to. And yeah, I can. Comfortably too."

"Then I say do it. Take the pressure off them."

"We're engaged, so it's gotta be a we thing."

"I'm on board. One hundred percent."

Sawyer nodded and looked over at Bob and Gladys. "I guess I need to have a serious conversation with Gladys now then."

"I'll let you do that on your own. Unless you want me to join."

"It's okay, I got it, darlin'." He got up from the table and pushed his chair in, adjusted his belt buckle, and said, "Wish me luck."

"Good luck, babe."

Much of the crowd had cleared out so Gladys wasn't hustling anymore when he approached her at the end of the bar. Marina couldn't hear the conversation but watched, sometimes swirling and sipping her drink. Gladys seemed saddened and shook her head no. Sawyer laid his hand on her shoulder and leaned down closer to her, still talking. Marina was anxious to hear all about her reaction. Bob walked over to Gladys, noticing she was getting upset. Gladys turned to talk to Bob and Bob shook his head no. Sawyer looked to be explaining and almost begging. Gladys and Bob discussed with each other while Sawyer looked at Marina, frustrated. Gladys grabbed hold of Sawyer's arm to get his attention, then Sawyer bear hugged her. Gladys was crying but Marina couldn't tell if they were happy or sad tears until Sawyer released her and shook Bob's hand. Gladys and Bob hugged each other and Sawyer walked back to Marina, giving two thumbs up on his way.

"You and I get everything free here from now on. The band too. Bonus!" He sat and scooched in his chair and Marina laughed.

"I'm guessing it went well?"

"Yeah, I had to explain and convince. Hell, I practically begged. They trust me and they know I don't have any hidden agendas. They know another opportunity like this probably won't come up to help them out. They're in debt with this place so I made a deal with them to not charge rent for a year so they can get caught up and where they need to be. She seemed relieved after she finally accepted the offer."

"I can imagine. I'm sure they were letting their pride get in the way at first. This is such a kind thing for you to do, Sawyer. Nobody has a bigger heart than you. It's just your nature."

"I believe you do too, darlin'. That's why we were made for each other."

"You're right about that." They shared a long, tender kiss before watching Gladys and Bob pour drinks for the four of them for a toast.

The guys played a few more songs before calling it a night.

CHAPTER 6

On the Line

Light rays beamed above the pastures from the clouds as the sun rose. Tails swished as the horses grazed. Sawyer had just turned them out. Marina carried a basket of sheets out to the clothesline and was pinning them up to finish drying. The breeze flittered the linens, which clung to Marina's blue plaid sundress. Sawyer saw her out there, the mango hue from the rising sun bouncing from her golden-honey hair. He slowly walked toward her, pushing linens out of his way. She spotted him as she bent down to pick up a clip that she'd dropped. The bright light at his back, light-washed jeans and barefoot, a white fitted t-shirt; he took her breath away. As she stood, he smiled and cradled her face in his hands. Their lips mingled and she grabbed him by the hips, pulling him closer. Together, they glowed as if they were in a spotlight. The world rotated around them at that moment.

"You're absolutely beautiful." He pushed her hair out of her face and tucked it behind her shoulder. She lifted to her toes, wrapping her arms around his neck as grassy shadows danced around them. The quiet country surrounded them; the only sound was of leaves rustling in the trees.

He spent the first half of the day building a porch swing in the garage. He had set aside a space just for carpentry. She went out to let him know lunch was ready and saw him covered in sawdust. It was all over in his hair and on his clothes.

"Hey, baby. Good timing. You wanna hold this so I can screw it together?"

"Sure." She tightly pressed the beautifully sanded boards together. "This is going to be beautiful. Are you hanging it on the front porch or out back?"

"I figured I'd hang it out front so we can drink our coffee overlooking the field across the road. We can have a drink in the evening after the sun sets too." He looked up and smiled at her.

"That's perfect. Watching sunsets with you will be even cozier now." She nodded.

"A couple more screws and it's done. Oh, and the chain."

She helped him finish it. It was simple but beautiful. She couldn't wait to relax on it with him.

"What else do you wanna do today after lunch?" He stood and untangled a long line of chains.

"I think we should plant the garden. The seedlings are big enough now."

"Sounds good. Let's go hang this so we can eat and get planting that garden."

She loved that he loved spending quality time together. They didn't have to be doing much of anything to enjoy each other's company. It had always been that way.

They planted okra, berry vines, herbs, and other seedlings before visiting the garden center at the hardware store. They shopped for tomatoes, peppers, and lettuce; the plants that grow better for her already started. They bought lavender and marigolds to plant between all the veggies to help deter bugs and lemongrass to plant next to the porch by where the swing would hang.

When they returned home, they hauled everything to the garden from the truck bed together. He knelt to his knees as she sat on the ground to plant.

"Think it's mean to enjoy seeing the pissed-off look on Shanda's face every time we go to the hardware store together?" he asked.

She laughed. "No, not really. To be honest, I kinda like it too. I hope she tells your ex every time."

He laughed and nodded. "Fair enough. I'm sure she does." He swung his ball cap around backward as clouds passed in front of the sun.

"That slight breeze felt nice," she mentioned as she brushed her hands together.

"I'm thinking the pool sounds nice." He stood, brushing the knees of his jeans off, offering her a hand, which she gladly accepted.

"It does, actually." She held his hand as they entered the pool and patio area.

"I'll go get my suit." She started to pull away but he pulled her to him.

"For what?" he asked softly, staring at her for a brief second before peeling his sweaty t-shirt off. He tossed it over toward a patio chair but it missed. He unbuttoned his jeans and stripped them off and she couldn't help but just watch him, her heart racing. He flung his ball cap over with his clothes then stripped her shirt off her. Up over her head it went before joining his clothes on the concrete. She shimmied her shorts down her legs and flung them with her foot. Stripped down to their underwear, they walked into the water, which was barely cool enough to be satisfying. The aquamarine water swirled around their waists as Sawyer took off his briefs and wrang the water out of them above the surface before tossing them out of the pool. They slapped the concrete with a wet *thud*. Marina looked around, surprised that he was nude in the pool.

"I'll have you comfortable being naked around here in no time." He smirked, trying to coax her into stripping naked. "We've got acres surrounding us, baby. Ain't nobody gonna see."

She couldn't resist that sexy grin of his. Her panties joined his briefs then he unhooked her bra and flung it. She pressed her chest against his as he held her close by the small of her back. He hoisted her up, her legs wrapping around his hips. Her arms embraced his neck as she pressed her lips to his. They sunk further into the water together. Her long, flowing hair floated along the water's surface as she ran her fingers through his. Her eyes connected with his glacier blues, her fingertips caressing his scruffy face. His thumb separated her lips before he kissed her so heatedly, passionately; down her neck, then down her chest, her hands pressing against his shoulders to arch herself backward. Her heels squeezed onto his rear like spurs into a bronco's sides. Fingernails clung to his shoulder blades as she pulled herself back up, her teeth gripping his bottom lip. She knew that always drove him wild. With her back now against the wall of the pool, they indulged in one another. The temperature of the water rose with their heated passion as light shimmered atop of the water. There was a subtle breeze, just enough for the patio palm leaves to flutter.

CHAPTER 7

Moonshinin'

T he day was drawing to an end after a late dinner, the moon hanging brightly as Marina and Sawyer led the horses in for the night then sat together on the truck tailgate in the driveway. He unscrewed the lid to the jar of moonshine he had snagged from the barn fridge.

"You know we have a porch swing for this now, right?" Marina reminded as she let her flip-flops hit the ground.

"Old habits." He shrugged. "I kinda like the tailgate sometimes though. Reminds me of old times..." He paused, taking a sip, then looked at her. "Like the night we first kissed."

"Aww you're sentimental too. I love it."

He chuckled. "Have you given any thought to weddin' plannin'?" He took his boots and socks off and dropped them down to the dirt.

"Are you kidding? I've been brainstorming like crazy." Her feet crossed below the tailgate.

"Really? I assumed, but you haven't said anything."

"I know. I didn't want to seem too eager."

"Why not?" He laughed. "I'm excited too."

"You are? I didn't know guys got excited about weddings." She took his hand in hers then took a chug after him.

"Well, I am." He shrugged and smiled, staring at the droplet of moonshine upon her lip.

"So, you want me to talk to you about it?"

"Yeah, absolutely. We should plan it together. Although, whatever you want will happen."

She smiled wide, her cheeks almost squinting her eyes shut.

"I'd love to plan it together. I want you to have input on everything. It's *our* special day so I want us *both* to love everything about it." She squeezed his arm, resting her head on his shoulder.

"Baby, as long as you're there, it'll be perfect." He looked down at her as she looked up at him, gleaming with happiness.

"Wanna go for a ride?" he asked.

"In the truck?"

"Nah, horseback." He hopped off the tailgate and held his hand out for hers after setting the jar on the tailgate.

"Sure." She accepted his hand and slid herself off the tailgate.

She was about to slip her flip-flops back on when he said, "I'm ridin' barefoot."

She laughed and followed suit. She loved that he'd rather feel the Earth beneath his feet, the bottom of his denim pant legs all dirt. The exterior barn light lit up his broad, bare shoulders. He didn't wear tank tops often but she loved it when he did. They held hands all the way to the barn like giddy teenagers.

"Who do ya wanna ride?" he asked as he pulled the big barn door open. He turned to see her looking at him and smiling a sideways grin.

"My sense of humor is wearing off on you. I love it." He chuckled, then opened Tango's stall and Tango excitedly walked out himself. Sawyer grabbed a fistful of mane and hoisted himself up then helped her up behind him. She'd almost rather ride separately so she could watch him ride, yet she loved wrapping her arms around him and couldn't complain about her current situation. They rode through the field, enjoying one another's company in the quiet night air. She rested her head against his back on their way back to the barn. They could feel the moonshine kicking in by the time they slid off of Tango beneath the barn light. He shut Tango in the stall and pulled the barn door closed, then took Marina by the hand, led her to the grass just outside the pasture, and wrapped an arm around her lower back. They danced under the moon to no music, a blanket of stars shining down on their love, the steps choreographed from their souls.

The next night, after the music room was completely finished, he looked up at her in the bathroom mirror as she came through the doorway. She entered slowly, taking in the sight of him. His gray towel was tucked low and snugly around his waist, the top curvature of his hips showing. He turned around and softly kissed her, holding her face in his shaving creamed hands.

"Have you picked out a dress yet?" he asked before turning back to the mirror and tilting his head for the razor blade to scrape down below his jawbone.

"No. But I have saved a few photos of some I like. I can't wait to try some on. I probably need to decide on bridesmaids first though, so I know who to invite to come along. I wish our moms could both come. They got along so well at Easter. I don't want to rush anything though." She wiped the cream off her cheek.

"Well, I for one, can't wait to call you my wife. I don't wanna wait too long." He finished perfecting his manly scruff then clunked his razor on the side of the sink after rinsing it.

"Aww, I can't wait to call you my husband. Should we set a date then?"

"Yeah. Let's do it. How about soon? Maybe June?"

"I think June would be perfect. The first Saturday?" she suggested.

"That works for me. Are you okay with taking my last name?" He raised a brow at her in the mirror.

"Are you kidding? I'd be honored."

"Good. How big of a bridal party should we have?"

"I'm sure it would be hard to decide between the guys so

maybe you should ask them all." Her hand rested on his back as he washed his face off.

"I could do that. You have the same number of close girl-friends to pair them?"

"I do. I was going to have a hard time deciding who to ask."

"Large wedding party it is." He nodded.

"I might have a folder started for wedding stuff."

"Do ya now?" He chuckled.

"Yeah, I do," she admitted timidly.

"Good because I have one on my phone. What do ya say we shower then compare notes in bed?" He dried his dripping face off with the hand towel as she took off her clothes and stepped into the shower. He dropped his towel and quickly followed behind her. She turned the faucet on, the warm water raining down on the two of them. He held her close to him, his fingers trailing gentle lines up and down her spine as she dragged the bar of soap across his broad, muscular chest. The lather built quickly and she traded out the soap for the bare palm of her hand, wanting to feel his racing heartbeat beneath her fingers. The suds traveled down his washboard abs in slick, glistening trails, drawing her attention to his bellybutton, then further. Her hands followed. He grinned before using his body to press hers against the tile wall and crushing his enticing lips down upon hers, his tongue hungry and demanding. He could feel her wetness along his aroused length and almost fell to his knees at the sensation. He barely pulled his lips away to growl the words, "You're so fucking sexy."

She could've melted down that wall but she didn't want to escape his grip and she couldn't have pried her hands off of him if she wanted to. Her chin rested on his shoulder as she whispered, "I want you." Steam fogged the mirror and glass shower door as the sound of shampoo bottles hitting the shower floor echoed through the bathroom.

They got comfortable on the bed, blanket straightened beneath them, her folder opened and pages scattered about. He flipped through a country bridal magazine, lying on his stomach with his feet crossed.

"What are your thoughts on us guys wearing jeans for the wedding?"

"I wouldn't have expected anything else."

"We'll dress it up though. I was thinkin' I like these." He pointed out a pair in the magazine.

"I like those! Those would look great on you. Y'all can wear whatever you want. Be comfortable. I kinda want it to be a surprise. I don't wanna know what y'all are wearing ahead of time. Just like you won't see my dress ahead of time either. Do you have a preference on flowers?"

"I don't. I think some vines hanging would be a nice touch though at the altar. Maybe we could incorporate roses but in whatever colors go along with the color palette you wanna go with."

"I want teal for sure, if that's ok with you. You look amazing in it."

"Aww thanks. That's good because I was thinking a blue too."

"What other color? Have any ideas?" She flipped through pages and dog-eared one.

"You look gorgeous in anything, darlin'."

"Aww. Ooh, look! The sunset is so pretty!" She stretched upward to look out the bedroom window. He sat up and pulled the curtain back so they could watch the sun finish sinking below the tree line at the back of the cotton field across the road.

"You're breathtaking in these sunset colors, you know that?"

"Oh, Sawyer." She shied her face away. He tipped her chin toward his and gently kissed her soft lips.

"I think this yellow shining on you making you glow is a sign we should choose yellow in your bouquet."

"Sky colors it is then." She smiled and leaned over onto him. He wrapped his arm around her, keeping her close as they enjoyed the sailor's sky together. "I wanna have fun planning this; it's too special not to."

"Me too," he agreed. She scooched up near the pillows and he returned to his stomach in front of the magazine and turned the page, steady on his elbows.

"I know we already had fun in the shower but if you don't put more clothes on than just those briefs, we'll be going round two." She tried to resist but she peered over at him, her eyes moving up and down over the rim of her glasses.

"I'll put clothes on if you take those glasses off."

"They get you goin'?" She smirked.

"You know they do," he whispered as he crawled over top of her and took them off her face. He kissed her passionately as she leaned back, him straddling her carefully.

They didn't get much accomplished with wedding planning. Pages presenting floral and cake ideas lie about on the floor, the blanket covering half of the pages. The ceiling fan twirled, and papers crinkled, rolling and floating around on the floor. Sawyer and Marina lie on their backs staring up at the swirling shadow of the fan on the ceiling, overheating, breathing heavily. Wedding planning had taken root but would have to wait til tomorrow.

CHAPTER 8

Trouble 'n Plans

S awyer's elbows leaned on the kitchen countertop, a steaming coffee mug in one hand and his phone in the other.

"Mom. Mom. I know, I know, but I'm just...I don't think it's a good idea. Because. Oh, come on, Mom. You know what he was like when we were younger. Well, that's because he caused trouble. He was a bad influence, that's why we grew apart. I started using my head. I know we were close but Drew just...oh so you're saying he's changed? How much is the question."

Marina had come into the kitchen in a long t-shirt of Sawyer's. It didn't quite cover her whole rear so he paused as he stared at her when she reached up to get a cereal box down from the top shelf of the pantry.

Without taking his eyes off her, he continued his phone conversation.

"Yeah, Mom, I'm still here. Next time, ask me first, please. No, I'm not mad. And don't say you know my eyes are rolling right now. Yeah, yeah, love you too." His eyes did, indeed, roll. He ended the call and dropped his head. "Well shit."

"What was that about?" Marina shut the fridge door after getting out the milk.

"My mom told my cousin he should be one of my groomsmen without asking me."

"I take it that's a bad thing?" she asked with her mouth full of cereal.

"I don't know." He rubbed the back of his neck, aggravated. "I just can't believe Mom would do that. Ya know?" He slapped his hand on the counter like he had an idea. "I bet ya anything that he asked Mom to be a groomsman and she went along with it. She probably knew I'd turn him down."

"Would you have?"

"Probably. We had a lot of fun back in the day but trouble has followed him since before we were teens. Mom said he's changed but I can't picture Drew any other way."

"You think he'd mess up our big day?"

"Maybe not intentionally. He makes me nervous because he doesn't think before he does stupid shit. I'm sure he'll be making a move on my bride at least."

"Oh, Sawyer, you don't have to worry about that. Not ever."

"Aww, I trust you, baby. It's me I don't trust because I'll jack his jaw if he does. Cousin or not." Sawyer hugged her tight.

"How about we go into town? We can go get fancy coffee and just hang out for a while."

"I'll take ya shopping too. That'll put me in a better mood."

They enjoyed their fancy coffee at the coffee shop out at a patio table then went to a clothing shop. He enjoyed watching her try on items and even tried to sneak into the dressing room with her but she giggled, pushing him back out. After, they enjoyed lunch at the deli cafe before heading home.

Later that afternoon, Sawyer sat on the couch with a notebook and pen.

"So, I have a list of groomsmen. You have your list ready so we can match them up?"

"I sure do." Marina sat on the couch next to him with her own notebook.

"Okay, so I have Justin, Chris, Jake, Trev, and my cousin, Drew, thanks to my mom."

"I have Becka, Savannah, Raquel, Andrea, Bailey Rose, and Olivia. So, I have an extra. Well, shoot."

"It's okay, we'll figure it out. I actually thought about asking my dad since we're so close."

"I think that's a great idea. He would be honored."

"Okay, I'll do that then. It'll be hard to choose between the guys for best man, although I probably would've chosen Jake, so I'm gonna ask Dad to be."

"I'll ask Savannah to be my maid of honor."

"So, you want a big wedding or a small one?" he asked as he wrote his dad onto the list.

"I think a small one will do just fine."

"Sounds good to me. You want fancy or—"

She interrupted him with a head shake, "We don't need fancy. Let's save that for the honeymoon."

"Ahhh, okay! I like that." He gave her a kiss before continuing on.

"I love that you have a notebook for planning," she said, smiling.

"Yeah? Well, it's a lot of work. It shouldn't all be put on you to handle, unless of course, you'd rather do it yourself. I don't expect you to, though."

"I wouldn't mind if you didn't want to plan but I'm really glad you want to do it together. I love it, actually. I just know you're busy."

"I'm never too busy for you, baby. Don't ever forget that." He put his arm around her and kissed the top of her head.

"You're sweet. Are you taking time for a bachelor party before the wedding?" She looked down at her wedding magazine then over at him.

"I don't want one."

"What? Why not?"

"I don't need one. I see my friends whenever I want. I don't need any of that crap most grooms do. I have you." He patted her knee.

"Well, what about a day trip with the guys? Go fishing or something that you all like to do."

"I could do that. I don't like the term bachelor party though. I haven't been a bachelor since the day you and I first kissed."

"Aww. Good, because I can't stand the thought of some half-naked woman all up on you."

"Oh, I wouldn't do that to you. I don't want anyone but you. Don't care to look at anyone else."

He tipped her chin up and looked her in the eyes.

"I trust you." She kissed him.

"What about you?" he asked, flipping through his notebook.

"Well, maybe a relaxing paddleboarding and yoga weekend. Spa too, maybe. You should do a whole weekend. All of you guys have been working really hard on the music room addition. Now that it's done, y'all should relax and reward yourselves."

"Yeah, maybe we should." He leaned back with his arms behind his head. "A relaxing weekend before our big day is probably a good idea. We should plan our parties for the same time frame. That way we only have to miss each other for one weekend."

"I like the way you think. Looking at the calendar, it would probably have to be three weeks before the wedding, which is approaching very quickly. Are we sticking with the first weekend in June for the date?" She flipped through her planning calendar.

"Yeah, I'm good with that. Let's run it by the wedding party after we ask them all to be in the wedding. It is kinda short notice. Hopefully, it all works out as planned."

"We can always change the date if we need to. We could push the wedding back a week or two. We need to think about a venue too." She set her pen down on top of her notebook on the coffee table.

"All I can think of is where I'm laying you down the night of our wedding." He attacked her with playful kisses. She leaned over, laughing as he wrapped his arms around her.

"Where would you like to go for our honeymoon?"

"What's your dream destination?" she asked.

"Wherever I can see happiness in your eyes."

"Sawyer, you're adorable. That's anywhere I'm with you. How long would we go for?"

"How long do you *want* to go for?"

"Depends on where we go."

He chuckled, "Okay, so why don't we each make a list of like five places we've always wanted to go and compare them?"

"Think we'll be wanting to visit the same places?"

"Possibly. I'm thinking we could go to two places. Spend four or five days at one, then go to the other."

"That sounds amazing! I'm so excited. Let's do that!"

He ripped a piece of paper in half and handed her a pen then went around to the other side of the coffee table and sat on the floor.

"Don't be cheatin'." He covered his paper with the side of his hand and kept looking up at her with a raised brow and serious face, making her laugh. He finished his list quickly. It was apparent that he had been pondering places for some time.

"Okay, I'm ready." He slapped the table.

"Gosh, that was quick! One second." She tapped the pen on her cheek, deep in thought for a moment, then wrote another place down. "I'm ready."

He sat next to her on the couch again and they uncovered their papers at the same time.

"No way! Three out of five match!" Marina was excited.

"Awesome! Let's pick two then save the other for when we get burned out with work and need a vacation."

"I think we both have the most expensive place on Earth on our list. Maybe we should save that one for later," Marina debated.

"Nah. Let's do it."

"Really?"

"Well, I know there's nobody I'd rather go there with and there isn't a more romantic time to go than a honeymoon."

"True." She smirked.

"Bora Bora it is!" He circled it on his list. "Which other? Maldives?"

"That's going to be a really expensive trip. You sure you wanna go to two places?"

"Don't you worry about it, darlin'. It's a special time for us. Let's splurge. Besides, I've been savin' for our wedding and honeymoon for eight months."

"But you just proposed four months ago..." She seemed confused.

He looked her in the eyes and smiled a sly, sideways grin and winked. He melted her heart and looked so damn sexy doing it.

CHAPTER 9

The One

"I'm so excited to try on bridesmaid dresses. I imagine you're stoked to try on wedding dresses." Raquel opened the bridal shop door for the other girls to enter first.

"You have no idea how excited I am." Marina looked around at all the dresses as they entered. "There's so many!"

"Dress shopping is so much more fun when you're marrying a man you're madly in love with." Becka took a dress on a hanger from a nearby rack and held it up.

"That's true. That one's pretty. Let's save it to try on." Marina looked it over and Becka flopped it over her arm as they kept browsing.

They picked out a few before Marina asked the bridal consultant about a couple of dresses she had photos of. They had the exact one that was her favorite. She tried that one on first. Raquel, Andrea, Becka, and Olivia waited in chairs just outside the dressing room. Marina came out from behind the curtain following the consultant and their jaws dropped. Based on the girls' reaction and how she herself felt and looked in that dress, she knew she had found the one.

"Yep. You found it." Becka stood and clapped.

"You're glowing in that dress." Olivia's hands flew to her face, excited.

"I agree. You look stunning." Raquel almost looked to be tearing up.

"I love it. I have a feeling you'll be picking this one." Andrea walked around her, checking out the dress.

"I think so too. I really love it." Marina admired it in the long mirror.

"Let's try these other few on before you make a final decision." The consultant held the curtain open for her.

Marina would come out, dress after dress, stand on the pedestal and turn. There were things she liked about each and things she wasn't so crazy about. After putting the first dress back on, she and the girls decided it was the one after all. It was perfect and no alterations were needed so the consultant packaged it up for her in a dress bag as she happily swiped her card.

The girls tried on dresses and they were all able to agree on the same style. Marina bought the girls' dresses, including dresses for the girls who weren't there, then they continued on to shoe shopping while in town.

Meanwhile, the guys tried on their attire at a different shop. They didn't take long and Sawyer picked up his dad and Drew's attire since they weren't in town. They stopped for lunch before hitting up a western hat and boot store that Sawyer frequented. He knew they would have all that they needed. They knew what they were going for so they just had to try things on and pick them up. It was a relief for all parties involved to have attire taken care of. They entered a music store and spent more time in there than they did buying their attire. Sawyer was having a great time testing out an electric guitar that caught his eye.

CHAPTER 10

Going Once? Going Twice? Sold!

"You're up early." Marina opened her right eye a crack to see Sawyer almost completely dressed.

"Well good mornin', baby. We might have to grab breakfast on the go."

"Huh?"

"We've only got a half hour before we need to leave. I'm gonna go hitch up the trailer while you get ready."

"Where are we going?"

"Today's the auction at the county fair."

"Oh! I completely forgot." She flipped the sheet back and landed her feet on the hardwood floor.

"Sorry I didn't wake you sooner, I just got up myself. I must have hit dismiss on my alarm."

"It's okay, I'll hustle."

They pulled into the red clay field next to the equestrian arena. It was busy already; horses were being unloaded from trailers and dirt was clouding the field as more trucks filled the space. The 4H barn was packed.

"I've never been to an animal auction before. I've been to fairs and rodeos before though."

"I've been to several. Most go well. It's hard to see the condition of them sometimes. Some owners are just desperate for money so let great animals go for cheap. Some trade for other animals. Many are auctioned by breeders though and even from 4H."

They held hands walking into the arena and scouted for good seating until Dave flagged them down from the stands. Sawyer waved and joined him only a few rows up from the ground. They greeted each other and sat, chatting while waiting for the auction to start.

"Looking for anything in particular today?" Dave asked.

"Not really. Calm trail riders would be ideal. You?"

"Oh, you know me, Sawyer..." He chuckled and gave Sawyer a shoulder pat. "I'm always up for a challenge. Hopefully, I'll find one for you to train."

"That would be ideal too." Sawyer adjusted his black cowboy hat.

The auctioneer took the podium and folks settled in.

"They always save the horses for last, unfortunately," Sawyer told Marina. After several heads of cattle went, a young stallion was brought out to open the horse auctions. He was a beautiful paint and acted a bit unruly on the lead. Dave bid and Sawyer chuckled and shook his head, knowing what the outcome would be if he won, which he did.

"Looks like not many were up for the challenge." Dave laughed, thrilled at his win.

"Congrats, Dave. Looks like *I'll* need to be up for that challenge." Sawyer patted the old man's back and laughed.

"I appreciate ya, Sawyer."

"The feeling's mutual, Dave."

"That stallion is beautiful." Marina admired the horse's beauty as it was quickly walked away from the center of the arena, its head thrown back with mane flying. A white Arabian was brought out next. A teenage girl a row down and a few seats over stood and started crying. She held her face in her hands as she bellowed "No, I can't do this to her."

Sawyer wrinkled his brows with concern.

"I hope she's okay." Marina stood as if to go check on her. Sawyer tapped Marina on the shoulder before she could get far, walking in front of her and over to the girl himself.

"You okay, Miss?"

The girl's father spoke up, "She'll be okay. That's her horse."

"Dad's making me sell her if I want a car. It's the only way I can pay for one myself."

"She'll need a car to have a job. That's just how it goes."

Sawyer felt pity for the sobbing girl as the auctioneer began rattling off dollar amounts. Sawyer looked back at Marina, who was watching with concern. Sawyer looked down at the horse, its head hanging low to the dirt. When the next dollar amount was announced, Sawyer placed a bid. The girl looked at him with panic in her eyes, like how dare he? Someone else bid but Sawyer outbid them and won. He winked at the girl and nodded. She quieted down, confused as Sawyer went back to his seat. The girl stared at him as he explained the situation and his plan to Marina.

Marina's arm wrapped around him. "That's so sweet of you, Sawyer."

There were only a few horses left to auction before they'd be allowed to claim their wins. Sawyer, Marina, and Dave walked down to the arena floor and Sawyer nodded to the young girl to follow him. She did so with hope gleaming in her eyes. She caught up to Sawyer and he gave her the ticket for her horse. She had no words, she just stared at it then up at him.

Her dad joined and asked, "What's going on?"

"I think this man just bought Willow and gave her back." She was frozen. Sawyer smiled and nodded.

"Well, that's awfully generous, cowboy, but that's not exactly teaching this young lady a lesson, now is it? She turns sixteen tomorrow and wants a car."

"If I may be so bold, sir, I understand the lesson, but I also know how hard it is to lose a pet. Some bonds shouldn't be broken."

"This man has a generous heart. He's always helping others out. It's in his blood, and I, for one, am very proud of him." Marina hugged Sawyer's arm.

"Please, let her accept her horse back as a birthday gift from a stranger. She shouldn't have to be without her horse on her birthday," Sawyer pleaded. The man looked at his daughter, who was fearful her father would reject the offer.

"We're about to move. We won't have a barn anyways," her dad reminded her. The girl hung her head and wiped a falling tear.

"Well, I happen to have an empty stall at my barn. How about the mare stays at my place but you come over any time you want to ride her? Would that work?"

The girl bear-hugged Sawyer, not wanting to let him go.

"I'm Sabrina. My mare's name is Willow. Promise I can ride her whenever I want?"

"Nice to meet you, Sabrina. I'm Sawyer, and yes, I promise." She let go of Sawyer and he handed her a business card from his wallet.

"This is the best birthday gift ever, Sawyer. Thank you so much. I don't know how I could ever repay you."

"That's the thing about gifts. They don't need to be repaid."

"That was kind of you. I appreciate you doing what I couldn't." Sabrina's dad shook Sawyer's hand.

"My pleasure. Sabrina, you want to load her up in my trailer?"

"Sure." She took the lead rope and led the mare, following Sawyer and Marina, to the truck.

"Dave, you need help?" Sawyer hollered back.

The paint stallion reared up, making all kinds of noise, and Sawyer had Marina help Sabrina so he could help Dave. The paint was loaded with Sawyer's expertise before he joined Marina at the truck.

"Can I come by tomorrow?" Sabrina asked. "I don't want Willow to think I've abandoned her."

"Yeah, sure." Sawyer smiled, assuming she would've wanted to.

"Thank you again. I'll bring feed for her, she's on a certain diet."

"Sounds good. Anytime is fine with us."

The next morning, Sawyer and Marina finished their chores and tied balloons to the Arabian's stall door. Marina baked a small cake for Sabrina and put it in the barn fridge. They were about to head to the house when Sabrina's dad pulled into the drive. They greeted Sabrina as she quickly bailed out of the truck.

"How's Willow?"

"She's great. She's made new friends already. I just turned her out but we can go get her." Sawyer waved for Sabrina to follow him and Marina out to the pasture fence. Her dad unloaded the feed before joining them. Sawyer didn't even have to whistle. The mare came running, tail held up high, the moment she saw Sabrina. They embraced just inside the gate. Such a heartwarming moment told Sawyer he had done the right thing.

"We have a little surprise for you," Marina told her excitedly.

"Really?" Sabrina and her dad followed Marina and Sawyer to the barn and she lit up when she saw the colorful balloons floating. Her hands covered her mouth. Such a small gesture meant the world to her. As if buying her horse back for her wasn't enough, they made her birthday even more special. She embraced them both with a big thankful hug. Marina got the cake out of the fridge and set it at the table where they all sat for a small celebration.

CHAPTER 11

Idea in the Making

"Damn, baby, whatchu cookin'? It smells delicious in here," Sawyer said as he came through the front door and slung his boots off. He hung his hat and tousled his hair spikes as he entered the kitchen.

"Chicken chimichangas. Kind of my own recipe."

"I can already tell they'll be a favorite." He wrapped his arms around her, nestling a kiss upon the side of Marina's neck.

"Did you have a good day?" she asked, turning to him.

"I did, but it's much better now that I can see your beautiful face."

"Aww." She kissed him on his soft lips.

"How was your day?" He popped a piece of diced tomato into his mouth.

"Lazy." She smiled and popped another piece of tomato into his mouth. "But so much better now that you're home."

"Wanna be lazy together?" He pulled her close against his pelvis to distract her as he snuck open the oven door to snoop. She pushed it shut and grabbed the front of his shirt, her eyes connecting with his. He snickered as his lips melted with hers in front of the oven heat.

"I would love to be lazy with you tonight, right after dinner, but I have something to talk to you about at the table."

He leaned back and looked at her, worried. "Uh oh."

"You don't have to be worried. It's an idea that I want to run by you."

"Okay...I'm curious now." He raised a brow and the timer on the oven beeped until she pushed the button. He grabbed the pot holder off the countertop and whipped the oven door open.

"You hungry?" She laughed.

"Yeah! I skipped lunch." He set the pan on the stove and flopped the pot holder down on the countertop as he shut the oven door.

"These look amazing."

"Thanks. I hope you like them." She got plates down from the cabinet and handed him one.

"Oh, I'm sure I will." They fixed their plates and sat together at the table.

"So, let's hear this idea." He shoveled food into his mouth like he hadn't eaten in a week.

"Well, after the auction and the relay race, I got thinkin'..." she hesitated, watching him.

"Don't be shy, baby. Tell me," he said with his mouth full. She was surprised at his sudden lack of manners, but laughed. She didn't mind one bit.

"These are great by the way," he said before shoveling another bite.

"Thanks. I'm glad you're enjoying them. Anyways, I thought maybe I could sell my other house and buy the land that's for sale behind yours."

"For what?" he asked nonchalantly with a shoulder shrug.

"Maybe to start a therapy program. Ya know, with horses and kids, veterans, emotionally traumatized folks, physically challenged too..." Marina folded her hands together on the table. "What do you think? Be honest."

Sawyer put his fork down and took a drink of water before answering, "I think that's a great idea."

"But it would...wait. What?"

"I think it's a great idea. I'm proud of you."

"You are? For what?"

"For wanting to reach out and help others and sacrificing something of yours to do it. It's admirable." He picked up his fork and ate another bite, not able to hold off long on the deliciousness.

"Thank you. That means a lot."

"I mean it. I want to make sure wedding planning comes first though and I don't want you to get stressed out because both things should be fun." Sawyer took her hand in his.

"Oh, I agree, absolutely. Would you want to do this with me?" she asked.

"Absolutely."

"Really?" She could barely contain the excitement bubbling in her chest.

"Baby, I'll support you always. I've always got your back. If this is something you're passionate about, let's do it."

"You'll train horses?"

"Of course. Whatever you need me to do to achieve your goals, I'm here for you." He reached over the table and gave her a kiss.

"Thank you for being so supportive. I know you work hard already so if you don't have time—"

He put a finger to her lips, "I'll make time. You don't worry about that, darlin'. Just promise the wedding planning comes first. I don't want you getting stressed out."

She took his hand and looked at him softly. "I promise. The wedding *should* come first."

"I'd do anything for you. This is a great idea though. I'm thinking we could buy some horses at auction and give them some TLC, train them to be companions, whether they're able to be ridden or not. Simple trail riding stuff for most, a sanctuary for others. Yeah, hell yeah. Let's roll with it."

"Should we plan a special occasion? " she asked excitedly.

"How about a charity ball?"

"Yes! A ball! I love it! I love you." She leaned in for a kiss and squeezed the hand of her amazing man.

"I love you too. I can't wait to see you all dolled up."

CHAPTER 12

Charity Ball

She painted her lips a light, peachy pink and placed a jeweled clip in her hair along the right side above her ear. That lip color looked enticing against her tan skin and golden hair. She batted her long lashes as she stood back from the mirror, examining her evening gown's fit. She had never been to an event this extravagant before besides her senior prom, but as an adult, this felt different; more important. A dress this elegant had never caressed her skin before. The event was for a good cause and she worried she wouldn't act sophisticated enough and would embarrass Sawyer. Upon exhaling a deep, nervous breath with her eyes closed, Sawyer knocked gently on the bathroom door. It startled her and she answered quickly, "I'm ready!"

He chuckled, "You're okay, darlin', take your time. Just checking to see if you need help with a zipper or anything... zipping up...or down."

"Thanks, but I'm good," she opened the door and his jaw dropped. He stumbled backward a step.

"Do I look fancy enough?" She pulled her hair over to one shoulder, the side opposite the clip, exposing a halter strap. He looked her up and down and swallowed hard with his lips parted. Her fitted silver gown drew attention to her low v-cut cleavage;

the *V* traveled nearly to her navel. The deep slit up to the front of her hip allowed her tan leg to poke through when she walked. Strappy silver heels showed off her light-pink-glitter nail polish, which closely matched her lipstick. She twirled slowly for him to see there was no zipper to be zipped up or down, for the dress was backless. He looked dapper himself, pulling off a black tux very well. It was snug where his muscles were biggest and she found that incredibly sexy.

"You haven't said anything." She looked down at herself then back at him as he stared at her and swallowed again.

"That tux looks incredible on you." She looked him over.

He cleared his throat. "I'm speechless. That dress was made just for you."

"You like?" She smirked.

"You have no idea. There won't be a soul there that can even come close to how beautiful you are."

"You're sweet." She smiled and reached up for a kiss. He watched her walk out of the bedroom and she had to ask if he was coming or not as she fetched her silver-sequined clutch from the end table near the front door. He joined her, taking her arm in his. Her thin heels balanced carefully down the porch steps, him alongside her for support. Neither one of them could wait to show the other off.

She carefully stepped out of her SUV when Sawyer opened the passenger door. Her dress touched the ground as she took his arm. They walked close together up to the entrance; they looked like movie stars walking the red carpet.

"I hope this charity ball we put together is a big success," Marina said upon entering the five-star hotel conference hall, arm-in-arm with Sawyer.

"I hope so too, baby."

They were handed champagne flutes when greeted by the staff. The white lights, the chandelier, the flowing white tablecloths, and the classical band were all so beautiful. There was a waterfall wall at the entrance and a small platform with a podium stage and microphone at the front of the conference room.

"I guess it's time to welcome everyone." Sawyer then asked for her to join him, but after nervously looking around the room, she politely declined. He handed her his champagne flute then stepped up and tapped the microphone as guests finished trickling in. Champaign was being handed out around the room from trays by staff. He looked so handsome up there in his black and white tux. He didn't even wear a cowboy hat. He had spiked his hair up a little and it paired so well with his suit.

"Welcome, everyone. Good evening. Thank you for joining Marina and I for this special occasion. I want to start by explaining our purpose for this charity ball. First of all, everyone likes a good excuse to dress up every now and then, am I right?" The guests cheered. "Marina came up with the wonderful idea to start a therapy program with horses, which will not only benefit auction-rescued horses but also children and veterans. This program will provide emotional support as well as physical therapy. The bond between humans and horses is quite therapeutic in itself. Our plan is to hire a few qualified staff members to take care of the animals on a daily basis: a physical therapist, an emotional support coach, a veterinarian when needed, and I will train the horses myself, without compensation of course. Marina will be in charge of running the program. This is a way we can reach out to help others, both human and equine. This charity event is more of a fundraiser tonight to help get the ball rolling, but we offer our program as a charity so the program is free to those who sign up. Any donations made tonight, or any time in the future, will be used for business-related activity: to help with payroll, horse care and feed, riding equipment, and vet care. These donations are also, obviously, tax deductible, as we will be a nonprofit organization. Marina selflessly sold her former home to purchase the land and I'm paying to have stables, the arena, and fencing built. She and I will buy the horses from auctions and rehabilitate them, if need be, before training them to be perfect companions. She and I will keep our regular jobs as well as run this organization together. I'll be moving my office to a space in the stables and working between there and our home. As of tonight, we're getting the word out to recruit those in need of companionship and therapy. There's a list of charities that I donate to and hold dear to my heart on the donation table up front, some that are run by some of you here tonight. I encourage you all to donate to at least one before leaving. I'd appreciate it and I know they would as well. I appreciate the returned support in making my lady's vision come to light. I'm extremely proud of her. I look forward to working with her every day." He proudly smiled at her across the room. "I hope you all enjoy yourselves this evening, and on behalf of Marina and myself, we want to thank each and every one of you for your generosity. Thank you." He nodded and stepped down as guests clapped. He walked straight over to Marina and pulled her into his side.

"That was perfect, Sawyer. Thank you." She took his hand as he reached for her to dance with him.

"It's difficult to concentrate on the purpose of this evening when you look like that in this dress," he whispered next to her neck.

"It's that distracting?" She smiled, slyly.

He looked straight into her eyes as they swayed as one to the music and said, "I wanna let that dress hit the floor."

"Oh? Well, that will have to wait until we get home, mister."

"Will it though?" He chuckled when she laughed. "I can't wait to get home. I'm going to take pleasure in indulging in you."

She glanced away and did that sultry lip bite that drove him wild. She couldn't help it; it was like an instinct whenever he would talk dirty to her. The floor flourished with couples dancing, gowns sparkling, and suits swaying. The event was a success, the whole evening was. It was a night to remember.

As they rode home after thanking everyone again, her dress sparkled in the headlights of every passing car and his white button down shone almost as brightly, his jacket having been discarded in the back seat for a more comfortable drive. The slit in her dress rode even higher on her thigh the longer they drove. Her eyes were roaming him as much as his hands were her. His fingers felt her leg skin peeking through that slit. His white dress shirt clung tight to his large biceps.

"We should've auctioned off a date with you," Marina told him on the drive.

"Nah, you would've earned more." His hand rested on her leg. "You make me wanna pull this truck over."

"As much as I'd love a woodsy déjà vu, I can't be snagging this dress on tree bark."

He ran his fingers through his hair as his attention went back to the road.

"We've only got a few more minutes til we're home. I suppose I can wait."

She smiled at him and was just dying on the inside to rip his clothes off. She loved that he desired her so. His tie was now undone, hanging from either side of his collar. His shirt was now only half-buttoned, his tan chest peering through. Boy, did he know how to tease...He definitely had a head start on stripping clothing articles.

Dirt clouded the driveway beneath the headlight beams until the truck tires stopped and the engine shut off. They practically stumbled over each other as they rushed through the front door and he kicked it shut behind them as their lips firmly tangled before she shoved him up against the wall. Buttons flew as she ripped his dress shirt open the rest of the way. No time was wasted in dropping his dress pants to the floor. He stepped out of them and kicked his dress shoes off as he pulled her halter strap up and over her head. Slowing down for a brief moment, he slowly slid her dress down, his breath upon the side of her face. A tingle raced up her spine. Sliding her heels off, she stepped over the discarded dress as he whipped her around and pressed her against the wall. Kissing down to her navel, her hands in his hair, breathing deeper, her head leaning back against the wall, he raised back up and looked deep into her eyes. Their foreheads rested against one another for a few moments before he took her by the hand and led her to the bedroom.

The next morning, she opened her eyes to the sound of a bird chirping just outside the bedroom window. She rolled over to see Sawyer wasn't in bed. There was a note on his pillow that read "Come join me for coffee on the swing." An instant smile spread on her face and she grabbed his white dress shirt from the top of his dresser before pouring a cup of coffee in the kitchen. Barefoot and her long hair a tousled, uncombed mess, she stepped out onto the front porch. He paused, his cup having just pulled away from his mouth, and swallowed a gulp as he took her in.

"I love that you put on my dress shirt this morning. It looks so damn sexy on you." He grinned and patted the swing next to him for her to sit. Her cheeks raised with her smile as she sat, careful not to spill her coffee on herself. He put an arm around her.

"I'm sure I look a mess."

"Nah, darlin', you look perfect, as always."

"I'm surprised you put shorts on over your briefs." She snickered as she took a sip.

He looked straight ahead at the field across the road. "Well, I did chores already and figured I probably shouldn't do them in just my underwear. The horses might get jealous."

"Oh my God, Sawyer!" She playfully slapped his chest and laughed after almost spitting her coffee out. He laughed and gave her a kiss on her coffee-tainted lips.

"You're even witty first thing in the morning before you finish your first cup of coffee." She leaned against him.

"You like it." He laughed.

"Of course I do. I like that I can never predict what's about to come out of your mouth."

"That's probably scary in public though, huh?"

"Absolutely." She laughed. "Or when you send me short video clips. I can't open them if I'm around anyone."

"Well, I can predict that you'll laugh every time."

"You know it."

It was going to be a muggy day. Haze had already settled afar just above the cotton. Their skin was beginning to stick together as they cuddled on the swing for a while, listening to the birds chirp.

CHAPTER 13

Stuck in the Mud

C hores were finished, and horses were all turned out to the pastures. Marina was about to spray the mud off her boots at the outdoor spigot until Sawyer said, "Let's stay muddy. What do ya say?"

"What?" She asked as she turned the faucet off.

"I'm gonna get the Jeep. We're goin' muddin'!" He headed for the driveway.

"You're gonna get your pretty Jeep all muddy?"

"Why not?" he hollered back over his shoulder. "It'll wash!"

She looked around at all the mud puddles the torrential rainstorm left during the night.

"Don't be a stick in the mud, darlin'." He laughed as he climbed into the Jeep, retrieved the key from its spot under the seat, and started it up. She threw her hands in the air, surrendering to his spontaneity, and joined him. He spun mud from the tires, driving from the driveway to the field. She held on to the "Oh Shit!" handle, as he called it, with one hand while holding on to his hand with her other. He had her laughing with his "Yee haw!" as they flung mud above the Jeep roof. It splattered the entire windshield, the furiously swiping wipers only smearing mud across the window, making visibility almost impossible. It was all fun and games and laughter until the tires suddenly sank. They spun in place, shooting a roostertail of mud a good twenty feet into the air.

"Well shit," Sawyer grumbled, hanging his head and smacking the steering wheel. He tried rocking it out but wasn't successful. Marina slid over and tried to rock it with her window down as Sawyer went behind the Jeep to push. Still no luck. He went up to the window, his arms resting on the door frame.

"Well, that was fun." Marina snickered.

He laughed. "It was! But now we can't get the bitch out."

"The truck would get stuck too, wouldn't it?" she asked.

"Oh, yeah. The weight would sink it quickly. It's up to my ankles." He paused and looked at her with wide eyes. "I have an idea! Stay here, I'll be right back." He waded through ankle-deep, and in some spots deeper, mud back to the barn. She waited in the Jeep, windows down, skin glistening with sweat. There was a slight breeze but it was still a warm day. A good ten or maybe fifteen minutes passed before she looked in the side mirror and saw Dixie galloping through the field with Sawyer on her back. She laughed and leaned out the window.

"Yeah, baby!" She shouted. Dixie slowed to a trot before stopping behind the Jeep. Sawyer slid off her and hooked a thick leather strap to the harness he had put on her up at the barn. He tied the other end of the strap to the hitch on the Jeep and Marina put it in gear. Sawyer stayed alongside Dixie, coaxing her to pull.

"Should I get out?" Marina asked.

"Nah, she's got the horsepower. Your tiny bit of weight is nothin'."

A few tugs and the Jeep's tires were out of the ruts.

"Yes! Good girl!" He patted Dixie on the side of her neck.

"Thank you, Dixie!"

"You ridin' or drivin'?" he asked.

"I think I'll take my chances with the real horsepower." She exited the Jeep.

"Oh, ouch." He chuckled. "Nothin' wrong with Blue here." He tapped the hood of the mud-covered Jeep before getting in.

Marina climbed onto Dixie's back and situated herself, which was slightly challenging without a saddle.

"Sorry, baby, I should've helped you up there," he said before starting the Jeep.

"It's okay, I need practice anyways, she's growin' like a weed."

"It's a good thing too. We needed her today. I'll meet ya back at the barn. Wanna race?" He revved the engine and raised his brows.

"Why not? Let's do it."

"Yeah?"

She grabbed fists full of mane and clicked her tongue. Dixie started trotting.

Sawyer whipped the Jeep around and gassed it, mud flying yet again. Hooves clopped then began beating the ground like bass drums, her fluffy white hooves were complete mud. Dixie had a more graceful canter than Marina anticipated, and they barely beat Sawyer back to the barn by seconds. She slid down Dixie's side as Sawyer got out of the Jeep.

"I love adventures with you," he said, pulling her to him. She wrapped her arms around his neck.

"Every second with you is an adventure. I'm so glad you keep me on my toes. I love that you're far from dull and boring." She raised to the toes of her muddy boots and kissed her rugged man.

"I love that you go along with random fun." He placed his cowboy hat upon her head.

CHAPTER 14

Helping Hands

Marina brought bottled water out to the guys. They were working hard, sweating in the heat and humidity, hammering away. The sound of power tools rang through the air, thundering in her ears as she approached them with the cooler. Sawdust flew, floating down upon her hair and sundress. She didn't mind. Seeing her man all sweaty, his glistening skin being beaten upon by the sun, was totally worth it. Justin and the band had all come, pitching in to help build the new stables. Sawyer had hired a small contracting crew to help build the shell since the building was projected to be huge, but he was one to do at least some of the work himself.

"Aww thanks, baby." Sawyer hugged Marina, his sweat moistening her skin.

Boards fell loudly behind Sawyer and a round of laughter rang through the air.

"No horsin' around, y'all. I don't have insurance to cover your asses." Sawyer bantered before pouring ice water down his dry throat.

All the guys were a sight to be seen. She was looking at a country cowboy hunk calendar; a magazine spread of in-shape testosterone. They grabbed water bottles from the cooler.

Justin held one to the back of his neck. "I don't know how y'all work out in this heat on your ranches every day."

"It's not even summertime yet." Sawyer chuckled.

"Ya get used to it, office boy." Chris teased.

"Pencil pusher having a hard time keepin' up, is he?" Trev asked as he dropped his hammer and joined in the ribbing.

"He's out here helping take the load off y'all and, to be fair, I'm an office boy too," Sawyer reminded.

"I give him credit for puttin' up with your asses." Jake laughed.

"Yeah, that's the biggest challenge." Justin chuckled.

Sawyer cracked open another water and took his black cowboy hat off.

"This here is how we cowboys cool down." He closed his eyes and poured the water over his head. It ran down his face, his lips, his sleek chest...good God he was a sight.

Marina stared at him, mouth gaping open like it was the first time she had ever seen him shirtless and dripping wet.

Five guys out there working up a sweat, wearing just jeans and boots...what a view it was. Their shirts were laid over saw horses and lumber, covered in sawdust and dampened with sweat. Cowboy hats and baseball caps shadowed their faces.

"You guys want lunch?" Marina asked, trying not to make it obvious that she was staring. She couldn't help it. She felt as though she needed to pour water over herself at that point.

"You guys hungry?" Sawyer asked, tossing the empty water bottles into the cooler.

"Starving." Trev nodded.

"I could eat," Justin agreed.

"I think we've all worked up an appetite." Chris re-tied his light brown man-bun and scratched sawdust from his short beard. He was an attractive guy, tall and broad. If he had tattoos, he would look more like a biker than a rancher.

Jake looked around where the saws were set up. "Yo, we're out of screws."

"We just opened a bucket," Trev said as he looked around.

"This bucket?" Sawyer held up an almost-empty plastic bucket that had two lonely screws rolling around in it, tinging together.

"Well shit." Trev readjusted his ball cap and shielded his eyes from the sun.

"I can go buy more and grab pizzas or something," Marina volunteered.

"You don't have to, baby. I can go."

"Really, I don't mind."

"Hey, Sawyer we need the concrete bags too," Chris reminded.

"Thanks, I forgot to get those this morning. Why don't you and I go together?" Sawyer pulled Marina in for a kiss. She felt dainty amongst so much muscle.

"You'd be better at loading those concrete bags than I would." She smiled, her arms wrapped around his sweaty back. He was so drenched that her hands slipped right down to his belt loops.

"We'll be back soon, guys." Sawyer snatched his shirt off the rail and put it on while on their way to the truck.

They retrieved what items they needed at the hardware store and, of course, Shanda was the cashier. She gave Marina a dirty look and smiled all flirty at Sawyer, who paid her no attention. He was his polite, delightful self, as was Marina. Sawyer swiped his card then pushed the flat cart out to the truck, Marina walking alongside him.

Marina loaded the buckets of screws and nails into the truck as Sawyer tossed the concrete bags in the truck bed like they were bags of flour. Three female employees were gathered at the door watching him. They turned back inside when Sawyer flipped up the tailgate and got in the truck. Marina loved that she was claimed by this man whom other women drooled over. Better yet, she was happy that he treated her like a queen and made her happier than she had ever been. She was proud to be his. She looked over at him as he drove out of the parking lot and thought about how lucky she was to have such a wonderful man.

On their drive home, they passed an overgrown fenced yard on the corner of a dirt road. The weeds were tall around the outside, not much shorter inside the fence. Two alpacas and a pony looked rough for wear. They caught Marina's attention.

"Sawyer, slow down a second, please." She sat forward, looking out her window back at the tiny pasture yard. He slowed down.

"What did you see?"

"Animals. They look to be in rough shape." She answered as Sawyer pulled over and rolled the truck to a stop, pea gravel shifting under the tires. "They look thin." Sawyer leaned over and looked out her window over her shoulder after Marina expressed her concern.

"They do, don't they?"

"Should we knock on the door?"

"And say what, baby? It looks like you starve your animals. Feed 'em?"

"I don't know, but we can't just do nothing."

"I can make a phone call and have them checked up on. Maybe I can send Doc and he can pretend he showed up at the wrong address for a house call or something."

"Really? Think he'd agree to that?"

"Maybe. Worth a try." He shrugged.

"Thank you, Sawyer."

"Of course." He kissed her forehead before driving off.

They picked up pizzas before heading back to the property where the guys were leaning against Chris's truck, taking a break in the shade.

"We'll get the concrete out of the truck after we eat." Sawyer set the pizza boxes on the tailgate and the guys behaved like vultures going after fresh roadkill.

"Should I get napkins from the house?" Marina asked as Trev wiped his hand on his jeans.

"Oh, baby. You're so cute." Sawyer pecked her cheek, a pizza slice in his hand and a mouthful of pizza. She rolled her eyes, smiling and shaking her head before walking around the truck to get her water from the cup holder in the console.

"After we eat and unload the concrete, let's work on getting that small quarantine pen built." Sawyer said quietly and pointed over to the area in which he wanted it.

"Sure thing." Jake didn't question the change in plans. Sawyer always had a smart strategy, no matter the job at hand.

Marina ate with the guys then drove the truck back to the house to do work around there for a while. The guys worked fast to put up the round pen. It was getting dark when they finished, having worked straight through supper time.

Sawyer was totally beat when he got home. He showered and went straight to bed. He had fallen asleep by the time Marina got out of the shower. The lamp on her side of the bed was still on, so she switched it off and crawled into the satin sheets, snuggling against his warm back. He let out a sigh as he rolled over and scooped her to his chest without waking. His arm rested under her as if he were a pillow, and her head tucked beneath his jaw. She felt instantly relaxed in his arms. The rhythm of his heart beating put her to sleep like a lullaby.

Sawyer was already gone when she woke the next morning. She drank her coffee out on the porch swing. The warmth from her mug humidified her already-warm face, adding to the insane amount of moisture already in the air, which only got worse as the sun rose. She got dressed and twisted her hair up into a messy bun before joining the guys over at the property, ready to work in her jean shorts and tank top.

"Good morning', Marina," Chris greeted her before starting the saw back up.

"Good morning!" she hollered back as she approached Jake, who was loading a nail gun.

"Where's Sawyer?" she asked, her hands tucked into her back pockets.

"He uh...ran an errand. He should be back soon." Jake smirked then got back to nailing.

Marina knew that he knew something she didn't. She gave a nod and asked, "So what can I help with?"

"You any good with post-hole diggers?" Justin asked as he handed the tool to her along with a pair of work gloves.

"I can handle that."

"Follow me." Justin measured out and marked the ground where Marina would be digging holes.

"Actually, how about we trade? I'm sure you can read Sawyer's map and measurements just as well as I can. I'll dig." He took the post-hole diggers and handed her the map.

"I can handle it, Justin."

"Oh, I know, but that wouldn't be the gentlemanly thing to do." He patted her on the shoulder and slammed the diggers into the red soil.

"Hey, y'all got a whole pen put up yesterday?" Marina noticed the fenced-in area.

"We did."

"I assumed y'all would finish the main fencing first. Hmm..." Marina pondered.

Justin looked over at Jake and shrugged as Sawyer pulled into the drive, hauling a horse trailer. The dust settled as Sawyer made his way around to the back of the trailer and Marina shielded the sun from her eyes above her sunglasses.

"Marina, baby. Come here."

She set the blueprint map on the ground, pinning it with a fist-sized stone, and trekked across the dirt field to the truck.

"Good morning, babe." She greeted him with a soft kiss and tight hug. His white t-shirt was a little dirty, and his jeans were too. He wore it well. He handed her a fancy coffee he'd picked up while in town.

"So, I stopped over at that place with the alpacas you saw."

"Really? Did you talk to anyone?"

"I did. An elderly man came to the door. He was grumpy at

first and threatened to get his 12-gauge but I assured him I was no threat."

"Oh, my goodness!" Her brows rose high with surprise.

Sawyer chuckled, "It's okay. Everything's okay. He said the animals were his wife's and he had refused to take care of them, but when she passed away a couple of months ago...well, it's been hard on him to go out to take care of them like he should. Honestly, I think maybe it was harder emotionally than physically but he held on to them because they were hers. I offered to buy them. He refused."

Marina's eyes lost their glimmer.

"I told him they need to be looked after better, vet care and different feed. He said he can't afford it and finally agreed to sell them to me."

"Wait! Really? You bought them for real?"

"I did, just for you. I couldn't turn the old man in for animal neglect and I couldn't leave them there like that. You were right, they are thin. I hope you know a thing or two about alpacas because I don't." He laughed as she flung her arms around his neck. She held on tight, fighting to not squeal like a little girl on Christmas morning.

"You're the most wonderful man, Sawyer. I love you so much."

"I love you too. I'd do anything for you. Even almost have a 12-gauge aimed at my face."

She laughed. "I wouldn't want you risking your life. Not for alpacas."

"Well, there was the pony too though." He chuckled and opened the trailer door. The pony trotted on down the ramp but the alpacas stayed huddled in a corner at the front of the trailer.

"Yeah, so I don't think they like me too much. I might have to have the guys help out."

"You're a horse trainer, and a great one too, can't you do your magical little whistle or something to coax them out?" She stood at the ramp, looking in at the thin-framed frightened animals. "Is this why you guys built the quarantine pen first?"

"Yes, ma'am. We're working on the lean-to for it today so they have shelter till we get the stables finished."

Chris had a hold of the pony, petting it. "He got a name?" Chris hollered.

"I'd say no. The old man said his wife called them all Baby, but there's only one *Baby* around here." Sawyer slapped Marina's rear.

"I get to name them?" she asked excitedly.

"Absolutely."

"Hmmm..." She thought for a moment. One alpaca was dark brown and the other a light tan. The pony was a dark bay and hyper too. "Espresso." She pointed to the pony.

"I'm thinkin' snip-snip," Sawyer joked, pointing out that the pony was not a gelding.

The guys laughed and Marina shook her head, smiling.

"Mocha and Latte." She nodded at the alpacas and walked up the ramp. They shied at first but Marina stayed to the side, careful not to corner them, and held out a hand as she drew closer. Sawyer was ready to step in if he had to and Trev came over just in case the animals got rowdy. Marina was patient and spoke softly to the animals, knowing they were unsure of her intentions. They eventually allowed her to get close and calmly usher them down the ramp.

"Well look at you..." Sawyer was impressed. "I draw the line at pigs though. Seriously."

She smiled and tipped his hat back enough to express a thankful kiss.

CHAPTER 15

Coffee with Who?

Marina strolled the sidewalk uptown and hit the bakery up for a donut and one to take back to Sawyer. She looked both ways and crossed the street to Chillax-a-latte Café for a fancy coffee. The barista greeted her and asked if she wanted her usual.

"Yes, please. I'll need Sawyer's too." Marina paid and stood at the counter waiting for their coffee. The shop was busy but Marina was patient.

"Excuse me. Excuse me, ma'am." A brunette woman was trying to get Marina's attention. Marina turned around and smiled. The woman waved her over so Marina made her way across the café.

"I just love your wedge sandals. Where'd you get them?" the woman asked.

"Thank you. My fiancé bought them for me, I'm not sure where though. I'm sorry."

"You're fiancé? Congrats."

"Thanks."

"I'm Joselyn. I go by Jos usually." She shook Marina's hand.

"Marina. So, are you from around here?"

"Yeah, I don't come in here as much anymore but I craved it today."

"My fiancé works in the office space across from here so we frequent this café."

"Justin?"

"You know Justin?"

"I do. He's a good guy."

"He is, yeah. Actually—"

"Marina," the barista called out before she could finish. "Sawyer's is ready too."

Marina excused herself and went up to the counter to get their coffee. She returned to Joselyn's little table but remained standing.

"Sawyer? *He's* your fiancé?" Joselyn asked with piqued interest.

"Yep. That's him. You know him?"

"I've heard of him, perhaps through Justin. I've seen him enter the office from here. He's an attractive man. You're a lucky girl."

"Aww thank you. He really is. He's amazing all around."

"Would you happen to be busy this evening? Care to have dinner? That probably sounds odd but I don't have many friends around here."

"Well, I would love to, except I picked up a shift tonight."

"You're engaged to the infamous Sawyer yet you're working?" Joselyn was sincerely confused.

"Yes," Marina answered slowly, curious as to what she meant by that comment. "I didn't realize he was infamous."

"Well, I heard he's really well off, so I'm just curious as to why you're working."

Marina's head tilted sideways. "I've always worked. I like to, actually. He told me I don't need to but I refuse to use him that way. I'd rather contribute, ya know? Pull my own weight. I've learned to never rely solely on a man financially but I don't think

I'll ever have to worry about that with him. He respects how I feel about it."

"Wow, well good for you. I wish you the best. Where do you work?"

"Backcountry Bar. Just once in a while on really busy evenings. We're friends with the folks who run it and I like to help them out."

"I see. Well, maybe I'll see you here more often."

"I'm sure you will. I better get this home to Sawyer before the ice melts. It was nice to meet you." Marina took the donut box off the table and carried the coffee in a drink carrier. A gentleman held the door open for her as she left.

A week later, Marina made a stop at the coffee shop to meet Becka. They sat chatting for a while before Joselyn walked in. Marina waved at her politely and Jos lifted her bougie sunglasses to the top of her head before walking up to the counter to order.

"I had a green facial mask on and he came into the room. I thought for sure I'd scare him and he'd run for the hills, never to return, but he told me I'll never scare him off no matter what I do or look like."

"Well yeah because you two aren't just lusting after each other, you're so deeply in love."

"We really are." Marina's chin rested in her hands, elbows on the table.

"So..." Becka took a sip of her iced chai. "You've been wearing skirts a lot lately. Is that a new one? I haven't seen it before."

"Yeah, well I've found that they're easily accessible...ya know," she spoke quietly. "Sawyer gets horny so easily and it's *hard* to calm him down. Never know when he's going to spontaneously want a piece of cake," she said, twisting the conversation into incognito style as Jos was approaching their table. Marina assumed Jos heard every word but Jos walked past like she hadn't to get napkins, then back to the counter.

Becka waited till she passed their table before leaning forward and asking, "Does he know you wear skirts and dresses for that reason?"

"I think he's figured it out," she mumbled with a giggle. "I noticed the way he'd look at me when I dressed up as if he adored me. When I wear cut-offs, he gets that sultry-smoldering look on his face. When I dress cozy, just lounging, he has that adoring face that turns sultry when we start cuddling."

"It doesn't matter what you wear, you're sexy to him no matter what. Might as well be comfortable."

"He sure makes me feel that way, so I pick cozy skirts." She giggled. "He's such a sexual creature, only when he's around me of course, but it's like, all the time. I love it."

Jos got her coffee and came over to greet the girls.

"Becka, this is Joselyn. We met last week when I stopped in."

Jos pulled up a chair, inviting herself to join.

"How's your fiancé doing?" Jos asked with a smartass grin.

Becka caught on to negative vibes immediately.

"He's great. It was difficult to leave him this morning, out there training a horse shirtless."

"Ooh..." Becka made Marina laugh.

"Yeah, I can imagine." Jos rubbed the back of her neck then looked at Marina with envy.

"What do you do?" Becka asked Jos.

"Right now, I'm working on photography projects. Oh, hey! Would your man be willing to do some photo shoots? He certainly has the body for it." She held back a smirk.

Becka kicked Marina under the table.

"Um. What kind of shoots?" Marina was hesitant and cleared her throat.

"Maybe sexy cowboy shoots or whatever else he'd feel comfortable doing."

"I can ask but I doubt he would."

"Yeah, ask him and let me know. The last I remember, he wasn't shy."

"Sure." Marina nodded but she did not plan to ask him.

Jos told the girls to have a good day before leaving and Becka tapped Marina's arm. "What the hell was that?"

"She did seem bizarre. Hmm, odd." Marina watched Jos walk to her car.

"Um, yeah, why's she so interested in your man? And how does she know he isn't shy?"

"No idea. She said she knew of him but now I'm wondering how and to what extent."

"Might have to find out." Becka raised her brows and crossed her arms.

"Yeah, I have every intention to. I might not come here for a while; I'd rather dodge her."

Marina pulled into the driveway and carried the coffee and donut box from the car to the porch but heard the sound of metal banging further up the drive in the circle beyond the garage near the barn.

"Shit!" Sawyer was laying under the big lawnmower, which was jacked up.

She saw jeans and boots, that was it from that angle. She walked back around after setting stuff down on the step and asked, "You okay, babe?"

His knees were up and he was shirtless when he slid out from under the mower, wearing grease on his face, hands, and bare chest. He was dirty from lying in the dirt.

"Yeah, I'm ok. Just pissed off." He sat up and rested his forearms on his knees.

"What happened to the mower?" she asked, crouching down in front of him.

"I hit a metal crowbar on the edge of the yard over there and it bent the damn blade." He pointed over toward the barn.

"It needs a new blade?"

"Yeah, I can't bend this one back."

"Why was there a crowbar in the grass?"

"My guess?" With raised brows, he pointed at Whiskey, who was rolling in the grass in the front yard. She giggled.

"But that little shit sure is cute." He shook his head, still pissed.

"I can go buy one if you text me what size I need."

"It's okay, I can go to town. You just got home."

"I don't mind. Besides, you're a filthy mess."

He looked down at his chest and arms as he stood. "So?" He shrugged.

"So...as hot as you look, how about you take a coffee break?" She stood and pointed to the porch.

"Ooh, donuts too?" Brushing dirt off his butt, he bee-lined for the pastry.

"It's all yours, I ate mine. Oh, hey, by the way, how do you know Joselyn?" she asked, a hand casually resting on the mower.

He picked up his coffee and started chugging. "Who?" He opened the donut box and sat on the porch to eat it.

"Joselyn. I met her at the coffee shop a week or so ago and saw her again today when I met with Becka.

"I don't know a Joselyn." He shook his head with a mouthful.

"Well, she said she knows *of* you, and she claims to know Justin too. A client maybe?"

"Doesn't ring a bell."

"She's attractive, our age, brunette."

"No idea who she is, baby."

"Hmm, okay. No biggy, I just wondered how she knew you guys. She sure seemed interested in how you're doing."

"Sorry, darlin'. I don't know. Are you sure you're okay with going back uptown? I can shower—"

"It's fine, I don't mind. I'm taking my coffee with me though." She walked up to the porch to get it. He gently grabbed her wrist when she reached within arm's length and pulled her to him.

"Thanks for the treats." He kissed her with wet coffee lips laced with maple icing.

"You bet. I'm always thinkin' of you, cowboy." She winked at him.

"Likewise. Hey, you wanna take trouble with you?" He smiled a wide, fake smile.

"Why? He's probably filthy. I don't want him in my car."

"Take my truck. A ride will be good for him."

"You just need a break from his chaos, don't ya?" She laughed.

He nodded yes with a mouthful.

"I'll grab his leash."

Sawyer reached up onto the porch behind him and handed Marina the leash.

"You had it ready? You were planning on him getting out today I'm guessing."

"I thought about taking him on a walk when I got done with the mower. A ride will work though."

"Will they let him in the store?"

"Yep. I took him there a few days ago."

"Did you really or are you desperate?"

"Both." He chugged his coffee.

She laughed and hollered for Whiskey, who came running, his spotted ears flapping.

"If he's naughty, you're gonna owe me," Marina teased.

"Deal." He smiled, counting on it as she loaded Whiskey into the truck.

CHAPTER 16
Strummin' Surprises

T hursday, the barn note read, "You're stuck with me today" and Sawyer worked from home. They had coffee together out on the porch swing before he worked on the laptop for a bit at the kitchen table.

"This client makes me wanna start drinkin'." He rubbed the top of his head, frustrated, and sighed.

"Aww, I'm sorry. We can get drunk together later tonight." She laughed.

"I'm drunk on your love, baby. Oh! That gives me an idea!" He darted for the music room and hollered back, "I'm gonna put this new room to use!"

He had been in there for a couple of hours. Marina had gone for a ride on Legend and was getting hungry by the time she returned. She hosed Legend down and turned him out to pasture then came in to make lunch. Marina knocked on the music room door as Sawyer strummed his guitar and then jotted down notes.

"Yeah, baby. Come on in," he hollered. She could barely hear his voice through the thickly-padded wall.

Upon entering she asked, "Whatcha doin'?" and walked around to his front side as he sat on a chair with his guitar on his lap.

"Just writing a song." He put the pen down on the sheet music template page then carefully laid his guitar on the floor.

She straddled his lap, arms around his neck. "What's the song about?" She spoke softly.

"I can't tell ya."

"Why not?"

"Well, because I'm writing it for you."

"Really? That's so sweet! Oh, come on, tell me."

"Nope."

"Pretty please?" She batted her eyes.

"Not even with a cherry on top." He sported a sexy, sideways grin.

She wrinkled her nose at him. He laughed and gave her a kiss. "Although tempting, you'll find out soon enough, darlin'. It'll be a surprise."

"You gonna sing it to me in bed or at the bar?"

"The bar, so everyone can hear it. Then I'll sing it to you in bed." He winked.

She giggled as he peppered kisses down her neck.

"I meant to tell you lunch is ready. You're very distracting though."

"I've got lunch right here." He bit her neck.

"No, I'm dessert. Let's go eat lunch."

While eating at the table, Gladys called Sawyer's phone. His hands were messy with buffalo sauce from the chicken wings he was eating so he swiped his phone and tapped the speakerphone with his pinky knuckle.

"Yes, ma'am?" He continued tearing meat off the bone with his teeth.

"Hey there, Sawyer. I have a favor to ask of you."

"Consider it done."

"You haven't heard what it is though yet." Her drawl might have given Sawyer's a run for his money.

"Gladys, it doesn't matter, you know that. Whatcha need?"

"Oh, Sawyer, you're such a dear. Well, sadly one of the usual bikers passed away yesterday. One of the guys just called asking to get ahold of you. They were hoping you'd be so kind as to play here at the bar on Sunday after the funeral."

"Wow, that's horrible news! I'm so sorry to hear that. Of course we'll play. I'll let the guys know and we'll practice tonight instead. Who was it that passed?"

"Thank you, Sawyer. I knew I could count on you. It was old Billy. Apparently, he had a heart attack. His wife thought he fell asleep in his recliner late watching TV but he had passed. So sad. They figure he didn't suffer though."

"Wow, that's crazy. He seemed like a rough tough guy."

"He was healthy...besides all the beer." She chuckled fondly. "He would appreciate you boys playing in his honor, I'm sure."

"Well, it's an honor to be asked to play for him. I'm still surprised though that he passed away. Thanks for asking, Gladys."

"Thank you, Sawyer. You're a good man."

"Yes, ma'am. You're welcome." He hit end on the call and sat back in his chair.

"That's so sad." Marina didn't know what else to say.

"I guess we just never know when it's our time," he replied as he wiped his hands on a napkin.

That evening, the band came over to rehearse a few songs they hadn't played together before. These songs seemed fitting for the celebration of life they would be playing for. Marina sat in on their practice session, perched on a stool against the wall to keep out the way. The music room wasn't extremely spacious, just enough room for all the guys to set up. They would play the songs on the wireless speaker then they'd look up the melody of their particular instrument on their phones. They played along twice to each song and had the music practically memorized already. Marina was amazed at how musically inclined they all were and how they worked as a perfect team. They didn't even practice that long, they all had plans with their ladies. They had plans for the following night as well, except Trev and Trina, so the two of them made plans to have lunch with Marina and Sawyer.

CHAPTER 17

Play Ball!

S awyer and Marina met Trev and Trina for a late lunch Friday evening downtown by the boardwalk. The baseball stadium was nearby which prompted the restaurant to be sports-themed. They served the best burgers and Cajun fries. Sawyer and Trev only had one beer but the girls had a couple of drinks. The weather was ideal, warm but not too hot and muggy; a slight breeze floated through the outdoor balcony overlooking the water where they'd been seated.

Marina had the giggles; she often did once she hit her second drink. She sat sideways in her chair, legs over the arm, and crept her toes up Sawyer's leg under the table edge. His left elbow rested on the chair arm, his hand on his chin, and his right arm on her legs. Her toes crept to the inside of his thigh and he quickly peered over at her then back at Trev who was sharing a story. Sawyer was having a difficult time focusing on Trev's words. He readjusted his posture in his seat and cleared his throat. When she reached his groin, he squirmed, almost spilling his water.

"You okay?" Trev asked, mid-story.

"Mmmhmm, I'm listening."

Marina covered her mouth with her fisted hand, trying not to laugh. He'd run a hand through his hair, then rub his chin scruff, rub his chest, stretch, and put his hands behind his head. She loved it when he did that, his biceps bulged even bigger. He couldn't sit still. Her toes gripped at his zipper and he looked over at her. She looked back at him and bit her bottom lip, causing him to pinch the bridge of his nose and clench his eyes shut for a moment. Trev's story seemed to drag on and Sawyer couldn't have repeated a word of it, he was too distracted. The girls would chime in and giggle, Marina fully aware that she was driving Sawyer absolutely crazy. His knee started bouncing and she loved the telltale sign that she was getting under his skin. Her toes were becoming more aggressive and his breaths grew deeper and slower. He inhaled through his mouth twice before slapping the chair arm and pointing out the time.

"Trina, you said you have a hair appointment today, yeah?" Sawyer reminded.

"I do. I have about a half hour before we'll have to leave though." She looked at the time on her phone.

"I actually have an errand to run that I forgot about so..." Sawyer scooched his chair back from the table. "This was fun, guys."

"Yeah, we'll have to do it again soon." Trev stood from the table and handed Trina her purse as she stood. Marina gave Trina a hug while Sawyer sat as long as possible before standing to give Trev a shoulder pat. Sawyer took Marina by the hand on their way out to the truck, practically dragging her along, their flip-flops flapping. They waved at their friends and he squeezed her hand tightly before opening her door.

"You, Miss Marina, are a naughty tease." He shut her door after she climbed inside. She found it quite amusing, barely keeping from laughing.

He got in and started the truck then looked over at her. She was already staring at him with a sideways grin. He bit the inside of his cheek and didn't say a word. Driving out of the parking lot, she asked, "What's your errand?"

"I don't have one."

"But you said"—she paused—"Oh! So, you—"

"You were driving me crazy, Marina," he interrupted, looking out the driver's side window.

She giggled. "Was that okay?"

He looked over at her and raised his brows with his chin tucked then chuckled. "I liked that you were playing ball."

She laughed a cute, tipsy laugh.

"I think that last drink did you in, didn't it?" he asked.

"Maybe." She pointed to a car wash and he seemed confused. "Your truck is dirty. You should wash it."

With turned in brows, he nodded. "Okay." He turned into the car wash.

As soon as he paid and the truck started moving along the tracks, she got handsy. His shorts rode up a couple of inches from his knee and her hand was running up under them, inching higher and higher. He slid down in his seat a little, looking at her like he was inviting whatever was going to happen next. Her nails dug into his thigh just before she leaned in and unbuttoned his shorts. He looked around, scouting for spectators. With one hand down the front of his shorts and the other up the sleeve of his t-shirt, she kissed him; an aggressive mouthful of tongue. He tightly wrapped her hair up in his hand. That drove her wild. She pushed his chest, pressing his back against the seat. With his hand still wrapped in her hair, she went down on him. He tipped his head back against his seat, closed his eyes, and gripped the steering wheel. Rainbow suds covered the windows, rubber squeaked against the truck's metal sides, and giant brushes spun. The loudness of water spraying, rinsing the suds down the windshield, didn't cover the sound of his breathing. As the driers fired up, she sat up and he released her hair.

"So that's why you wanted to hit the car wash."

"Mmhmm. I've always wanted to mess around in a car wash."

"Really? Well, I'm not complaining. It wasn't my truck that was dirty though." He wore a big grin.

"This is what happens when I have a drink or two."

"Well, again, baby, I'm not complaining. You had three though. Jesus, I need a drink now." He laughed. "You're just full of surprises. I owe you."

"I'll hold you to that."

CHAPTER 18

Dissin' Dixie

Marina had her girlfriends over to chill poolside after going out for lunch. Sawyer and the guys had been working over at the property but brought tools and such back to the house. As the girls came inside to change, Sawyer and the guys were outside cleaning up. Dusty and paint splattered, they cleaned and put away tools and threw away the trash they'd brought back with them.

"Hey, Sawyer, did you get that errand run yesterday?" Trev hollered over the sound of water spraying against a paint roller he was cleaning.

"Yep. Mission accomplished." He smirked.

Jake found a football in the garage when he and Sawyer were on their way through to add paint trays to the trash.

"Go long!" Jake hollered from the garage. Sawyer turned and saw a football coming at him so he dropped the trays and caught it.

"Dude, what the hell?" Chris laughed.

Trev shut off the hose and hollered, "I'm open!" He dropped the roller to the ground and put his hands up. Sawyer tossed it at him as the girls exited the house and stepped onto the porch.

"Ooh, y'all out here lookin' all hot playin' football all messy," Raquel flirted.

"You girls wanna play?" Sawyer asked as Trev tossed the ball toward them. Marina caught it but almost fumbled. She looked at the girls and shrugged in question.

"Sure," they all agreed.

"Four against four? Guys vs girls?" Chris suggested.

"Sounds fun." Andrea tied her shoes that she had only loosely slid on. Others let their flip-flops fly.

"I'm game." Becka clapped her hands, ready to roll and eyeing Jake. Marina noticed and smiled. Jake was really attractive, even Marina thought so.

They all walked over to the side yard, which was more rectangular, and the guys lined up against the girls after using a paint stick to draw touchdown lines.

"We tacklin'?" Trev asked.

"Why not?" Sawyer answered with a cheeky smile, then winked at Marina. She laughed and flipped her wavy ponytail back behind her.

"I don't see us girls tackling any of the guys, to be honest." Andrea laughed, already feeling defeated.

"You girls can play the pansy way if you'd like and just two-hand touch or whatever." Chris shrugged, teasing.

"I think that's a challenge." Becka put her tough-girl look on.

The girls chose to play offense first, Raquel giving it a good throw. Trev stumbled backward, blades of grass flying, but he caught it and then ran forward. He was quick too, darting around the girls who were all trying to run for him. The guys blocked well and Trev was able to run it on in for points.

"Ugh!" Andrea had been on his heels the whole time, her dark brown ponytail flying behind her. They lined back up and Jake gave it a good throw, but Marina was quick to intercept it in front of Chris and took off running, the girls cheering and the guys cussing. Sawyer was coming after her fast. She contracted the giggles, which slowed her a bit, and he tackled her to the ground, careful not to hurt her as she screeched. She was giggling so hard she snorted, causing Sawyer to laugh. He, of course, stole a kiss while she was pinned beneath him on the ground. He discretely pulled her skirt back down in place so her panties didn't show when he took her hand and pulled her to her feet.

Becka threw the next turn, which Andrea caught and began to run with, but Chris tagged her shoulders like a gentleman, even after Raquel tried slamming into him. Sawyer played quarterback after a few downs of the girls not gaining yardage. He told the guys, "Y'all better go long." And as the girls went running after the guys, he threw a Hail Mary. Marina just missed it and almost crashed into Jake, who was reaching out for it. It bounced and tumbled into the pasture, just under the fence as Dixie was nearing with curiosity. She excitedly galloped to it and kicked it with a fluffy front hoof. Everyone cheered and laughed, but it went further into the pasture and she chased it. She continued to kick it, then picked it up with her teeth, whipping it back and forth and up and down, her mane flying, and deflated it as Sawyer climbed the fence to go retrieve it from her.

He threw his hands into the air. "Well shit! There goes our game, y'all. Sorry. It was fun while it lasted." Everyone booed for the game ending but laughed at the horse, who stood with her head hanging low, staring at the dead football like she had lost a best friend.

"Aww. Poor Dixie." Marina puckered her lips as she watched her horse's ego deflate.

CHAPTER 19
Biker Down

S
awyer rushed in the door, later than he had expected to return home.

"Hey, darlin'! Sorry I'm late." He darted over to her on the couch for a kiss then to the bedroom. I'll be ready in like five minutes." He stripped his shirt off and threw it into the hamper, then snatched another from his dresser.

"You're playing tonight, right? It's Sunday."

"Yes ma'am. I wouldn't miss this memorial."

"How did your appointment go?"

"Great! I've got the paperwork ready and it's in the truck. How was your day?" He pulled the clean shirt down over his torso.

"Uneventful. That appointment took a while."

"Just had to make sure all the fine print was good so I had an attorney friend meet me at my office to go over it. It's good to go." He put on a button-up shirt over his white t-shirt while in the doorway, then put his white cowboy hat on from the hook by the door before fetching his guitar from the music room.

Marina was waiting in her sundress on the couch with Whiskey lying at her feet.

"Can I help you with anything?"

"Nah, baby, I'm ready. Thanks though. Actually...I better put more deodorant on." He came out to the living room carrying his guitar case and set it by the door. He ran back into the bathroom to quickly apply deodorant then back out he came.

"Well, don't you look purdy? As usual." He smiled and winked, chewing gum.

She stood and joined him at the door as she slid her shoes on. "Thank you. You look handsome, as always."

He gave her rear a tap as she headed out the door ahead of him then he whistled for Whiskey to follow.

There had to be a good two dozen motorcycles parked in front of Backcountry. The rest of the band beat Sawyer and Marina there. Sawyer lugged his guitar in and Marina carried a manilla folder. Whiskey wasted no time greeting everyone and sniffing under tables for crumbs. Sawyer took his guitar to the stage then he and Marina met Bob and Gladys up at the bar with the folder.

"This paperwork is for y'all. I had an attorney look everything over but, of course, you're more than welcome to as well."

"I'll go ahead and sign it, Sawyer. I trust ya." Gladys took the folder.

"Take your time. I'm not rushin' anything. You two sit and go over it whenever y'all get time."

"Will do." Bob nodded. "Thanks again, cowboy."

"You betcha. You expect this crowd to get wild this evening?"

"Nah. They're grieving. They usually don't get really rowdy even when they're celebratin'." Bob polished a squeaking glass before setting it on the shelf behind him.

"You two want drinks?" Gladys asked, getting glasses down.

"I suppose we'll need one for the dedication cheers," Marina shrugged.

"You got it."

Marina took her drink to a table near the stage and Sawyer sat on a stage stool with his. The band was set up and Marina called Whiskey over to her so he wasn't a distraction. She picked him up and held him on her lap. He lay there calmly, panting from all the excitement.

"I can't say we've ever played for a celebration of life memorial before but we're honored to be asked to do so. Man, to be honest, I'm not sure what to say. I'm so sorry about Billy's passing. He was a cool guy, always polite, and had a fiery spirit. He was a funny old guy who always had a story to tell. I only had the pleasure of chatting with him a few times but those conversations were memorable. We all enjoyed his company and now he'll be making jokes in the sky, making everyone up there laugh too. We lost a good soul here, but Heaven gained him. We've got the perfect song, but first, we'll raise our drinks for a toast." Sawyer raised his ice-jingling glass of golden liquid as the crowd raised their beers. "To Billy! Fly high, brother."

They dove right into *Give Heaven Some Hell* by HARDY.

"That song was the perfect tribute. Fits Billy to a T," Bob shouted from behind the bar. The crowd agreed.

Next, they played *Drink A Beer* by Luke Bryan and *People Are Crazy* by Billy Currington. Billy's biker friends requested a few songs that Billy enjoyed and the band played those as well.

"I have a feeling Uber will be busy tonight," Sawyer joked as the band packed up. Gladys and Bob joined Marina at her table and Sawyer came over and pulled out a chair and sat backward on it.

"I think it was a nice send-off tonight," Gladys told him. "You boys would've made Billy proud."

"Thanks. I'm sure he saw it all." Sawyer nodded with a smile.

"Bob and I glanced these over in the office real quick. Everything looks good from what we can tell. We trust you. We signed them." Gladys slid the folder across the table to Sawyer.

"You sure? I want y'all to be sure about this before I turn it in."

"We're sure. We won't be offered a get-out-of-jail-free card again. We can't pass this opportunity up." She smiled and took Bob's hand on the tabletop.

"I don't want y'all to feel forced, by any means. I just don't want y'all to be struggling or lose this place we all love."

"We appreciate that. We appreciate y'all feeling like this place is worth keepin'. There's nobody on this planet we'd trust more than you, Sawyer. We appreciate you offering us this generous deal. You'll be savin' us," Bob agreed.

"Okay then." Sawyer wiped his sweaty palms on the thighs of his jeans and pulled the paper out to sign it. He scratched his signature across the paper and slapped the pen down on the folder, then clapped his hands and shouted, "We own a bar!"

Marina laughed and high-fived him.

Gladys and Bob laughed and offered them another round of drinks to celebrate. The four of them clinked glasses.

CHAPTER 20

All Is White Gold

Marina was looking in the display case at the wedding bands as Sawyer rubbed her back looking alongside her, both of them with a coffee in hand.

"Ooh, I like this one! I think it would match my engagement ring perfectly. What do you think, babe?"

"I think it's beautiful and probably what I would've picked for you myself."

"Yeah?"

"Yeah. I like it. That would look great on you. It's whatever you want, baby. You're the one who's gonna be wearing it." He saw the gleam in her eyes in the reflection of the glass countertops.

"Can I see this one please?" Marina asked the young lady behind the jewelry counter.

"Absolutely." She took it out of the case and carefully handed it to Marina. Sawyer politely took it from Marina and placed it on her finger.

"It looks perfect," he said.

"I think so too." She smiled at him and couldn't keep that smile from reaching her eyes.

"You have exquisite taste," the woman told Marina, then

glanced at Sawyer with batting, flirty eyes. Marina definitely noticed that she wasn't referring to the ring and thought to herself *here we go again, having to fight women off with a stick* but Sawyer paid the woman no attention so Marina didn't mind.

"Thanks, I think so too." Marina smiled, side-hugging Sawyer, then slid the ring off. She looked at the price tag and her eyes instantly grew huge. If she had taken a drink of her coffee right then, she would've spit it across the counter.

"I should probably keep looking though." She reluctantly handed it back to the woman.

"You sure?" Sawyer asked.

Marina nodded and took a sip as she slowly walked along the display case. He could tell she was looking at tags.

"Marina, if that's the ring you want—"

She shook her head no.

"Hey...Marina, I'm serious."

"There's no reason to spend that much on a ring. I can keep looking. I'm sure they'll have something similar for less. Let's go look for yours first while I think about it."

"I hoped you wouldn't be looking at price tags but you are, aren't you? Please don't."

She was quiet as they stepped over to the men's counter.

"Marina, I'm serious."

"Sawyer, I heard you, Love. I can't justify the cost—"

"Nope. No ma'am," he interrupted, shaking his head.

She tilted her head and exhaled.

"Darlin', we're not getting into an argument about this. I saw your face when you saw that ring and again when you had it on your finger. I plan on only doing this once. I don't want you to forever regret not getting the one you fell in love with."

She looked away, biting the inside of her cheek in thought. "Let's look for yours first, okay? Besides, as long as I'm married to you, that's all that really matters. I'm not a materialistic girl, you know that." She wrapped her arms around him.

"I love that you're sensible when it comes to money but this is a once-in-a-lifetime deal." He looked in the case with her. It seemed as though for a simple guy he was particular in what he was looking for in a ring. He called the woman over to have her pull two out of the case.

"Which one you like?" he asked Marina, holding them both.

"You're the one gonna be wearing it," she said with a wink. He chuckled and put one on, then the other.

"I like the first one." He decided quickly.

"Me too," Marina agreed.

"Okay, you sure?" the woman asked.

"Yes, ma'am. I'll be wearing it forever so that's the one I want." Sawyer kissed Marina on top of the head.

"Okay, I'll box it up. Does it need to be resized?"

"Nope, it's perfect. Thanks." He took Marina by the hand and they walked back over to the ladies' counter. She browsed a bit but looked back over at that first ring a couple of times. She seemed indecisive so Sawyer waved at the woman and, as Marina leaned over looking through the glass, he pointed above Marina at the ring she had tried on. She obviously had her heart set on it. The woman took that one back out of the case and Marina's eyes followed it. She looked at Sawyer and he nodded.

"Baby, if that ring was half that price, would you even have to consider it? Is it the one you'd choose?"

"Yes, absolutely but—"

"No buts, baby. It's yours." Marina's jaw was loose, her expression that of shock, knowing full well that ring was the tag price.

"It looked perfect with your engagement ring and I can tell your heart and mind are set on it. My baby gets what she desires." He embraced her.

"Does it need to be resized?" the woman asked.

"Actually, no, it's a perfect fit."

"See, it was meant to be." Sawyer smiled.

The woman boxed their rings up, put them in a jewelry bag, and cashed them out. Marina lifted to her toes, kissing him passionately before they left the store. Sawyer thanked the woman again on their way out, jewelry bag and coffee in one hand, the other around Marina.

"Now I think you need a black cowgirl hat to match my hat." He pointed down the street to the Western store.

CHAPTER 21

The Weekend

The next week flew by. Wedding plans were all set in stone and building on the property was well underway. Anticipation for a relaxing weekend had finally come to a peak as the guys pulled into the drive one by one. Sawyer hauled a big cooler to the truck and Chris let down the tailgate for Sawyer to slide the cooler in. They each loaded a bag into the back of the truck.

"Hope Dad's flight comes in on time."

"Drew gonna be with him?" Chris asked as he slammed the tailgate up.

"Yeah, supposed to be."

"You don't sound thrilled." Trev laughed.

"He's a cool guy, he really is. He's just a bit rowdy. Bad influence. But we're adults and I have a mind of my own. He's not causing trouble this weekend."

"So, he and your dad flying back together too, or is Drew staying here with you for the next couple weeks before the wedding?" Jake asked, snickering as he laid fishing poles in the back.

"Screw you, Jake." Sawyer plunked Justin's bag in the truck bed. The guys had a good laugh at Sawyer's expense; Drew's too.

Marina dragged her suitcase out onto the deck and Sawyer ran up the steps to retrieve it from her, noticing that she must have been so excited to get out the door that she didn't zip it up all the way. She had packed one of his t-shirts and it was sticking out of the corner of her suitcase. He smiled, loving that she was taking something that smelled like him for comfort. On the weekends, she usually threw one on while they lounged and had coffee together before chores. He tucked it in and zipped up the bag as the first of her girlfriends pulled in and Trev showed them where to park. The guys were taking two vehicles since they all owned trucks, so the rest of the vehicles were parked alongside the barn.

"Is that Bailey Rose? Oh, my goodness, she came!" Marina was excited and ran to give her a hug. Bailey had rented a large SUV from the airport so all the girls could fit into it for the drive. The other girls pulled in soon after.

Sawyer and Chris loaded all the girls' bags into the SUV for the ladies, like the gentlemen they were. Everyone was introduced to each other.

"You lock up the house, baby?" Sawyer asked as he loaded the last bag.

"Yes, sir, I did."

"I locked the barn up. I'm paying Sabrina to take care of the horses while we're gone and she couldn't be more excited."

"That's great. She'll be fine."

"I left Doc's number, and Dave's too, in case she needs anything. She should be set though. Bob and Gladys have Whiskey, they came early this morning and picked him up while you were in the shower. They're getting an order together for booze for the reception. They offered to bartend as our wedding gift from them."

"Awesome! That's wonderful of them. They're just the sweetest. I hope you accepted, that'll be the last task checked off our list."

"I sure did. Things have fallen into place, darlin', so you relax this weekend. All is taken care of."

"We ready to go, cowboy?" Justin hollered from the passenger side of Sawyer's truck.

"Yeah, hold your horses. Gotta tell my woman goodbye." He pulled Marina close to him and held her face in his hands as she wrapped her arms around him. "I don't want to let you go," he told her.

"I don't want you to."

"This could take a while." Jake got into the truck.

Sawyer's black tank top was already hot from the sun. He wore plaid cargo shorts to match with black flip-flops. He didn't look much like a cowboy heading out for his weekend. Her sundress flowed with the breeze, wrapping slightly against his leg.

"You have no idea how much I'm going to miss you." He looked down into her eyes.

"Oh, I'll miss you just as much. This is going to be so hard being apart from you."

"It's only three days. We can do it. Have fun with the girls and relax." He moved her hair out of her face.

"I will. I hope you have fun too."

"I'll try. I'm gonna miss holding you at night."

Chris rolled his eyes and spoke up and said, "You can hold Justin."

"Man, what the hell?" Justin yelled back. The girls were cracking up.

"Nah, he'd enjoy that." Sawyer winked at Justin and blew him a convincing air smooch.

The guys laughed as Justin shook his head and mumbled, "Y'all are assholes."

"Oh my God, you guys are crazy." Savannah was amused.

"They're crazy asses but I love 'em like family." Sawyer laughed.

"Well, all of you crazy asses be careful." Marina smiled and tugged his short chin scruff.

"We will. You girls be careful too. God, I'm gonna miss you."

"I'm gonna miss you too." Marina lifted to her toes as he

passionately kissed her. He bent her backward slightly, a hand on her face and the other around the small of her back. They had a difficult time parting but had to in order for Sawyer to get to the airport. They weren't going to be more than two hours away from each other the whole weekend, but being apart for three days would be the longest they had been apart since she moved into his house.

"My oh my...he's a cowboy god!" Bailey Rose was practically drooling as she rested her chin on her hand, watching them out the car window.

"Oh, he's fine all right. Great guy too," Raquel agreed.

"Mmmhmm." Andrea stared.

"That southern accent too." Olivia fanned her face.

"I admit I'm a bit jealous," Savannah confessed.

CHAPTER 22
The Girls

O n the drive, the girls gushed over how sexy Sawyer is and how they envied that passionate goodbye kiss.

"Gosh, it's so hard to leave him." Marina kept looking up at her rearview mirror like she expected him to be chasing after her.

"I totally understand that," Bailey Rose agreed. Marina wasn't sure Bailey Rose would be able to attend, but Bailey had let Savannah know she was able to pull something off last-minute. Marina welcomed the surprise with excitement. They had been friends since middle school, closer as adults, even though they lived so far away from each other.

"The weekend is all planned out, ladies. The beach house looks awesome and all, but I hope you girls are prepared for a day of paddleboarding and beachin' it for our first day. Tomorrow, we have a yoga retreat, then Sunday morning is the spa before we head home." Savannah had planned and reserved the weekend since she agreed to be the maid of honor, although Sawyer insisted on paying for it. Marina gave her ideas and Savannah made it happen.

. . .

Paddleboarding:

When they arrived at the beach, they checked into their rental house. They hauled in their bags and situated before heading to the water for their paddleboard rentals. The water was calm so paddling was easy. They saw a pod of dolphins surfacing several yards away and admired pelicans' graceful glides above the water.

"You expect Sawyer to go all out this weekend?" Savannah asked.

"You mean like, getting wasted and being around half-naked chicks? Nah, he's not that way. He told me he didn't want all that. He said he actually didn't need a party weekend at all and he doesn't consider himself a bachelor so he hates that term. I convinced him to relax and spend time with the guys."

"He sees the guys pretty often, with the exception of his dad and Drew, but they're usually working or strumming," Becka said.

"Yeah, but they never go fishing together. I'm sure music is fun but they just need some relaxing outdoor time. They don't all go do that sort of thing together as a group. He said Drew is trouble but I know Sawyer, he'll make sure things go smoothly."

"I was gonna say we could've set you up with some hunk fun this weekend but ya don't need it." Olivia laughed.

"You're right. I'm about to marry one. He's all kinds of fun every day. I'm the luckiest girl alive."

"Yes, you are," Bailey Rose agreed.

"If we were all single and all the groomsmen were single too, we could've had a rockin' weekend all together. Those guys are all pretty good lookin'," Andrea remarked.

"They are. Mine's the hottest though." Marina proudly smiled, making the girls laugh.

They took a rest, floating on the paddleboards while their paddles lay unused at their sides.

"So, flowers all chosen and set?" Savannah asked.

"Yep. They'll be beautiful. Bartending is now set too. The guys know a live band that they used to go watch so Sawyer has hired them for the wedding and reception. I've even ordered the cake from our favorite bakery in town. I chose a photographer, another friend of mine since Andrea here is *in* the wedding, and I know the photos will turn out great. We're having our favorite deli café in town cater, the one I took you girls to that Sawyer takes me to lunch to sometimes, so food is taken care of."

"Oh, that's awesome! I love that place too." Raquel seemed excited as her legs dangled into the water. "They have a great menu, plus they'll have options for the vegans and picky eaters."

"Exactly. Easy peasy."

"So, you want us to help decorate the night before? Not sure which venue you ended up choosing," Andrea offered.

"Well, the beach would be too hot and I decided not to deal with all the sand. We thought about a lake, but mosquitos would be an issue. We ended up choosing to have it at home."

"Home?" Olivia asked.

"Yep. Well, actually over at the stables on the property. We're going to decorate the barn inside and out with white lights. It'll be climate-controlled, too. The space will be wide enough for the reception and it will have a rustic country look. It fits us both perfectly. We'll have the wedding there too, but outside. Hopefully, the stables will be finished by then and it will be spacious and beautiful. Our blueprints call for what we call 'dressing stalls' and we can use them as dressing rooms. We're thinking we could use it for a wedding venue to rent out later on but we know we want it fit for our wedding now for sure. I'm sure it will seem pretty upper-class for the horses."

"It'll be beautiful. I can't wait to see it all finished," Becka said, swishing her hands in the water.

"Me too, I'm excited. If y'all want to help decorate, that would be great. Thanks for offering."

"Yeah, absolutely. It'll be fun. The guys helping too?" Savannah asked.

"I think so. I heard Sawyer talking to Justin about it on the phone one night."

"Sweet! Eye candy!" They all laughed as they balanced to stand back up on their boards and paddle back.

They dined at a beachfront restaurant, eating with their toes digging into the sand at the picnic table. They sipped cocktails and chatted under that large umbrella, enjoying the ocean-front breeze and the fresh salty air.

"So...Marina..." Olivia's brows raised and a grin spread across her face.

"What?" Marina smiled back and took a drink.

"Oh, come on! You know what. We're all dying to know."

"Know what?" Marina moved the blue umbrella in her cocktail out of her way and took another drink.

"How's the sex?" Raquel blurted.

Marina laughed, nearly choking on her drink. "How do you think it is?" She smirked, which turned into the biggest uncontrollable smile.

"Smokin!" Bailey Rose laughed and slapped her hand on her leg.

"Oh yeah!" Marina nodded dramatically. "Seriously, he's amazing." She still couldn't keep a straight face.

"Ugh, so jealous." Bailey Rose twirled her hair.

"I mean, he's perfect in every way." Marina looked up like she was daydreaming for dramatic effect.

"I have no doubt he is at that too." Becka giggled.

"Right!" Savannah agreed.

"I was so excited to meet him in person, not gonna lie. The way he walks in those tight jeans and that southern accent. I think if he were a male stripper, his stage name would be Thunder Thighs. There is a God after all," Bailey Rose commented, blushing cheeks and all, making the girls laugh.

"It feels nice to be proud of my man and brag."

"I bet, especially after the last loser." Becka devoured the last bite of dessert on the table. Marina loved her bluntness and couldn't disagree.

"Sawyer is a world of difference. I can't wait to pledge the rest of my life to him. That man *is* my life."

"Aww, that's so sweet." Raquel squealed.

"Honestly, I can't believe nobody asked about the sex sooner." Andrea shrugged. She was no stranger to directness.

"Right!" Olivia laughed.

"I'm so glad to be sharing my special day with you ladies. You're all just the best. I love all of you." Marina held her hands out on the table and they all joined hands.

"We're thrilled that you asked us. It means the world." Savannah squeezed Marina's hand.

"It's our privilege, really. We're honored," Andrea said as she raised a glass. "To Marina on her big day and the fun we're going to have this weekend!"

"To Marina!" they cheered and their glasses tinged.

The girls walked down to the beach just outside the rental house before dusk and sprawled their beach towels out on the sand, securing the corners. They took a few fun group photos before settling in on their towels to watch the sunset.

"I usually bring a good book to the beach," Becka mentioned.

"I usually write when I'm at the beach." Raquel relaxed, stretching her legs out in front of her. Marina laid on her stomach and adjusted the cheeks of her suit bottoms.

"Sawyer and I have been to the beach a couple of times. We had a great time. And you know what's nice? He doesn't even check out other chicks! His attention is always on me, or he's overlooking the water, or free diving in the shallows. I'm still not used to that."

"I bet that does seem nice." Bailey Rose was aware of how disrespectful Derrick had been.

"I think you and I have had more beach days since you've been with Sawyer than we ever did before," Becka realized.

"Yeah, I think you're right. I'm allowed out of the house without a guilt trip," Marina said.

"I'm so glad you don't have to deal with that anymore. You have freedom," Savannah remarked.

"Thanks."

"Although, we all know you'd rather spend every second with that man." Raquel chuckled.

"Wouldn't you?" Andrea laughed. "I mean, seriously."

"I know I do, but I do love spending time with you girls. I love that I can do both. That's the way it should be. He has his music and I have my girl time, usually when the guys are rehearsing. It works out."

The sky struck brilliant sorbet colors as the sun sank below the horizon.

"Did you get him a wedding gift?" Raquel inquired.

"I did and I'm really excited about it. So, a few days before our wedding the guys will be playing at the bar, of course. I've arranged for a music producer to come scout them. Well, not really scout, but listen to them live. I sent a recording already without Sawer knowing. I hope he'll be okay with that. He's been writing his own music but he won't show me or let me listen; except for the song he sang when he proposed."

Maybe he's writing a surprise for you for your wedding gift." Becka perked up at the thought.

"Aww, that would be amazing. I think he is, actually. He said he was writing me a surprise but I didn't think about it being a wedding gift." Marina loved the thought and hoped Becka was right.

"That would be the best gift. Straight from the heart," Savannah agreed.

"You have to let us know what he does for you. I'm already dying of curiosity." Bailey Rose adjusted her adorable sunhat that wasn't really needed anymore.

"Oh, I absolutely will. Maybe we'll all find out at the same time the night of our bridal party." Marina sat up and brushed the sand off her feet.

"You ladies wanna hit the water?" Becka stood, ready to cool off.

"Sure! It's muggy." Andrea and the rest of the girls hopped up and left footprints in the sand leading down to the water.

"Watch for fins above the water, y'all!" Marina warned, alarming Bailey Rose.

The night was humid but the stars were still visible as darkness began to take over. After cooling off, they lay on their backs looking up at the sky and pointing out the constellations.

Yoga:

"Were we supposed to bring our own yoga mats? Because I didn't bring mine." Andrea asked, opening the door for the rest of the girls.

"Nope, they provide everything," Marina replied as she breezed through the door with a thankful smile.

"I'm ready to get super relaxed." Becka was excited as they approached the front desk.

The receptionist got the girls all set in the private room a few minutes before the instructor came in. She was a fit and well-conditioned woman.

A water fountain in the front and center of the room, plants everywhere, the essential oils diffusing, and the meditation music were instantly calming. The whole yoga experience was silent besides the music and the soft voice of the instructor. They stretched and held each pose just as instructed.

As an added bonus, the studio offered smoothies after their session and each of them grabbed a different flavor, swapping them around so they could each try a little of every option; most of them were pretty good, but a couple of them were total duds. Overall, they decided the adventure had been worth it as they headed to a nearby tiki bar and grill on the beach...their stomachs growled with hunger.

The reviews said they served the best mahi and ahi tuna

around. They ordered fruity tropical drinks with umbrellas and sat up at the bar to eat.

"I know this isn't the Caribbean but to me, not having traveled this far south before, it feels like a tropical vacation." Bailey Rose happily took her cocktail from the bartender.

"It's a popular vacation spot. It gets touristy in the spring and summer so beach traffic becomes a bitch," Marina explained, dipping a bite of tuna in wasabi.

"I miss being on the water like we used to back in the day, Marina. You and I would have our happy asses in the water day in and day out." Olivia reminisced.

"Me too. Those were some good times. I'm thankful for all those memories and the snorkeling trips we took. Great experiences with great friends. I will never again night snorkel though." Marina noted.

"Oh, for sure!" Olivia knew exactly what Marina was talking about. "Lobsters, barracuda, and sharks, oh my!"

"I remember the one y'all dragged me on. I'm so glad you did too because that was one hell of a trip. It was just as amazing as you claimed it would be and I made a new friend out of it," Savannah recalled, referring to Marina having taken her on a trip where she became friends with Olivia. "The food, the beach, hiking the rainforest...everything about Costa Rica, even the dry forest camp without air conditioning, was fun."

"Those showers were the coldest our bodies had ever endured. We had to check for scorpions in our beds and suitcases too. Our crazy wardrobe fashion show was epic though. There wasn't even alcohol involved, we were just crazy," Marina reminded.

"Fashion show?" Raquel insisted on more information.

"Oh my gosh, yes! Bras, jean shorts, and high heels that we bought in town were the fad that night in our bunk room. We even had a theme song."

"Ooh and there at the dry forest when we told Savannah the lizard on the trail was called a skank and she hollered to the hiking group that there was a colorful skank...oh my God we were dying!" Olivia could barely contain herself.

"You mean a skink?" Andrea asked, confused.

The three girls nodded yes but they were laughing so hard they couldn't speak. Marina actually had tears because she was laughing so hard.

"You girls suck," Savannah cackled. "That was so embarrassing."

"We're never going to let you live that down either." Marina could barely breathe from suffocating laughter.

"Some real bonding happened on that trip." Olivia calmed enough to take a bite of her nachos.

"Wish I could've seen that. Sounds hilarious." Bailey Rose sounded bummed to have missed out.

"Oh, I can picture it." Raquel reached down the bar for the salsa.

"Yep, me too." Andrea giggled.

"There's a picture somewhere..." Olivia shrugged, teasing the fact that she was in possession of it.

After they ate, they watched the sunset, laughing and telling memorable stories in umbrella chairs facing the water. They would get giggling so hard there were tears once again. The alcohol may have been a contributing factor to some extent. The stories of Marina and Savannah as kids and growing up together were precious, funny too.

"Oh my God, Savannah was a handful when she was little. One time she gave me a black eye while we sat watching a movie together. Just punched me right in the face. We fought sometimes like crazy and other times we were best friends, making up our own games to keep us entertained."

"Some things never change," Savannah said with a straight face before busting out laughing.

"Really though, we had some great times. I wish we lived closer so we could make more memories to laugh our asses off about later." Marina side hugged Savannah.

"Well this weekend can be one of them," Savannah said sweetly before adding with laughter. "I'm sure I'll do something stupid this weekend we can all laugh at before we head back home."

Andrea colorfully described the Hell she went through growing up with brothers, but it was comical.

"My brothers used to dissect frogs and stab them with sticks then throw them at me. They'd chase me all over the yard. They were such assholes. Still are. Pretty sure I'm scarred for life. I probably should've been in therapy."

"Eeww, glad I had a sister." Raquel chuckled.

They sat out there with sleepy giggles until they were almost too tired to walk back to the beach house.

Spa:

Spa morning turned out to be the ultimate relaxation.

"It's been so long since I've been to a spa," Savannah mentioned as she changed into a lush white robe in the fitting room.

"Me too. I think the time Olivia and I went to the one in Alabama at the casino was the last time I went. That place was nice, too," Marina recalled as she came out in her robe.

"This place is nicer." Olivia looked around at the metal artwork on the walls.

"I can't wait for the pedicure." Marina looked down at her feet with a grimace. "I'm in desperate need, my heels are getting rough."

"We haven't done a pedicure in a while," Becka agreed.

"The massage is what I'm needing." Savannah rubbed her own shoulder and neck.

"I get those at home." Marina teased proudly.

"Oh, I bet you do!" Raquel laughed.

"He's probably better at it than the masseuses here," Bailey Rose muttered, raising her brows.

Marina smiled and nodded. "Oh, he is, and they always lead to other things, if ya know what I mean."

Back knots from their paddleboarding exertion were kneaded out and feet were massaged with pedicures. Manicures were needed of course to match their pretty toes. There were so many nail polish colors to choose from.

"What a great idea to use essential oils as fragrance!" Andrea checked out the wooden diffuser on an entry table.

"This cucumber water is amazing too," Raquel poured the girls each a glass.

Their hair was wrapped up into white towels while relaxing with cucumbers on their eyes for a while before their facials. They all decided to take advantage of having free range of the place so onward to the sauna they proceeded.

"This sauna is really working up a sweat. Whew." Raquel wiped her face off with a hand towel.

"It feels great though. It's a good sweat. Sawyer and I need to come do this together."

"Guys in saunas...that's hot. We should've told the guys to join us," Bailey Rose said excitedly.

"That would be a hot sight, all those guys in here in just towels that could slip off at any second because they're too sweaty to keep them on," Olivia daydreamed, her words coming out slower as her daydream lingered. The girls agreed, laughing.

After speculating 'beneath the towels' in guy chat, they hit the showers to cool off. A dip in the spa pool was relaxing, the water-falls and tranquil music constrained their voices to a low volume. They experienced the whole works. The girls felt absolutely pampered. Sawyer insisted on splurging for the girls' weekend and sprang for the ultimate package. All of the girls got along great, which made the weekend even better. They all had so much in common; from taste in music to hobbies, foods, and fun things they liked to do. The car ride back was a karaoke party with windows down and the wind in their hair as they passed around snacks.

"I hope the guys got along as well as we all did this weekend. Wonder what they did besides fishing," Marina pondered out loud.

"Hopefully kept Drew out of trouble." Becka laughed, scrolling through a playlist.

They speculated how drunk the groom-to-be would end up and what shape he would be in when they returned.

CHAPTER 23

The Guys

Deep-Sea:

The guys went to a different beach farther east and chartered a deep-sea fishing boat for the day.

"I haven't done this in forever. It's nice to get back out here," Sawyer said, hoisting the cooler onto the boat. "What the hell got packed in this cooler, y'all? It's heavy as hell."

"You packed a shit-ton of water," Justin reminded.

"I packed a shit-ton of beer." Chris laughed.

"I put a pack of sports drinks in too," Jake admitted.

"Jesus, y'all should've helped lift this then."

"You've got the muscles. You'll be alright." Drew patted his shoulder, walking by with his fishing pole.

"Who's got the sunscreen?" Justin dug around in a bag they took onto the boat containing their wallets, phones, and keys.

"Sunscreen?" Sawyer asked with a wrinkled nose.

"Yeah, I packed it. There it is." He opened it up and squirted a glob in his hand then rubbed it on his arms and legs where his tank top and shorts didn't cover. He offered it to the guys but Chris was the only one who accepted.

"Why the hell not? My shoulders always burn." He smeared

some on his shoulders and the rest of the guys shook their heads. They were already tan enough; they wouldn't burn and Trev and Tom wore long-sleeved sun shirts.

The salty breeze blowing in their faces on the ride out of the bay felt refreshing as the waves slapped up against the boat's sides. The fishing boat was large, fitting all of the guys comfortably along with the captain. They packed food so they didn't have to head in till dusk if they chose. They began the day catching mainly snapper and Trev caught an impressive mahi. It was nearly three feet long and was the brightest yellow, green and blue. Justin made sure to snap a picture of Trev with the brilliant fish. Tom caught a sailfish mid-day, it thrashed about in and out of the water, proving difficult to reel in even with help from Sawyer. It took half the guys to get it up on deck once it reached deck level.

"Man, I don't know about y'all but I've worked up an appetite." Sawyer cleaned his hands off.

"Yep. Let's eat." Jake set down his pole then the others followed suit.

As they finished eating lunch out of the cooler, a pelican landed on the boat wanting bait fish.

"Got any herring in that bait, Captain?" Sawyer asked, poking his head around the doorframe of the cabin.

The captain dug one out of a cooler and handed it to Sawyer, who tossed it to the pelican then wiped his hand on his shorts. That large throat gulped it down quickly and off the bird flew, flapping its wide wingspan. The guys watched it fly away before grabbing their poles.

Sawyer tossed a line out baited with a large bait fish in hopes of catching something big. He helped Chris reel in a large grouper and Drew hollered that Sawyer's rod had a catch. Sawyer rushed back to it as Drew finished helping Chris. Jake jumped over a tackle box to help Sawyer who had a fighter on the end of his line.

"I'm grabbing the net!" Tom hollered as he rushed about the deck but the shark he reeled up wasn't going to fit in that net.

"Don't bother, Dad. We got it." Sawyer carefully lowered the shark to the deck and held it still with one hand as he straddled it and released the hook from its mouth with the other. Justin videoed and took pics more than he fished, which was great to have fun times to look back on. Sawyer got the little four-foot bull shark tossed back into the water pretty quickly. He wasted no time so it didn't stress too badly. Marina had a soft spot for sharks so Sawyer knew she would've appreciated the release.

"You caught a nice grouper! That thing is huge!" Jake helped toss it into the big fish cooler.

"Hell yeah! I'm about worn out." Chris retired his pole for the day and sat with a beer. They caught a few more snappers and decided to head in with their catches.

"Wanna stay at the beach tonight or y'all wanna grab a bite and head up to the lake house? I know a guy that owns a big condo here. He said just call if we wanna stay and he'll bring us the key." Sawyer unloaded the cooler, with Chris' help this time, onto the dock from the boat.

"I think if that condo has a grill we should stay. We can clean these fish and make our own supper tonight." Chris grunted as they lugged the cooler back toward the truck.

"I'm game for whatever." Trev shrugged.

"Stop at the liquor store on our way?" Drew pleaded with a wide grin.

Sawyer laughed and nodded, not the least bit surprised at Drew's request. "I'll call the guy for the key and we'll swing by the store. We need stuff to go with these fish anyways."

"You really plan to be cooking all weekend, son? Thought we were doing that at the lake house?" Tom mentioned, putting the tacklebox into the back of the truck.

"I don't mind cooking, Dad. Even on vacation."

"Okay. Up to you. I was planning to treat everyone to dinner tonight."

"Dad, you don't need to do that. I mean, unless you really

want to. I don't wanna rain on your parade but it's not necessary. I don't want these fish going to waste either."

"Oh, no, Sawyer. I just figured if we went out, I'd take care of the check, that's all. You paid for our flight and the boat today, the lake house, Marina's weekend, the whole nine yards. It's the least I could do."

Sawyer patted his dad on the back and said, "I appreciate that, Dad. Tell ya what...you can pay at the store when we stop. Would that make ya feel better?"

"I suppose it would." Tom and Sawyer chuckled as rods were loaded. They shopped for items they needed at the store before meeting the condo owner for the key.

Grilled fish and veggies were on the menu that night. The weather was ideal with a slight breeze so they ate at the big patio table on the balcony, overlooking the ocean. The sun was lowering to the west, a bright orange sky just above the sand dunes.

Chris dug hot peppers out of a jar and popped a few in his mouth before offering them to the guys, challenge and mischief glistening in his eyes. Jake was the only one to take him up on the offer. The others stared, waiting for a reaction because they knew they were flaming hot. Jake tried to power through for a good ten seconds before he jumped up, ran to the kitchen, spit it into the sink, and stuck his face under cold running water, rinsing his mouth.

When he could speak again, he yelled, "What the hell, dude?"

"You eat a lot of spicy shit," Sawyer told Chris, laughing.

"Nothin' an antacid won't fix." Chris shrugged.

"More like an entire bottle of antacids. I bet your burps are a lingering Hell," Drew commented, fishing the smallest one he could find out of the jar and biting into it. At least he didn't have to go rinse his face in the sink.

"Your asshole made of steel?" Jake asked, his brows down-turned as he came back out onto the patio. "Seriously, not cool, man."

"Y'all are sissies." Chris ate another.

"Ya know? We could've gone to the Florida Keys," Trev mentioned once all the laughing quieted.

"I thought about it. I figured since we only had three days, I didn't want half of it to be driving. Could've flown, I guess. Too far away from Marina though." Sawyer accepted a drink Drew handed him.

"Oh, lord, dude. Seriously?" Jake laughed and shook his head. "To be honest, I'm enjoying this break from my girlfriend. She's so clingy when we're alone."

"Hey, what if something happened and I wasn't close enough to get to her in time?" Sawyer took a sip.

"Understandable." Tom understood where Sawyer was coming from.

"It's sweet that you worry about her so much." Justin popped open a beer.

"Can't help it, but I'm sure she's fine. I hope she's having a great time." Sawyer swirled his whiskey before gulping it.

"Anybody else whooped? Seriously, I am exhausted. I think I'm gonna shower and go to bed." Chris got up from the patio table and scooched in his chair. It was barely dark.

"Yeah, that sun out on the water did me in. Probably should've drank more water than beer," Drew agreed.

"You gotta call your woman yet, son?" Tom asked, getting up from the table.

"Nah, we agreed to just have friend time the whole weekend, so I won't bother her."

"It's killin' ya, isn't it?" Jake laughed.

"Yep," Sawyer sat back in his chair, relaxed, and chugged the rest of his whiskey, "Y'all just let me know when the shower is free."

Lake House:

The next morning, the guys loaded up and drove two hours back north to the lake house Sawyer had rented.

"Wow, this view is awesome. You guys wanna get the canoes out on the water?" Jake still held his fishing gear as he looked out the French doors at the lakefront view.

"Sure! I'm up for fishing again." Justin plopped his bag down in a bedroom doorway.

"We have an odd number so I'll take the beer and fish coolers in mine," Drew volunteered.

"Deal." Chris laughed, popping open another beer.

They made their way out the back door, barely bothering to drop their bags first, and fished from the canoes for a couple of hours. The water was a calm, quiet flow and they caught a few keepers, enough for them to make a meal out of, then went back to shore to clean the fish for meal prep.

"Grillin' these zucchinis too?" Justin asked as he dug through the fridge.

"Hell, yeah." Sawyer prepped the filets in foil with butter and seasoning then got olive oil, salt, and pepper from the cabinet for the veggies. "The darker they get, the better they taste. Wanna start up the grill, Dad?"

"Sure thing."

They gathered at the picnic table out back of the lake house facing the water.

"Man, this is a great view. I could get used to eating dinner at a place like this every night," Drew said before Chris asked him to pass the veggies.

"Yeah, it's nice being out on the water. Mosquitoes might carry our asses away before dark though." Jake stood to fetch the salt and pepper from the center of the table.

"This is the perfect environment for song writing. Kinda gets your head in the game." Trev tossed the idea to Sawyer and the guys.

"Maybe we can come up with some ideas for a song before the weekend is over," Sawyer told him.

After their mid-day dinner of more fish, joking, storytelling, and talking music, they rested in lawn chairs down by the water's edge at the bottom of the hill. Bare feet nestled in the sand, lawn chairs on the grassy edge, shirtless, wearing just shorts with a beer in their hand.

"This is the life, man. Beats going to work anyday." Drew twisted the cap of a beer bottle.

"Ya just gotta like what ya do for work. Work, no matter what kind it is, will get stressful but having a job you don't really need a break from...well that's just the way to do it," Sawyer said and Tom agreed.

It was a hot, muggy day so they'd dip in the water every so often. There was a floating dock several yards out. The guys were doing flips off it and cannonballing into the refreshing water, competing for the biggest splash. The echoes from their hollering and splashes rang wide. They were relaxing, floating in shallow water when a boat slowly moved through just outside of the no-wake zone. Sawyer walked out of the water and sat back down in his lawn chair all wet, aviator glasses shielding his eyes, water dripping down his tan skin. Jake followed him out slowly, noticing the boat that the guys were watching.

"Who's this?" he asked, walking backward then stopped. It turned around in the no-wake zone and came up to the dock slowly as the engine shut off. There were three girls aboard, young, probably early twenties. They all wore bikinis and waved at the guys but didn't get off the boat.

"Ladies." Drew nodded, greeting them as he walked down the creaking dock toward them. He was all about it.

"You boys looking to have a good time?" one girl asked loudly as she flipped her straight, blonde hair behind her shoulder.

Sawyer shook his head no with a straight face and Jake laughed at his reaction. There would be no temptation on Sawyer's part. There was no chance he wouldn't be on his best behavior.

Trev told the girls, "Thanks anyways, ladies but we're having a guys' weekend. Besides, we're all spoken for."

"No girls allowed!" Tom waved and smiled politely. Jake

joined Sawyer up at the chairs and dug through the cooler of ice so loudly for a beer that they couldn't hear what was being said down at the dock temporarily.

"Who's the hottie in the chair with the glasses?" the brunette asked Chris, who was in the water near the dock.

"That there is the groom-to-be."

"Y'all need some bachelor party entertainment?" she asked, dancing around.

Drew had a begging look on his face when he looked over at Chris. Drew and Justin were the only single guys.

"We're good, ladies, but thanks for the offer." Justin waved and walked to the beach to join Sawyer and Jake.

"What do *they* want?" Sawyer asked.

"Apparently, you." Justin laughed.

Sawyer took down his glasses and scowled at Justin.

"Well, I don't want them. Not to be rude, but they need to go." He put his glasses back on and tipped his head back.

Jake motioned to Chris, who was still in the water, to get the girls gone. Chris nodded and briefly spoke to the girls without the guys on shore able to hear. The boat engine started back up and the girls headed away from the dock, smiling and waving as Drew aided in giving it a good shove.

"Damn, we could've had some fun!" Drew walked back along the dock toward the guys on shore.

"I'm cool with just relaxing with y'all. Don't need other females around. This is a guy's weekend. Besides, the only female I wanna look at and have fun with is Marina."

"Aww. Dude, you sound so sappy," Drew teased Sawyer as he dried off with a towel.

"Don't care." Sawyer's eyebrows raised above the rim of his sunglasses as he shrugged a shoulder. Drew raised his hands, surrendering to Sawyer's wishes.

The other guys joined from the water as Jake and Tom started a bonfire and as the sun sank behind the trees across the lake, leaving streaks of orange across the sky.

Drew plopped into a chair and asked, "So, Cuz, when do I get to meet this woman that's got you all down on solid ground?"

"Hopefully she'll be back when we get back and I'll introduce y'all before I take y'all to the airport the next morning."

"Sweet. I can't be letting my cuz marry a woman I've never met. She must be real special."

"Oh, she is." Sawyer smirked and lifted his sunglasses to rest upon his head.

"I gotta say, he's a lucky man," Jake spoke up.

"Yeah?" Drew questioned, tipping his head to the side.

Jake nodded and Justin grinned then said, "She's not just smokin' hot but she's wonderful. She's perfect for Sawyer."

"Thanks, guys." Sawyer rested his arms behind his head, smiling.

"So, if y'all break up, I can—" Justin started but was interrupted by Sawyer.

"Don't even finish that sentence." He glared to get his point across but couldn't keep a straight face. "She really is perfect though."

"Actually, we all like her. We approve," Chris agreed. "Shoulda brought your guitar, Sawyer. I can drum on anything with sticks."

They shared about old times as they sat around the fire, passing a couple of moonshine jars around. Their laughter echoed across the lake as crickets and frogs competed for a voice.

Bar Bash:

The next morning was slightly cooler due to a short-lived storm during the night. The guys made breakfast and challenged each other to cornhole. They set up two sets then the guys who sat out to keep score would play the winners. All the guys were good sports, shaking hands or fist bumping, nobody was too competitive, just wanted to have fun. They even lost track of score in their last game.

"I don't know about y'all but I feel like I got some sun this weekend. I better stick to drinking water today." Chris checked out his red shoulders that his tank top didn't cover. "Glad I put that sunscreen on too. Man, I'd be a lobster. I slept great though. Those bunks are pretty comfy."

Sawyer, Justin, and Tom just glared at him.

"Glad somebody got to sleep," Tom mumbled. The four of them had shared one bedroom while the others shared the other room.

"You snored like a son of a bitch all night." Sawyer looked tired even getting the words out.

"Really? I didn't hear a damn thing." Chris shrugged.

"It was probably all those damn peppers trying to escape out his throat," Justin teased.

"Might wanna stay in the shade more, too." Trev laughed.

"Yeah, well, it must be nice to not have to worry about burnin'." Chris readjusted his man-bun.

"What do ya mean?" Trev asked with a crooked brow.

"You don't burn, dude. You're half black, you're already pretty dark."

"Doesn't mean I can't burn. I was smart and wore a sun shirt on the boat, you dumbass. That's where you screwed up." Trev shook his head, throwing a stick at Chris which he dodged, making the guys chuckle.

"This cowboy doesn't burn either." Justin patted Sawyer's shoulder as he handed him the cornhole bags.

"His tan ass is always shirtless. You know, Sawyer, you're gonna look like the leather on a saddle twenty years from now," Chris joked.

Sawyer threw his head back, laughing a loud roar. "You're a dick, Chris." He tossed a bag and landed it on the board.

"I'm sure you don't wanna sound like leather when she's ridin' you," Chris added.

"Damn!" Jake shouted before tossing.

"Maybe I oughta quit layin' out by the pool naked then." Sawyer tossed a bag, landing it in the hole.

"Remind me to call before stopping over in the summer," Trev joked.

"I'm not shy, either." Sawyer did a quick raise of his brow then laughed.

"We know." Chris laughed with his head down.

Justin cleared his throat and asked, "So, Marina lay out there naked too?"

Sawyer tossed a crappy throw, totally missing the board as he whipped his head around and scowled at Justin. "Dude."

"Hey, can't blame the dude for askin'." Drew laughed. "I really gotta see this chick. When we pull in, one of y'all point her out."

"You'll know why he's missin' her so badly. She's on fire!" Jake exclaimed.

"I wouldn't be goin' and flirtin' with her though," Trev warned.

"I'm getting hungry, boys. What's for lunch today?" Tom handed the bags over to Drew.

"I think I'm all seafood spent. How about burgers or something?" Sawyer fist-bumped Jake on a good game before plopping the bags down on the board.

"There's a good burger joint here on the other side of the lake. They have Cajun fries too," Justin noted.

"Sold!" Sawyer grabbed his white tank top from the back of a lawn chair and put it on as the guys stood there, confused and still holding the cornhole bags.

"I guess we're going now." Tom laughed. "When my son is ready to eat, he's ready to eat now."

The guys loaded up in the trucks and Justin navigated them along an old paved path leading into the woods behind the lake.

The lakeside burger joint was a great spot. It was an old rustic place in the shade. Big live oaks draped with hanging moss stood near the water's edge. The wood siding on the little restaurant was tainted green along the bottom and it looked to be needing an updated roof.

"I used to go to summer camp up here. Good times." Justin reached across the picnic table for one of Sawyer's fries.

"Summer camp, huh? Like kayaking and boy scout stuff?" Sawyer asked.

"Yeah, I had a blast. This place has the best ice cream, too. Homemade."

"No shit? We might need to try it." Sawyer leaned back, already feeling full.

"It's happening." Chris went back in to order some for all of them.

The guys talked about the wedding and plans for the honeymoon.

"We decided to go to two places for our honeymoon," Sawyer said, eyeing the ice cream Chris was balancing on his way back to the table.

"So two destinations? Wow! That's gonna be a blast." Jake was excited for them.

"Nice! Where'd y'all choose to go?" Tom asked, helping Chris pass around the ice cream.

"Bora Bora and the Maldives. I'm so excited." Sawyer nodded with a smile as he took ice cream from Chris.

"Damn! I wanna go." Trev licked the side of his ice cream bowl where it was dripping.

"No shit, me too. I'm your office bitch. Don't I get a vacation?" Justin asked, his ice cream half gone already.

"If you went on vacation, I wouldn't have a bitch in the office," Sawyer said, making everyone laugh.

They reminisced about old times when Drew used to do stupid stuff and get Sawyer in trouble.

"Hey, Sawyer, remember that time your mom made pumpkin pies and said we couldn't eat them until after we cleaned our plates during Thanksgiving dinner? Then you got in trouble for a half eaten slice but you blamed the dog and it was actually me. Your mom was so pissed."

"I remember, Drew. I didn't get any pie the whole Thanksgiving break because of that."

"Your mom ever find out it was me out there cow tippin' that night, not you?"

"No, she didn't. I got in trouble for it though, she thought I was lying."

"She ever find out it was me who went to the door naked when the church folk rang the doorbell at your house on Easter?"

Sawyer shook his head as the guys cracked up.

"She was forever pissed about the whole train track ordeal. I was grounded for a month." Sawyer pointed a finger at Drew from across the table.

"What happened at the tracks?" Chris was dying to know.

"Drew hoarded firecrackers and fireworks from the Fourth of July and set them off on the tracks as the train was coming through. Scared the shit out of that poor engineer. I was there but didn't stop him." Sawyer chugged water.

"Oh, geez." Tom dropped his head.

"You did try." Drew shrugged and snickered.

"A lot of good it did. You never listened to me. That engineer called the cops and the cops came out to the house. Mom hunted us down as we were coming back through the woods. She whooped my ass because you said I did it. The time you stole my neighbor's car to go meet a girl at the convenience store at midnight was a memorable one."

"I was only gone a couple of hours. I returned the car so I was just borrowing it, technically."

"I was late-night fishing down at the lake with a friend so I got blamed for that, just so ya know."

"I mean...I borrowed a car before and returned it...without the person's knowledge," Chris laughed.

"Were you only fourteen?" Sawyer asked, his arms crossed.

"Oh, shit." Chris wore a surprised look on his face.

Tom was now realizing half of the things Sawyer got in trouble for as a teenager were Drew's doing.

"Gosh, son, I didn't realize it was Drew who did all that. I'm so sorry." Tom couldn't help but chuckle after apologizing. Sawyer nodded and they all had a good laugh while eating the best ice cream around.

They went back to the lake house and cleaned up, packed all their stuff, and loaded the trucks.

"We passed a couple of bars in town earlier. What's a bachelor weekend without hitting at least one?" Drew tried convincing.

"Any of 'em have live music?" Chris asked, his arm resting up on the truck bed.

"You plan to play? We didn't bring our instruments," Trev reminded him.

"Nah, but listening gives us something to do." Chris shrugged.

"What do ya say, Sawyer?" Drew asked.

"I guess we could grab a beer and listen to some music. I don't wanna get back too late though. I wanna see Marina before she goes to bed."

"It's not like you wouldn't wake her up," Jake joked.

"True." Sawyer smirked.

The guys changed into jeans, t-shirts, their cowboy hats and boots then went into town. They jammed the whole way there.

Upon entering the bar Drew chose, he bumped elbows with Justin and told him Sawyer had a surprise coming. Justin seemed confused but shrugged it off. He assumed maybe the band was the surprise. The guys got drinks up at the bar and sat at a big round table as the band started up.

"It's weird sitting on this side." Sawyer scooched his chair in.

"Yeah, it is," Trev agreed, looking at the stage.

A few minutes in, Chris said, "They're not bad." He nodded, pleasantly surprised, and the guys agreed.

The place was low-lit with neon lights everywhere and old rusty tin signs and license plates hanging on the walls. It wasn't very busy, either.

"We hear there's a groom-to-be in the house tonight," the singer said into the microphone.

Sawyer looked around but the singer pointed to him. He looked confused, looking around at the guys, then over at Drew, remembering it was Drew's idea to go to that bar in particular.

Justin got his phone out of his back pocket and mumbled, "Oh shit."

"What did you do?" Sawyer asked sternly, his brows turned in, staring at Drew.

Drew had a smart-ass grin across his face when, from the back room came a brunette in skimpy lingerie, heels, and a garter belt as the band resumed playing.

Sawyer turned his head away, shaking it. "Drew, I'm gonna kill you."

"Come on, Sawyer. It's a bachelor party!" He stood and yelled, "Yee-Haw!"

The guys all looked at each other, wondering if they should intervene.

She walked around behind Sawyer, who wore a scowl on his face, and grabbed his hat to put it on her own head. Without looking at her, he snatched it back and said, "Nope." He set it on the table and snarled at his cousin, "Drew, get her gone."

His whiskey burned on the way down and he slammed the glass down on the table.

She was dancing around provocatively at their table and glided a hand over Sawyer's shoulder. He cringed and told Drew, "This isn't cool. You knew I didn't want this."

"Oh, lighten up. Have some fun."

"I was, with you guys. Now I'm pissed off." He stood and turned around to the woman who was dancing seductively with her back to him. Jake's chair scooched back as he stood.

"Sorry, ma'am but I don't want this kind of party, so you'll need to go or we will." Sawyer put his hat on that he had just snatched off the table and adjusted it on his head. As he went to step away, she turned around in front of him and Sawyer's eyes grew large. He was instantly fuming.

"Gabby? You gotta be fucking kidding me!" He turned back toward the table and nodded for the guys to follow.

"You do this shit on purpose?" He got in Drew's face.

"What? Yeah, I hired her. You know her?"

"She's my ex!" Sawyer shouted at him then marched to the exit door. The guys were all speechless.

"Seriously?" Drew was unaware and it was obvious to the guys that hiring her in particular wasn't intentional.

"Oh, shit. This ain't cool, man." Trev got up and scooched his seat in. The rest of the guys followed in a rush, not bothering with the chairs.

Drew apologized to Gabby before catching up. Sawyer was waiting for him outside, kicking up dirt.

"Dude, I tried to do something fun and exciting for you. Why are you so pissed?" Drew shouted.

"I knew you coming here would be trouble."

"To the bar?"

"Here, to Florida, for the wedding. Trouble doesn't just follow you, Drew, you create it."

"What the hell?"

"I respect Marina. She wouldn't want this and I didn't want or need it either. I told y'all that. This may be how you roll but it's not how I roll. Everything was going great; we had a great weekend and everyone got along just fine. Then you had to go and fuck it all up."

"Whoa, Sawyer, calm down." Jake grabbed Sawyer's arm but Sawyer jerked it away.

"I've never seen you this pissed before, dude." Drew was starting to realize how serious Sawyer was.

"I have!" Jake nodded.

Sawyer let out a few huffs as he paced near his truck. Tom went and checked on him and told him to cool off in the truck in the a.c. for a few minutes.

Tom came back over to the guys and told Drew to ride back with Chris then said, "I understand what you were trying to do, Drew, but you should've run this by the rest of us before setting it up. We would've talked you out of it."

"Yeah, I guess I should've. I didn't know he'd get this mad."

"Sawyer's a one-lady kind of man. Not to mention the fact that the chick you hired is his ex that wants him back," Justin explained.

"Oh...shit."

"Poor Sawyer didn't even get to get wasted." Trev laughed then stopped with pursed lips when everyone looked at him, unamused.

"I think it's time we call it a night. It's getting dark and he'd rather not be too late getting back. Don't wanna keep poking the bear," Tom suggested. Jake was usually good at calming Sawyer down so he and Justin and Tom rode with Sawyer.

"I think he feels bad." Tom tried to smooth it over for Drew once they got in the truck. Sawyer didn't say a word.

"He probably just wanted to take part in the whole party planning thing or put a fun spin on the end of the weekend. You said he's like that so it's just Drew being Drew," Justin added passively.

Still, Sawyer said nothing. He tossed his hat up onto the dash and rubbed his chin.

"You gonna tell Marina?" Jake asked after several moments of silence.

"Yep."

"Well, that's good. I hope it goes smoothly."

"I guess we'll find out, won't we? We don't keep things from each other. Dad, I need Drew to keep his big mouth shut till I can tell her."

"I'll let him know not to say anything. You want him and me to stay at a hotel tonight, son?"

"No, Dad. Just keep him away from me till we leave for the airport in the morning."

"He was trying to have harmless fun," Tom said.

"Harmless? To whom, him? He might have just cost me the love of my life. If she doesn't understand that I didn't want this, I'll never forgive him."

"He's your cousin," Tom reminded.

"I don't give a shit."

It was a quiet ride the rest of the way home.

CHAPTER 24

Damage Control

T he girls had returned home and unloaded their bags before the guys pulled in. Sawyer's truck pulled in first. The guys helped the girls load bags into their vehicles before unloading their own. The exterior barn lights lit up the drive. Sawyer scooped Marina up in the most romantic embrace; as if they had been apart for months or years instead of a few short days.

When their lips finally parted, he said in a deep voice, "God, I missed you."

She lay a hand upon the side of his face, staring into those glacier-blue eyes, and said, "That was the hardest three days of my life being away from you."

"We tried to keep her occupied." Raquel snickered.

"It was really hard for me too, baby." He swept her hair out of her face. "I'm so happy to have you back in my arms."

"There's no place I'd rather be."

They looked at each other as light illuminated them. The rest of the guys pulled into the driveway in Chris's truck.

"What's Chris pointing at?" Marina asked, watching the guys park.

"I don't know. Maybe he's pointing you out to Drew."

"Hey, Drew, give them a sec." Chris halted Drew so Sawyer and Marina could greet each other. The guys unloaded the truck in the meantime.

"Did you guys have fun?" Marina asked, feeling down Sawyer's chest slowly.

"We did."

"Some of us tried more than others," Drew said as he cautiously walked by with his bag to take it to the house. That smartass grin made Sawyer even more furious.

Sawyer could've thrown daggers with the glare he gave Drew, his eyes on his cousin until he reached the steps to the house. Tom hung his head. It was as if Drew hadn't heard a word he'd said.

"What was that about?" Marina asked, but Sawyer just shook his head, blowing it off. "I sense tension. Everything ok?"

"It will be. All is good, baby. Nothin' to worry about." He kissed her forehead. "You girls have a good time?"

"We did. It was really relaxing. I'm glad to be home with you though."

"Mmm, me too." He kissed her again before nodding to the ladies and taking Marina's bag to the porch.

"It's getting late, we should be going." Savannah gave Marina a hug and the rest of the ladies followed suit.

"You girls sure y'all don't want to stay?" Marina asked.

"You two need some time together and y'all already have guests." Andrea threw a quick floppy wave, politely dismissing Marina's invite.

The guys said goodbye before heading out and Tom and Drew were already in the house by the time Sawyer and Marina made it inside. They were having a quiet conversation in the kitchen. Their conversation cut off when Sawyer came into the room.

"I'm sure you two are looking forward to some alone time, so Drew and I are gonna settle in. Guest room ready?" Tom asked in an attempt to lure Drew away from Sawyer.

"It should be good to go, Dad."

Drew approached Marina and told her, "You have the most beautiful eyes."

"Thank you. I like you already."

"Sawyer speaks so highly of you. He missed you like crazy and I can see why."

Marina looked over at Sawyer, who stared at Drew, unamused at his flirting and ass-kissing attempts.

"That's so kind of you, Drew." She flashed a charming smile.

"Sawyer and the guys weren't exaggerating, you're stunning." He smiled a sly flirty smile and Sawyer scowled and rolled his eyes, tongue in cheek. He knew Drew was trying to irritate him.

"Aww, that's sweet, thank you." Then she turned to Sawyer. "Oh, you guys..." She shied a smile, blushing.

"You trying to earn brownie points or get your ass kicked?" Tom asked Drew as he nodded for him to go to the guest room instead of provoking Sawyer.

"It's a pleasure to meet you, Marina." Drew shook her hand.

"The pleasure is all mine." She politely smiled.

"I believe you guys should be set. I'm going to take a shower and settle in myself. Help yourselves to whatever you need. Let me know if y'all need anything, just knock first," Sawyer offered as he took Marina by the hand and said goodnight to Tom and Drew then led her to their room. He kicked the door and, as it was closing, took hold of her, kissing her almost aggressively.

The next morning, Sawyer and Marina woke first. Sawyer threw on a pair of workout shorts as Marina straightened the straps on the sundress that she had pulled on over her head. They quietly made their way to the kitchen to start coffee.

"It's strange not tripping over Whiskey the last few days," Marina whispered as she reached for mugs. Sawyer chuckled in agreement and she poured two cups, handing one to him as Tom came out of the guest room, closing the door behind him.

"Morning, Dad."

"Morning, you two. Y'all are up earlier than I thought you'd be."

"Sawyer's always up early." She wrapped one arm around him from behind as she held her coffee with the other hand. His hand held hers against his stomach as he drank his coffee.

"Coffee?" Marina offered.

"Of course. I'll get it, you two look cozy." Tom smiled.

"Drew sleeping still?" Sawyer asked nonchalantly.

"He is. I think he had a few too many beers yesterday."

"Yeah, he should sleep it off then." Sawyer was starting to feel nervous about Drew saying something to Marina before he would get a chance to in private. He'd wanted that first night back with Marina to be drama-free.

"You guys hungry? I can make breakfast." Marina opened the fridge and took out the eggs.

"Sure. I'll cook with you." Sawyer snuck a kiss onto her neck. She loved it when he did that.

"I'm so glad you two love birds are tying the knot. Your mama is just as happy about it too."

"Aww that's so sweet, Tom." Marina gave him a hug as he leaned against the counter. Sawyer's mood changed slightly when Drew came out of the room and entered the kitchen from the hall. In fact, Sawyer turned away, rolling his eyes.

"Good morning," Marina greeted with a smile.

"Mornin'." Drew rubbed his eyes, trying to wake up. Tom poured Drew a cup of coffee, trying to keep out of the way of the chefs.

"Can I help with anything?" Tom asked as Drew went over and sat at the table.

"Nah, Dad, we got it. Thanks though." Sawyer cracked open an egg and dropped it into the heating pan.

Tom joined Drew at the table, coffee in hand.

As they all ate at the table together, they chatted about what they did over the weekend and the good food they ate.

Before they were finished eating, Drew asked Sawyer, "You get that lap dance last night after all?"

Marina smiled until she looked over at Sawyer, who had stopped chewing and was staring across the table at Drew.

"Babe, it's ok. It was to be expected that we wouldn't be able to keep our hands off each other last night." Marina blew it off.

"Drew, why don't you and I clear the table and clean up since they did the cookin'?" Tom stood and put a hand on Drew's shoulder.

Sawyer's heart was racing and his nostrils were flaring. Marina sat drinking her coffee, one knee up in her chair and skirt pulled down, facing Sawyer.

"Babe. You okay?" She laid a hand on his arm.

He turned to her. "I'm good." He kissed her forehead. "It's just disrespectful to talk about you that way," he said softly. She had no idea he was capable of harboring this kind of heated anger.

"Y'all are guys. As long as you're bragging and not bitching, I'm okay with it." She smiled.

"Oh, baby, there's absolutely nothing to bitch about. No doubt you're brag-worthy. I just don't wanna share our intimacy with anyone, ya know? It's between us." He rubbed her knee.

"You're too sweet. Such a gentleman." She leaned in for a kiss on his lips. "But just so ya know, when the girls asked how the sex is, I didn't downplay it," she whispered.

He laughed, "I don't mind *you* talking and bragging."

"Good." She bit her lip, which made him laugh again. "I better help them." She set her mug on the table and put her leg down.

"Nah, you sit your pretty self right there. I got it." He went to the kitchen to help the guys clean up.

"Yeah, you've got quite the gentleman all right." Drew stepped to the side to let Sawyer in by the sink to wash a plate off.

"I sure do," she agreed as she went into the other room.

Sawyer watched her go out then pushed Drew's shoulder and said in a low voice, "You better keep your big mouth shut if you know what's good for you."

"What?" Drew shrugged.

"I'll tell her myself about you hiring that stripper."

"You haven't yet, obviously."

"No, I didn't. I didn't want drama while y'all were here. I wanted to enjoy last night with her in case it caused an argument. Stop instigating."

"I think he's exaggerating," Drew told Tom, as if Sawyer wasn't standing right in front of him.

"Well, it's not your relationship so that's not your call to make," Tom said. "There's no reason to upset her. Maybe you shouldn't tell her," Tom added, looking at Sawyer.

"Oh, I'll tell her. I don't know how she'll react when I do, but I don't want to cause a scene in front of people. So, rein it in, Drew. Got it?"

"Okay, okay." Drew shrugged as Tom cleared his throat. Sawyer turned to see Marina in the doorway.

"Um...what time did you say y'all need to leave for the airport?" Marina asked, noticeably upset. She looked at Sawyer with disappointment in her eyes, her body feeling a little shaky, and the lump in her throat trying to consume her.

"Soon. You guys packed up?"

"Pretty much. I'll shower real quick." Tom quickly gathered his clothes in the guest room before heading to the shower.

Marina headed to the front door, Sawyer following her.

"I'm going out to do chores." Marina slid her shoes on by the door as Sawyer stood near her.

"I'll help you."

"No, it's okay. You shouldn't get dirty before going to the airport. Send your dad out for a hug before you leave?" Her fingers fumbled trying to tie her laces.

"Of course." He waited for a hug as she stood.

"Excuse me." Marina darted out the door and down the steps, not looking at him.

Sawyer blew out a huff and hit the doorway with his hand as she headed to the barn. He could tell she had heard something he was hoping she hadn't.

Tom found Marina leading Legend out to pasture as they were about to leave. He gave her a hug then she waved back at Drew, who was putting their bags in the truck.

Sawyer came out to tell her bye as Tom headed back to the truck. Marina closed the gate after releasing Legend.

"I'll be back soon, baby." He wrapped his arms around her and kissed her forehead but she couldn't look up at him. She barely hugged him back; her arms were slightly loose. He looked down at her and tipped her chin up.

"Hey, darlin', look at me."

She did, very briefly, before looking away again, tears welling in her eyes. He could see her heart breaking.

"I'd like to talk with you when I return."

She put her head down and nodded.

"I love you."

"I love you too." She held back the suffocating throat lump.

He was gone about an hour and when he returned, Whiskey in tow, her car was gone.

"Marina?" he hollered, entering the house. Whiskey ran inside, almost tripping him as he dropped his keys on the end table. His boots clunked the wood floor as he was on a mission to find her. Her purse was gone and their bedroom closet door was open, her bathroom sink toiletries and makeup were gone. He started to panic as he quickly searched the house; she wasn't there. He swiped his keys off the end table and called for Whiskey to follow him out the door. He was in such a rush, Whiskey almost accidentally got shut in the door. Maybe she went to the property. But why would she need to take her makeup?

"Fuck!" He slammed his truck door shut and drove over to the stables but her car wasn't there either. He paced, dirt stirring around him, debating on whether he should call her. He did. He needed to know where she was. She didn't answer, the call going straight to her voicemail. He was in full panic mode by this point. His heart was palpitating and he felt like his guts were being torn from his stomach. Whiskey jumped up at him, wanting to play.

He picked him up, his collar tag jingling, and asked, "What are we gonna do? Hmm? Where is she?" Whiskey whined with his ears perked and fluffy head tilted.

"This can't be happening." He and Whiskey got back into the truck and went home in case she came back. He called Bob and Gladys but they hadn't seen her. He rummaged through the office desk paperwork where he remembered her leaving her girlfriends' numbers in case he ever needed to get ahold of her and couldn't reach her on her phone. He found it but stared at it, his phone in his hand. He didn't want to invade her space if it was space that she needed but he had to make sure she was okay. He sat at the desk rubbing his face, taking deep breaths, running his fingers through his hair. He left the list of numbers with addresses on the top of his desk. His phone rang and, for a split-second, Sawyer thought it might be Marina. He frantically shuffled papers to find his phone and sighed when he saw the number.

"Hey, Dad," he answered.

"Hey, son. Just wanted to let you know we landed home safe and sound. I also wanted to say thank you for a fun weekend. It was great spending quality time with you. The guys too, of course."

"Wow, I guess that *was* a short flight. Glad you made it home safe, Dad. Thank you for coming along. I'm glad you did."

"You and Marina have a chat?"

"No. She's not here."

"Where'd she go?"

"I don't know but I'm worried. She packed a bag. I can't find her and she won't answer her phone."

"Oh, son, I'm so sorry." Tom sounded genuinely upset for Sawyer.

"I'm so pissed at Drew."

"I know you are. You handled him well this morning."

"Yeah, well, I wouldn't be right now if he were here."

"I know. Did you leave her a voicemail?"

"No. Should I call the girls?"

"I wouldn't. Let her cool down. Leave a voicemail and I'm sure she'll call you back."

"We've never had an argument or disagreement before. If I could just explain to her that nothing happened...I just need her to hear me out."

"She will, she will. Just give her some space. She'll be missing you and won't stay gone long."

"I hope you're right."

"Me too, son."

CHAPTER 25

Rock Bottom

Marina didn't return home that night. Sawyer lay on the bed on his back, staring at the swirling ceiling fan, arms up behind his head. His eyes would release a tear here and there, leaving a wet puddle on the silk pillowcase. He didn't bother wiping them away. He didn't sleep a wink, not even dozing off. Whiskey slept down on the floor on his doggy bed, dreaming and kicking. Sawyer would look at his phone once in a while, but no messages. He was feeling all emotions at once, angry at Drew, sad Marina had left, worried she wouldn't come back, and panicked because he hadn't had a chance to explain. He felt the urgent desperation to make things right. It was four a.m. and he decided to try calling her again. No answer, so he left a voicemail.

"Marina, baby. I understand you're upset right now, and rightfully so. Trust me, I am too. If you could just call me back so I know you're okay, I'd appreciate it. I don't mind giving you space but I'd really like a chance to explain what you heard. Please? I love you."

She had watched his number come up on her phone. She couldn't sleep either. She listened to the voicemail just minutes after he left it. Tears flowed down her cheeks again, her lashes soaked and sticking together.

Sawyer spent the day with the horses. He went to Dave's to work with the wild paint stallion Dave bought at the auction. It was a way for Sawyer to get out some frustration. He thought it would be a good distraction, but as he lunged the horse he kept feeling choked up. He got bucked off while saddle training and almost landed in the dirt because his head just wasn't in the game. He barely landed on his feet, scuffing dirt with his boots as he caught himself.

The band came over to rehearse that evening and they couldn't help but notice four empty beer bottles on the kitchen counter, one tipped over, as they made their way through to the music room. Sawyer would stop playing mid-song to check his phone. The guys pitied him, it was obviously killing him inside.

"Nothing yet?" Chris asked the fifth time Sawyer checked his phone.

"No. Sorry."

"You don't have to apologize, dude." Trev patted Sawyer on the shoulder as he left the music room to go get beers for them.

"Need a break?" Jake asked, setting his guitar down.

"I don't know." Sawyer rubbed his forehead with his palm.

Trev brought a beer in for each of them and handed them out. Sawyer chugged his within seconds then stood and said, "I'm gonna need something stronger." He left the room without another word.

The guys all looked at each other, worried. He came back in with a jar of pecan moonshine in one hand and a tall glass of whiskey in the other.

"Dude, you didn't drink that much all weekend," Chris pointed out, slightly exaggerating.

"Didn't have a good reason to. Until she hears me out, I don't wanna feel anything."

"You're gonna be so jacked up tonight." Trev laughed.

Chris elbowed him and shook his head.

"You want us to stop your binge drinking or just let ya regret it when you're puking your guts out later?" Jake asked as he picked his guitar back up. Sawyer just looked up at him as he set his guitar on his leg.

"Okay." Jake raised his brows.

"Hey this list of songs you sent us to practice tonight...we playing these at the bar Friday night?" Chris asked, scrolling through the list on his phone.

"Yep."

"You don't plan on her calling before then?"

"I don't know."

"Fifty bucks says he'll be drunk in the bathtub tonight," Trev muttered to Chris out of the corner of his mouth.

"I'll take that bet," Chris muttered back.

Sawyer did, in fact, get drunk that night. So much so that he fell asleep in the barn, sitting, leaning his back up against Tango, who was laying in his stall in the straw. Trev came over to check on him bright and early. After checking inside the house, he found him in the barn. He snapped a pic then started chores before waking him by accident. Sawyer heard the faucet turn on just outside of the barn. He turned the coffee pot on but it didn't play music like usual. He whacked the side of it with his hand and it played *Making Memories of Us* by Keith Urban. "Oh, great." He rolled his eyes and leaned against the doorway, waiting for the coffee to brew. He heard Trev around the corner so went outside, shielding his eyes from the sun with his forearm.

"You startled me." He squinted.

"Sorry, I didn't mean to wake ya."

"What are you doing' here?"

"Thought I'd check in on ya before heading over to the property. You Tango's new stablemate?" He laughed.

"He was nice enough to share his space last night. I probably vented to him too." Sawyer chuckled as he stretched.

"How you feelin'?"

"Like Hell."

"I figured. Are you able to be around power tools safely today?"

"I guess we'll find out. I need somethin' for this headache."

"There's a bottle of painkillers on top of the donut box in the barn. Pour ya some coffee too."

"Aww, you're such a sweetie. I didn't even notice the donuts." Sawyer gave him a hug and kissed the side of his head.

"Easy, buddy, I'm not sharing my stall with ya."

Sawyer laughed, walking back into the barn. He found a barn note from Marina next to the donuts that read "I just need some time alone" with a heart.

The guys were productive at the property. They kept Sawyer busy the entire day being one man down since Justin was out of town for the week. There was a muggy haze stretched far across the fields as they worked hard in the heat, the blazing sun beating down upon them, sapping their energy.

"Wanna grab a bite in town?" Jake asked Sawyer as they put tools in the stables for the evening.

"I think I might swim some laps and try calling Marina."

Jake dusted off his jeans. "You need to eat, dude. You didn't eat lunch today."

"I ate a donut this morning that Trev brought. I'm not hungry. Wasn't this morning either."

"All right, now I know you're worried sick because you're always hungry. Why don't you try calling her now while we finish cleaning up, then we'll go eat and you can swim laps before bed?"

"Fine. I don't know if I can eat but I'll go."

"You'll eat."

"I feel like I could puke."

"From drinking too much yesterday?"

"No."

"It's just a rough patch, a misunderstanding. Once you're able to explain, she'll come back."

Sawyer leaned against the building. "Think so?"

"You two were meant for each other. Yeah, I absolutely think so."

"I want to be cautiously optimistic. She isn't making it easy though."

Jake shook sawdust from his dark hair and neatly groomed short facial hair.

"I'm sure what she heard freaked her out." Sawyer pulled his phone from his back pocket and dialed Marina. Still no answer. "Shit." He shoved it back into his pocket.

"It's okay, man. It'll be all right. Let's go eat." Jake patted Sawyer's back as they headed to the truck.

"You guys comin' along?" Jake hollered at Chris and Trev. They nodded and joined.

Sawyer only ate a few bites, just enough to avoid a worse headache. He tried calling again, but no answer. Jake dropped him off at home and told him to call if he needed anything. He swam a few laps then tried watching TV while drinking but, somehow, everything he tried watching reminded him of her—if he could concentrate at all. He paced the hardwood floors barefoot, wearing gray sweat joggers and a white tank top, leaving a message for her again.

"Marina, baby, this is silly. Please just pick up the phone. I at least need to know you're okay. I swear I didn't let anything happen. Our wedding is approaching soon so we need to straighten this mess out. I refuse to lose you over this. Marina, this is killin' me. I love you."

The night dragged on for what seemed like an eternity. He worked out hard; tire flipping, battle ropes, treadmill, and weights. He was wet with perspiration, sweat marks on his tank top, as he sat on the porch swing with the entire bottle of whiskey. He took Tango out on a moonlit ride, took a sedative, then finished the bottle out poolside. He finally fell asleep shortly before dawn but was awakened by downpouring rain and thunder. His eyes opened to rain pelting his skin and he realized he was lying on the patio lounge. Thunder rolled and the dark sky flashed pink clouds. He had completely given in to defeat.

"Fuck it," he grumbled and closed his eyes, falling back asleep right there on the lounge chair in the rain. The wind picked up a bit; the empty bottle rolling across the concrete and into the pool. The sound of rain calmed him, it quieted the chaos consuming him. The sound of thunder became a distant rumble as the rain stopped. The clouds were clearing and the sun was trying to peek out.

"Rough night?" Chris asked, standing over Sawyer.

Sawyer squinted one eye open, peering at Chris. He grunted and inhaled a deep breath as he slowly and unsteadily sat up and tried to focus his eyesight. "What?"

"I asked if you had a rough night but you already answered." Chris hiked the thighs of his jeans up to squat down. He picked the in-tact whiskey bottle out of the pool. "Good thing you cut your hair. You'd look like a damn hobo right now."

Trev and Jake stood nearby, eyebrows raised.

"You out here during the storm?" Trev asked.

Sawyer looked around, confused.

"Your sweats are as soaked as the patio so I'm guessing so," Jake observed, refraining from smirking.

"How's your head, buddy?" Chris asked as if he were talking to a toddler while offering a hand to help him up, but Sawyer just scowled at him.

"Hurts."

"I bet."

"Little fuzzy too, is it?" Jake couldn't refrain from smirking any longer.

Sawyer rubbed his face in his hands in an attempt to gather himself.

"The sedative I assume you took finally kicked in I guess." Chris held up the empty bottle and looked at the guys. "I take it no call yet?" Chris pulled Sawyer up by the arm.

"Obviously not." He tried to fight the vertigo. Yawning, he

patted Chris's shoulder. "You guys are great friends, checking in on me."

"You'd do it for us, big guy." Chris almost knocked Sawyer off balance when he patted his back, "Whoa, okay, let's get you inside. Maybe some dry clothes too. Already had your shower."

Trev opened the back door for them.

"Wanna help him? I'll put on a pot of coffee." Chris detoured to the kitchen. Sawyer just sat on the edge of the bed and stared at the wall while Jake stood in the doorway with his arms crossed.

"Okay, so...I'm guessing jeans are in the closet?" Trev shrugged and pointed for Jake to grab jeans while he grabbed a t-shirt and boxer briefs from the dresser. They set the clothes next to Sawyer on the bed and stood staring at him.

"Hey, buddy. Wanna get dressed?" Jake nudged Sawyer's arm and Sawyer stripped off his joggers, so the guys turned to leave the room.

"Funny. Didn't you say that you didn't wanna show up here with Sawyer undressed at the pool?" Jake laughed at Trev.

"Technically he wasn't *naked* by the pool." Trev laughed.

"Oh, but he is now." Chris was headed their way from the kitchen but quickly stopped and covered his eyes as Sawyer left his bedroom naked. He walked right past Trev and Jake by the bedroom doorway and toward Chris, out to pour coffee, bare-assed.

"I swear he does this shit on purpose." Trev shook his head, rolling his eyes.

"Dude, he's out of it." Jake snickered then hollered, "Nice ass, buddy!"

"I wish Justin was here to see this." Chris laughed as all three of them saw Sawyer's bare tan cheeks enter the kitchen.

"He did say he isn't shy though. Think he's trying to get us to leave him alone?" Trev pondered aloud.

"I don't know. His thighs look bigger without pants on, don't they?" Chris scratched his beard, staring at Sawyer.

"Yesterday morning I found him asleep against his horse in

the barn." Trev grabbed the clean clothes off the bed and headed for the kitchen. "I have proof," he said over his shoulder.

"Jesus. Maybe we should track her down." Jake suggested.

"Well, he can't keep going like this. He can't even function enough to help us at the stables today. He needs to sleep this off," Chris agreed. "Maybe we should've left him sleeping by the pool."

Trev handed Sawyer his clothes without looking at him as Sawyer entered the living room with a cup of coffee in his hand. Sawyer took the briefs and put them on, then the t-shirt. "Hey, Sawyer, why don't you rest for a bit before going over to the property? We can handle it for a while. No offense, but you should shave soon too." Trev proceeded with caution.

Sawyer looked at Trev with swollen, bloodshot eyes then grunted. He walked back to the bedroom with his coffee, which he set on the nightstand before he crawled into bed, flopping the blanket over his head. The guys looked at each other, surprised he took them up on their offer. Sawyer wasn't the type to not pitch in and get the work done. Trev tossed the pair of jeans in on the end of the bed before they quietly left out the front door, letting Sawyer get some sleep.

"Damn, y'all. This isn't good."

"No, Trev, it's not. It's really bad. He could show up at the property later, forgetting to have put his pants on. We gotta do somethin'." Jake looked at Chris then at Trev and let out a sigh. "That cowboy has too big of a heart to be havin' it crushed. Marina hasn't been to the bar. Does anybody have her friends' numbers?"

Chris and Trev shook their heads.

"This is gonna be a long week," Chris said as he blew out a long breath.

CHAPTER 26
Sorting Out Feelings

M arina had done nothing but lounge in her pajamas with her hair up in a messy bun, sitting next to a box of tissues.

"Marina, are you sure you don't want to call him back?" Becka asked as they sat on the couch together.

"It's not that I don't want to hear his voice or understand what I heard, it's that I'm scared to know. What if some other woman laid her hands on my man? What if he enjoyed it? That would be even worse. What if—"

"Marina, boo," Becka interrupted. "That's just the thing. Why keep asking what if when you could just hear him out? Let him explain. I totally get the fact that you overheard what sounded like a secret he was keeping from you or whatever, but it sounds like he was planning to tell you, whatever it may be. He definitely wants you to know."

"I wish I would've heard every word they said. I never thought I'd have to worry about anything like this with him. He said he didn't want other females around for his weekend. I feel foolish and embarrassed that they weren't wanting me to know. I feel disrespected."

"Yeah, I understand that for sure. Even I wanna know what happened so I know it's eating at you."

"You want me off your couch, don't you?" Marina smiled.

"Nah, never. You can stay as long as you want. You know that."

"Thank you."

"I just don't want you missing out on the man of your dreams if it's just a simple misunderstanding, that's all. You two belong together."

"I think so too. I know we do. I can't imagine my life without him. That's why this is so hard. He knows how I feel about that topic though and I thought I knew how he felt about it. He's different from most other guys. At least I thought so."

"Maybe you should talk to him and his friends separately, make sure their stories add up."

"Maybe. That's not a bad idea. I hate that I'm not completely trusting him right now."

"I'm sure he was really going to tell you. He just should've done it right away."

"Yeah, he probably should've. But then again it would've ruined the wonderful night we had. I guess I understand *why* he didn't say anything right away." Marina dropped her head.

"It's been three days. Maybe you should call and let him know you're okay and staying here at least. Or text even." Becka stressed.

"Maybe I should. I'd rather not talk over the phone; I want to see his expressions if that makes sense. I asked for space but he just keeps calling."

"Text him then. Then maybe you can get a little sleep tonight, but do you really want him to leave you alone?"

"I bet he isn't sleeping either. No...yes...ugh I don't know...no."

"He's probably not sleeping. It's a good thing that he's being adamant, you're clearly extremely important to him. Hey, I have an idea. Why don't we go do painting with a twist tomorrow? Get our creative juices flowing. Maybe it'll help reset your mind and give some clarity, take your mind off the issue, at least for a little bit. Art is therapeutic for me."

"I guess we could do that." Marina's chin tipped upward.

"You don't even have to drink if you're still feeling nauseous. Just let all the pretty colors distract you."

"I think it sounds like just what I need."

She wept into her pillow that night more than she slept. Her mind was split, trying to decide how to handle the situation. She knew what she *should* do, but she was having trouble forcing herself to do it. She was afraid she was either overreacting or wouldn't want to hear the truth.

The next evening, the two of them sat with their color pallets at the table, canvases in front of them, chatting quietly between instructions. Brushing color strokes, the scratchy sound cutting the silence.

"Maybe I'm being too hard on him. I don't want him to think it's okay to disrespect me though. I am just so torn about everything."

"Well, you said Drew was a bad influence on Sawyer when they were younger and Sawyer was afraid of Drew causing trouble this weekend. Maybe Sawyer didn't have anything to do with what happened or didn't happen."

"I'm sure. It doesn't mean he didn't get involved though."

"Think the guys would be honest with you or cover for him?"

"I mean, I'm sure there's a bro code of some sort."

"You know I always stand behind you, no matter what decision you make, but...in this case, I really do think you should give him the benefit of the doubt. He's a great guy. He's never given you any reason to doubt him before."

"No, I know. You're right. I'm sure he'll be playing at the bar tomorrow night. He and I should probably talk afterward."

"Want me to go with you or are you working?"

"Gladys told me I could pick up a shift but I don't plan to.

You can go with me. In fact, I'd like that. If it gets busy, I'll jump in and help out."

"Sounds like a plan. I'm actually excited to hear them play."

"I'm surprised you haven't popped in to listen to them yet. You'll enjoy it. They're the best."

CHAPTER 27

Singing Out Feelings

F riday finally came. The guys had worked hard at the property all week. The stables and fences were finished and just the electrical and plumbing were left to do. It was an ideal stopping point so they got an hour in of rehearsal, showered, and changed clothes. Sawyer shaved because he really was starting to look homeless, then buttoned his light-washed distressed bootcut jeans. They were Marina's favorite. He pulled down an aqua t-shirt and dressed it up with the teal and black plaid button-up that she loved on him. He left it unbuttoned, the sleeves snugly wrapping his biceps. He took his black Stetson off the hook by the front door and grabbed his guitar case before heading to the bar.

The guys were setting up on stage by the time he got there; symbols screwed on, amps plugged in, microphone stands and barstools set just right.

"Think she'll show up?" Chris asked, digging for his drumsticks.

"She'll be here." Sawyer smiled with confidence.

"There's the Sawyer we know." Jake attached the shoulder strap to his electric guitar. "Glad you shaved, dude. You've dressed to impress."

"I'm desperate." He shrugged with hope in his blue eyes.

Trev plugged in his keyboard and spun his finger in the air for Bob to bring them a round.

"If you need advocates, we're here. Just say the word."

"I might have to take you up on that, Jake."

Some regulars started trickling in and taking seats at tables. Every time the door opened Sawyer would look up, hope and desperation beaming from his eyes, only to be repeatedly let down. The guys tuned their instruments then Sawyer stepped down from the stage and walked to the restroom just as Marina and Becka came through the doors. Jake noticed first. His eyes grew huge and he turned to the guys, pointing at her.

"Oh, shit! She came!" Chris was thrilled to see her. Jake jumped down and approached Marina at the table before she could sit.

"Marina, I just wanted to let you know that Sawyer's really messed up about you leaving. He's been trying to kill the pain but nothing's working. He's absolutely heartbroken and has hit rock bottom. He's really bad off, I mean, it's been *bad* this whole week. He's better today than he has been because he was hoping you'd show up tonight, but we even had to tell him to shave. I don't want to get all up in y'alls business, but if you could just hear him out...he didn't do anything wrong. I just wanted to tell you that. Howdy, Miss Becka." He tipped his hat to them and smiled before hustling back to the stage as Sawyer came out of the restroom.

He straightened his shirt coming down the hallway then looked up and saw Marina as he entered the bar space. He stopped, wanting to run straight to her, but didn't want to be rejected either. His heart raced. He smiled and tipped his hat before joining the guys on stage.

"Dude, what are you doing? Go!" Trev whispered to Sawyer.

"I don't wanna stick my foot in the flame. I wanna scoop her up but I don't know if that's what she wants."

"She came, didn't she? If I were you, I'd ride the lightning," Chris said as he got comfortable on his stool behind the drum set.

"Our fire isn't out yet; the spark is still there. It'll ignite again easily. Let's just play and see how it goes. Yeah?" Sawyer sat on his stool, adjusted his microphone, and rested his guitar on his leg. He took a drink of whiskey while the guys got situated.

Jake greeted everyone, which usually comes from Sawyer. He looked over at Sawyer, covered his mic, and whispered, "You good?"

Sawyer gave a nod and began to strum. They started on a calm note with *Something in the Orange* by Zach Bryan.

Justin stopped in halfway through that first song to hear the band play, returning to town just in time. He saw Marina at the table but didn't want to interrupt friend time since she was there with Becka, so he just grabbed a stool up at the bar. He nodded at the guys who nodded and smiled back.

The guys slid aside their stools to play *Whiskey Friends* by Morgan Wallen, which the crowd enjoyed.

He couldn't help but look at Marina often. Her pale pink sundress fit her body perfectly, snug up top and flared out at the waist. Her wavy honey hair flowed freely. He noticed how her lips matched her dress and the lighting danced on her tan skin, her shoulders glowing. Her dainty, slender fingers wrapped around her blue raspberry vodka lemonade and her fingers tapped the glass to the beat. She would look at him with longing in her eyes.

She still wanted him. God, she wanted him badly. She was struggling with not giving in and would have to look away but she couldn't look away for long. Her eyes were drawn to him, the same as they always had been.

Sawyer and Jake took their stools and sang *Man Made a Bar* by Morgan Wallen and Eric Church. It was always fun when they sang duets together. It seemed as though the guys themselves enjoyed it too. They complimented each other's voices well. *Drinking Songs* by Walker Hayes was a fun one that the guys stood to play; Jake sang background. Boot heels clunked the stage floor and the creaking wood was heard beneath the weight of dancing feet. Sawyer sang *Leave You Alone* by Kane Brown while Jake knocked that electric guitar playing out of the park.

Then, to her surprise, they played *F150-50* by Morgan Wallen, which was one Sawyer had said he didn't think he'd ever sing again. Marina knew he had a theme going on that night. The songs of choice were about her leaving, about them being apart. If she hadn't loved to hear his singing voice or watch him up on that stage, it would've been hard to listen to those songs.

Marina and Becka shared a pizza and Gladys brought them a second drink. With Gladys' hand on Marina's shoulder, she told her, "Honey, you let that man come after you." Marina just smiled at her and thanked her for the drink, then told Becka she'd be right back and went to the restroom. She leaned against the sink, palms pressed against the porcelain until her knuckles were white. She instantly regretted eating as the knot in her stomach grew. She looked in the mirror and took a few deep breaths, holding back tears which she thought were completely out of pure exhaustion, confused at her own feelings. Her heart and mind were battling.

She reapplied her lipstick, thinking maybe it would help her look like she was put together even though she was falling apart, then rejoined Becka at the table as the guys broke a minute to get another drink from Bob when offered.

The guys just had beers but Sawyer had another flaming drink on the rocks, which he blew the flame out on. He started up again with a solo acoustic version of *Love Like We Used To* by Troy Cartwright, then back with the guys for *Hungover and Hard Up* by Eric Church. He kept it slow for the next few: *Tonight, I Wanna Cry* by Keith Urban and *Mercy* by Brett Young.

Becka commented on how great the guys were but that they probably should go if they didn't want to drive in the severe weather they were supposed to be getting soon. As a patron left out the front door, they could hear thunder rumbling. Marina nodded to Becka and they stood, releasing their purse straps from the backs of their chairs.

"I know y'all wanna go before this storm hits, but we've only got one more song tonight. I've saved the best for last."

The girls had only taken a few steps from the table when the first few notes were strummed. As soon as those guitar strings started, they pulled at her heartstrings, stopping her in her tracks. She turned and looked at Sawyer, who was looking right at her. His right shoulder became the rhythm. Those glacier-blue eyes stole her delicate heart. *Wine into Water* by Morgan Wallen was her favorite song. It was about a man apologizing, sure, but the melody to that song was the most beautiful she had ever heard. They danced to it together often. She knew he had planned to steal her heart with it, that's why he played it and why he saved it for last.

"Are we going?" Becka asked, several feet from the table. Marina shook her head no, not taking her eyes off him. They sat back down, Marina folding her skirt beneath her legs as she sat. The rip in the knee of his jeans seemed slightly bigger than she remembered. He looked amazing, like always, but as he bounced his ripped-up knee and swayed seductively to the rhythm while completely feeling the music, it made her want to run to him. This man was feeling the music in his bones, his body language and the music expressed his emotions as clear as day, and they were nothing but strong. At one point, he wiped a single tear from his face. He radiated sadness and despair as he swayed with the melody. As soon as the last note rang, the girls got up and walked to the door. Sawyer stood and propped his guitar up against the stool, expecting her to stop for him to speak. She turned and looked back at him as Becka opened the door. The rain had begun falling, not a pouring rain yet, but the thunder growled loudly. He called for her, but the girls were already running for the car.

"Shit!"

"Go after her!" Trev yelled at him. Sawyer leaped off the stage and ran for the door. He busted through only to see taillights leaving the parking lot. The rain came down harder as the red burn of his heart's departure faded into the night. He went back in and rushed to pack his guitar.

Justin approached the stage as the guys packed up. "I need to come listen to you guys more often. Y'all rock! What's goin' on? Why'd she leave?"

"Dude, you've missed one hell of a week." Chris fumbled a symbol as he dropped the bolt he was unscrewing. It took a moment for the loud ringing to stop.

"You guys got this? I gotta go." Sawyer shut his guitar case and snapped the lock shut.

"Yeah, man. Go!" Jake encouraged. Justin held his arms out to his sides waiting for an explanation.

"Marina hasn't been home all week. She isn't talking to me."

"What? Why?"

"Long story," Sawyer huffed as he unplugged Trev's keyboard.

"It's not a long story. She overheard Sawyer telling Drew to keep his trap shut till he could tell her about the stripper." Jake closed his guitar case and they all rushed to load their equipment before the storm got worse.

"Oh, Shit! You explained to her nothing happened though, right?"

"No, she didn't give me the chance. But now I know she's staying with Becka. I gotta run home to get the address from the office. I'm going over there; I can't take it anymore." Sawyer jumped off the stage, guitar in tow.

Justin started helping the guys pack up on the stage and laughed. "Dude, I've watched you get pissed off at Drew like, five times. I laugh every time I play it."

Sawyer stopped halfway to the door. "What? What do you mean watched?"

"I videoed the whole thing."

"You what?" Chris asked, dropping his drumsticks as he shot to his feet.

"Yeah, I videoed at the bar that night. With my phone."

"Man, the shit we saw him do this week...I could strangle you right now," Trev told Justin.

Sawyer looked confused, brows furrowed.

"When the singer said there's a groom in the house and you asked Drew what he had done after Drew told me he had a surprise for you, I knew some shit was about to go down. Can't just *not* video it." Justin gave a blasé shrug and Sawyer ran to him for a man-hug.

"Justin, I love you. You're a lifesaver." Sawyer tousled Justin's curly brown hair.

"Really? Because I'm kinda pissed right now." Trev threw his arms to his sides.

"Okay..." Justin looked confused. "Y'all sounded great by the way!"

"Thanks!" Jake nodded.

"I just want to say thanks, guys, for helping me out this week. I know I was a total wreck, a complete pain in the ass. I appreciate you guys."

"Nah, pfffft." Jake waved like it was no big deal.

"No problem. No need to thank us. That's what good friends are for. We're just glad you had your shit together for us to all sound great tonight," Chris teased.

"Just make sure all that liver drowning was worth it. You keep that woman." Jake pointed to the door.

"I have every intention to. Text me that video. Now!" Sawyer ran out the door holding his hat onto his head.

CHAPTER 28

Pouring Out Feelings

S awyer stopped at the house and ran into the office. Papers shuffled as water dripped from his hat onto the desk. He found her friends list with numbers and addresses and folded it, shoved it in his pocket, then ran for the truck.

Windshield wipers were on high as visibility on the dirt road was not much farther than where the headlights shined. He took off his button-up shirt while driving and flung it in the passenger seat. He turned the dash defogger on to help clear the fogging windshield then took the damp paper from his back pocket and looked at the address before tossing it over where his shirt lay. He made it to the flower shop just before they locked the door.

Marina sat on Becka's couch, occasionally turning around to look out the window.

"It's really coming down," she said, watching the rain.

"Glad we got back when we did," Becka agreed, just before a loud crack of thunder echoed and a bolt of lightning ripped across the sky. A severe weather alert came over their phones.

"We're in a tornado watch now, too." Becka turned the TV

on and switched the channel to the local weather. Headlights reflected in the living room window, catching Marina's attention. She watched the truck go by, hoping it was Sawyer, but it wasn't.

"Maybe I should call him."

"If you want to, go ahead. He won't want you driving in this weather though."

"Maybe I should just go home."

"You're not driving in this."

"I'm a big girl, Becka. I've driven in worse."

* * *

Sawyer was almost to Becka's, but no text from Justin yet. He called Justin and asked him to resend it but Justin said he had been trying; the service wasn't allowing it to go through. He swore he would keep trying and sent it to Sawyer's email, just in case.

* * *

More headlights, not him though.

"He looked so good tonight." Marina rested her chin on her hand, her elbow on the couch arm.

"Mmhmm, and he played your favorite song."

"He did. It was beautiful. He was so sexy, moving with the rhythm."

"Yeah, he really gets into the music," Becka agreed, "Jake looked great too."

Marina smiled. "He did. I actually broke a promise to Sawyer though."

"How?"

"I promised him we'd always communicate if we were upset. I'm going to call him. I need to hear his explanation, no matter how hard it might be to hear. I've put him on ice long enough." The girls sat in silence while she started calling his phone, but another flash of headlights caught her attention. They suddenly shined through the window, changing direction. It was Sawyer pulling into the driveway, directly in front of the window. She jumped to her feet and tossed her phone on the couch as she looked out the front window.

"It's Sawyer!" She was nervous but happy he came; a bit relieved even. He got out of the truck as she stepped out the front door. There was only a small eve over the door where Marina stood. The storm was so intense that she was getting wet from the rain. He was in such a hurry that he didn't shut his truck door. The dome light stayed on and she could just barely hear the radio over the storm. He approached her and handed her a bouquet of multi-colored roses then immediately stepped back and kept his distance.

"Marina. I'd like to talk to you. Just give me a few minutes for a chance to explain what you heard." He almost had to yell over the loudness of the rain.

"I heard what sounded like you trying to hide something from me. Something you knew I wouldn't be okay with. That's not who we are."

He shook his head, rain pouring off his black hat. "No, baby. I wouldn't hide anything from you."

"I heard you tell Drew to shut his mouth about the stripper." Marina was starting to tear up.

He shook his head again.

"I heard you, Sawyer." The sound of her heart breaking was louder than the anger and confusion surrounding her.

"I know, but I wasn't trying to shut him up about..." He was getting frustrated, not knowing how to put it into words. He had thought about how he'd explain the situation a hundred times over but now that she was in front of him, he was so nervous. He was scared to screw things up worse. Charged particles absorbed the air, the tension similar to the moment right before lightning strikes. "I told him I wanted to tell you but not while they were there. I didn't want drama that first night back. I didn't want you and him fighting. Shit, I could barely look at him, I was so pissed at what he did." His aqua shirt was completely soaked and stuck to his skin, she could almost see through it. The clinging fabric outlined his pecs and it was almost as if he was shirtless.

"So, tell me what he did."

"He suggested we stop at a particular bar in town on our way back home that last night. He said they had live music so I told him we could go and listen and have one beer but I wanted to make it back before you went to bed. Then, apparently, he had this all planned. He told the band that was playing that I was the groom before we even got there and hired some chick." He stopped. Marina looked away, a tear dripping from her eye and racing several raindrops down her cheek. She was clouded by her thoughts, like a moth attracted to a flame.

"I didn't let anything happen, baby, I promise. I walked out. The guys followed. Drew and I had words in the parking lot."

"Did she touch you?" Marina's arms were crossed, bouquet in one hand, and she was still looking away.

"What?"

"Did she touch you?" Marina asked again.

"Her hand touched my shoulder but I moved away."

"Did you look at her? Did she have clothes on? I need to know these things, Sawyer."

He was nodding as she was asking.

"She had something on. I didn't look at her so I don't even know what exactly she was wearing. Peripheral vision, probably lingerie. What pissed me off most is that when I stood and told her either she or we were leavin'..." He hesitated.

"What, Sawyer? Say it."

"It was Gabby."

"What did you just say?" Marina's brows were raised and her jaw dropped, completely taken by surprise. She could feel static electricity in the air.

"It was Gabby."

"Your ex?" Marina was horrified, her fists balled at her sides.

"Drew didn't know so I don't know how that happened."

"Unbelievable!"

"I know, I'm so sorry, Marina. I didn't want anything like that to happen."

"Neither did I. I knew I didn't want to hear the truth."

Sawyer hung his head and checked his phone, which was getting drenched in his back pocket. No text. He closed his eyes and hung his head; afraid he was losing the battle with her imagination.

"You have somewhere else to be?" she asked.

"No, I'm waiting on the proof. Marina, there's no gray area when it comes to what happened the entire night. It's straight black and white. As soon as the issue arose, I put a stop to it. I shut it down fast, I diffused the situation before it started. Not only would I never do that to you, but it wasn't anything I wanted either. I told you that before. I made it clear to Drew that I wasn't cool with what he was trying to do; not just because you wouldn't be cool with it but because I had no interest in it. I refuse to do anything that would jeopardize us. If that chaps Drew's ass, so be it. I'll deal with him later. He should've known better. I need you to believe me when I tell you I'd never do that to you. Not ever. I love and respect you too much. I'd never lie to you; I'd never betray you or your trust. I don't ever want to look at another woman the way I look at you, not even for one stupid night out. There's no need because I have the most beautiful woman in the world. I know her heart and it feels like home. There's no place I'd rather be." A single tear slid down his face, trickling shame as he stood, vulnerable to his emotions. "I was trying to respect you needing time alone but...I've been trying to drown the pain of you leaving. I'm not numb like I thought I'd be. I still feel it all. I can't eat, I can't sleep. I don't even care about that but the thought of losing you is...it's killin' me. I know you have trust issues and I get it. I do understand. But I'm not him. Marina, I'm not like him. I'm a man of my word and I promise you I've told you the truth. I'm so sorry your heart is breaking because of me. I'm sorry I didn't tell you right away. I just missed you so much and I couldn't wait to kiss you, make love to you, and hold you all night. I was selfish."

"No, you weren't. I wanted all of that too. It may not have been your fault but..." She hesitated.

"I wish you wouldn't have overheard what you heard. I wish I wouldn't have said it. I'm mad at myself. I wish Drew wouldn't have kept trying to bring it up. Hell, I wish he wouldn't have done what he did. I knew he couldn't go the whole weekend without fucking it up because that's what he does. Always at my expense, ultimately, yours too. Ours. I'm sorry it happened, I'm sorry you overheard because I know it probably did sound like I was keeping a secret from you, but I had every intention of telling you as soon as they left. I am completely devoted to you in every way." He paused with a sniffle. "You're not saying anything. Honestly, it's scaring me."

She looked at him, not looking off into the distance or head down, but she was looking right at him.

"Marina, I'm beggin' you." He dropped to his knees in the mud that was puddling in the patchy grass. His head hung, defeated.

"Sawyer."

He looked woeful, his heart laid out on his sleeve, fully exposed. His words pervaded, silent tears flooding his face.

"I believe you."

He lifted his head, looking at her.

"You do?" His brows rose, his pleading eyes a bit brighter under the brim of his hat, the porch light shining on him.

"I do." She nodded and wiped her cheekbone with her hand.

Sawyer looked relieved as he stood. The rain was starting to let up a little, enough to hear that the song playing in his truck was *Silverado For Sale* and it reminded her of the time they made the pit stop in the woods and he took her against a big oak tree. She couldn't imagine not being with him; not waking to him, no more adventures, not making love to him...how well he treated her. This misunderstanding wasn't worth throwing it all away. She would never find anyone better than him. He was her everything. Here he was, pouring his feelings out as he groveled.

"Marina, I will love you through any storm but I'll never *be* your storm. We will weather them together." He had yet to approach her.

"I'm sorry I just ran away. I should've let you explain. You said you wanted to talk and I should've stayed."

"Why didn't you?"

"I guess I was scared."

"Of what, baby?" He sounded desperate.

"I don't know, scared of what might have happened, scared that you looked at or touched another woman in that way, the way you do me. I can't stand the thought. I hoped it wasn't something so horrible that I couldn't get over it and we ended up splitting up. I had found the perfect man and I...I just...I don't want to share you." She took a quivering deep breath while batting her wet eyes.

"Kinda like how I break dudes' noses over you?"

"Yeah, yeah..." She smiled, the first genuine smile she'd felt in days. "But I should've trusted what I felt in my heart because my imagination was playing evil tricks."

"I get it. You don't need to be sorry though. It's just you and me here in our own little universe. Always."

"Promise?"

"Oh, baby, I promise. You never have to worry about that with me. You can trust me, completely, wholeheartedly. You've become a part of me. I love you more than life itself."

They both could feel the magnetism pulling at the two of them. She wasn't going to fight it any longer. She ran to him, right into his arms.

"I love you, Sawyer."

He held her tight, his hat shielding her face from the rain. He felt instant emotional relief. He could take a deep breath again without feeling like his sadness was trying to suffocate him. He was less shaky with his nerves calming and his muscles felt more relaxed. His tears stopped flowing. There was no better feeling than having her arms wrapped around him. Marina looked up at him, into those eyes, and he kissed her ever so passionately. It was as though sparks flew as lightning ran through their veins and exited out their lips, melting them into each other. They stood there, kissing in the pouring rain, for what felt like an eternity, everlasting and not long enough all at once. She clung to him until her heart picked itself back up and welded together with the heat of him, until her lungs burned for oxygen as her firing neurons screamed for more, more, *more* of him, until she thought they might combust in the middle of that storm like burning stars...

"You have no idea how much I love you, Marina. Will you come home with me?"

"Yes." She nodded.

Becka quietly opened the door and set Marina's packed bag outside. Marina laughed and ran to the door, thanking Becka and giving her a big hug.

"We'll come get your car tomorrow." He took her by the hand as they walked to the truck and waved at Becka still standing in the doorway.

As soon as he backed out of the driveway, his phone dinged. It was the text from Justin coming through.

"Darlin' you know you could've stayed at the house and asked me to leave."

"It's your house. That wouldn't be right."

He took her hand on the console. "It's *our* house. As the man, I should be the one to leave. You shouldn't have to."

"That's sweet but I was in fight or flight mode anyway. I freaked out. I instantly thought that all men *are* the same after all and I was so disappointed based on what I did hear that I didn't want to listen to an explanation. I just didn't want to hear what you had to say because I was terrified of whether it was the truth or not. If you had lied, it would've changed the way I think of you and that would've destroyed me. I needed to listen though in order to sort my feelings out."

"I'd never lie to you. In fact, I'd like for you to watch this. That way you're never questioning me or questioning what really happened that night." He handed her his phone.

"Have you seen it?" She took the phone.

"No, but I was there. I wasn't drunk so I remember everything clearly."

She clicked on it but didn't press play yet. He looked over at her.

"I don't want you to think I don't trust you by playing this." She tried to hand his phone back.

"Baby, it would make me feel better if you do."

She hesitated then said, "Jake told me tonight at the bar that you didn't let anything happen. I guess I can trust them too, huh?"

"Absolutely. They're great guys. I told them that night that I was going to tell you."

"Okay then." She pressed play. It showed everything, from the minute Gabby walked out of the back room to Sawyer marching out of the bar. It showed Sawyer's reaction, facial expressions, him yelling, it showed it all, although it didn't show Gabby's face well from where Justin was sitting.

"Wow." Marina instantly exonerated him.

Sawyer looked over at her. "Yeah, it was a crazy night. I had no idea Justin had a video. He's been gone all week so I didn't find out he had this till we were about to leave the bar tonight. His text finally just came through."

"When you said you were waiting on the proof...I'm so sorry I doubted you. I completely overreacted. God, you were begging on your knees."

"It's okay."

"No. It's not. I should've known that you would put a stop to anything you weren't comfortable with and I should've known you wouldn't be comfortable with another female like that. I

169

should've known I could trust you completely. I feel horrible for being upset with you. I've been such a bitch."

He gently grabbed her chin, smiling. "No, no you haven't. Stubborn sure, but not a bitch. Don't be sorry, just promise me that we won't fight like this again. Promise we'll always talk out what's upsetting us. We have to communicate. Both of us."

"I promise. My scars sometimes show brightly, don't they?" She hung her head.

"Nah, but the stars in your eyes do." He smiled.

She flipped up the console and slid over next to him, her head against his shoulder and his arm around her all the way home.

"This was just a sad chapter, not our story. We can get through anything together, no matter how big or small or complicated. I'll do anything for you, *anything*, to make sure you stay, but of course, I'll never force it if you ever decide you want to leave. I need you though. I need you to know how much you mean to me."

"Oh, Sawyer, I don't wanna go anywhere. You're where I feel safe. I don't know why I needed time alone because I felt so empty when we were apart and I can't imagine life without you. I need you too. We can show each other just how much as soon as we get home, then you can hold me in your arms all night."

"I like the sound of that." He smiled, looking at those wide, bright eyes of hers.

CHAPTER 29

Waking

M arina woke up to those glacier-blues looking into her eyes. Sawyer stared deep into her soul.

"I'm gonna hold you in my arms in this bed we share together forever."

Nothing was more important than this promise that flowed from his lips. All of his promises. So far, he really had been a man of his word. She was glad she had watched that video. She knew for certain his words held weight so there was not a doubt in her mind she could trust him.

"I want nothing more." She smiled, holding his face in her hands as he leaned over her, running his hand through her hair next to her face as she rolled onto her back.

"I missed you." He got closer.

"I missed you too, so badly."

Their lips connected so softly and slowly. They were savoring every second. He took her hand and raised it above her head, up onto the silk pillow, his fingers interlocked with hers. Then the other. He held her hands there while crawling on top of her, never letting his lips leave hers. She wanted so badly to feel his warm body, every curve of every muscle. Those snug white boxer briefs rode high on his thick thighs. He lowered his torso further, against hers, while his rear remained higher. As he slowly kissed down the side of her neck, she wanted so badly to grab his ass and squeeze it, her nails sinking in, but he tightly held her wrists in place above her head. She was enjoying it, being pinned down, the forced cooperation. His monstrous thighs squeezed on either side of hers, his shoulders and biceps close to her face. Her back was arching as he kissed her breasts and the butterflies flittered within the pit of her stomach. She looked down at him and found him gazing back at her, his lips caressing her nipple. He let go of one of her wrists, just long enough to push down the front of his briefs. His tongue entered her mouth as he slowly inserted himself deep within her. He felt incredible. Holding himself slightly above her, he took his time, making sure she felt everything. He slid his hand down her slender arms and onto every inch of her body as she did his. She loved the way he looked her in the eyes when he made love to her. It set her heart on fire.

They cuddled on the couch that evening, relieved things were back to how they were supposed to be between the two of them. He didn't work the whole day. Nothing was as important to him as showing her that he was there in the present for their relationship.

"Do you think maybe you should call Drew? You guys should probably talk." Marina suggested.

"Yeah, I guess I should. I don't really want to."

"Do you have anyone to take his place as a groomsman?"

"Point taken." He huffed a long exhale as he sat up, took his phone off the coffee table, and dialed Drew. He put it on speakerphone even though Marina told him it wasn't necessary but he wanted to anyway. He rested his elbows on his knees.

Drew answered and Marina could hear the nervousness in his voice, "Hello?"

"Hey, you have a minute?"

"Uh, yeah."

"We should probably discuss last weekend, don't ya think?"

"I reckon we should, with the wedding coming up in a couple of weeks."

Sawyer rubbed his head, hesitating, "Look, man. We had a good time the whole weekend. I'm glad you were a part of it."

Marina looked at him, surprised he wasn't giving Drew hell.

"Yeah, I'm glad too, and look, I'm sorry I screwed up," Drew sounded sincere but Sawyer had a hard time wanting to accept his apology.

"I just wanted it to be like old times. I know there were never strippers involved in our shenanigans but I missed that carefree, rebellious feeling. We used to have fun."

"I've grown up, Drew. My advice is you should too."

"I know. You've always been a good influence, Sawyer. I've always been the one to get you into trouble. I'm sorry about that, even when we were younger, but I really do feel bad about our weekend. I didn't mean for things to turn out the way they did and I didn't know it would cause a rift between y'all. I thought you were just being a stick in the mud when you said you didn't want females involved in your weekend. I seriously didn't know it would be your ex either. That came as a shock to me too."

"How did that happen anyways?"

"I placed a public social media post and excluded you from it. She answered first and she was attractive so I hired her. She had mutual friends in common. It was a stupid move on my part."

"Yeah, she didn't hesitate to snag that opportunity. She always was an opportunist."

"So, your ex is a stripper now?"

"Not that I know of. Who the hell knows though. She just desperately wants me back. Not sure why since I've told her it'll never happen. Truthfully, she was a toxic thorn in my side and I'm embarrassed to have dated her."

"I heard you had a rough week. Jake texted me, bitchin' me out."

"Did he?" Sawyer laughed.

"Oh yeah, he did. Rightfully so."

"Well, you're lucky she forgave me, Drew. I'm thankful Justin took that video too. If I would've lost her...man, I don't know what I'd do."

Marina reached over, laying her hand on his thigh.

"I understand. I take full responsibility. I think I've learned a lesson this time. I need to be more like you."

"You can still be you, Drew, just don't drag others down with ya."

"Noted. Your buddies are good guys, they're fun. I owe Marina an apology. You've landed yourself a real catch by the way."

"Thanks. She's right here. I'm sure she'd appreciate that."

"Hi, Drew." Marina leaned in closer to the phone, twisting her arm with Sawyer's.

"Hey, Marina. I want to say I'm sorry. I really am, for everything. I didn't mean to cause you any pain. You or Sawyer. You guys are a perfect couple and I almost screwed that up. I'm an idiot."

"Nah, you were just trying to have fun. Now that you know where Sawyer and I stand on all that, we won't have to worry about it happening again, right?"

"Absolutely not, no, ma'am. I'll be on my best behavior."

"Thank you. We accept your apology, Drew."

"I appreciate that."

Sawyer scratched his jaw and said, "Yeah, I've seen your best behavior, Drew. I'm not convinced that's—"

"Yeah, yeah, you're funny," Drew interrupted Sawyer, laughing. "I hadn't called yet, even though I wanted to, because Jake told me to wait."

"Jake is my voice of reasoning. He talks me down when I get fuming pissed and he gives good advice. He's my wingman and a great guy, so if he gives you advice about something, please listen to him." Sawyer chuckled.

"Will do. Tell him thanks for the ass chewin'. It got me thinkin' and I realized I was wrong."

"I'll tell him."

"So, am I still a groomsman?"

Sawyer laughed before answering, "Yeah."

"Sweet! I won't let ya down again, cuz."

"I hope not. We'll have a good time."

"That's the plan. I'm lookin' forward to seeing ya get hitched."

"I'm looking forward to it too. We'll see ya in about two weeks."

"I wouldn't miss it."

"Do you feel better having talked to him?" Marina put her arm around Sawyer after he put his phone down on the coffee table.

"Yeah. I'm still pissed but I'll get over it. Now that I have you back, that's all that matters. At least he apologized. He meant it too."

"All is good again in our world." She felt his facial scruff as he smiled at her.

CHAPTER 30

Harley

The guys were unloading a trailer of hay into the new stables when a truck with a horse trailer pulled in.

"You expecting somebody?" Trev asked as he stacked a bale.

"No." Sawyer tossed a bale down and watched the truck stop.

A guy got out and went to the back of the trailer, so Sawyer jumped down off the trailer and took his work gloves off. He tucked them into his back jeans pocket and walked over to the trailer.

"Good mornin'. Can I help ya with somethin'?"

"Yeah, I got somethin' for ya." The guy handed Sawyer a set of papers.

"What's this?" He unfolded it and flipped through, quickly reading over it. Before he could ask any questions, the man dropped the back end of the trailer and stepped inside.

"Hey, I didn't—"

"Here ya go." The man stepped down the ramp holding the bridle of a black horse with a white blaze down its forehead and two front white socks. Hooves clunked loudly on the metal. With one raised brow and squinting the sun out of his eyes, Sawyer asked, "I didn't buy a horse, so what's goin' on?"

"He's yours." The guy clipped a lead rope to the bridle.

"Um, no, sir, I—"

"Yep. The paperwork says so."

"I skimmed it but—"

"This is Harley. Ol' Billy left him to you."

Sawyer tipped his head back, looking toward the sky, and chuckled. "That son of a bitch."

"I believe you're all set." The man shook Sawyer's hand and handed him the lead rope. He lifted the trailer ramp and slammed it shut.

"Thanks!" Sawyer led the horse to a gate and let him out into the round pen.

"You get a new horse?" Chris asked, taking a water break.

"Apparently so." He slapped the rolled-up papers in his hand. The guys stood, confused, watching the horse.

"That there is Harley. Billy's horse."

"Oh, shit! He left his horse to you?" Trev asked, surprised.

"Yeah, he's twenty years old according to these pedigree papers."

"Are you gonna keep him?" Jake asked before chugging water.

"Ya know, I'm thinkin' he might be a good therapy horse. He's the first addition to our nonprofit."

Chris clapped his hands, a grin all but swallowing his face. "All right, congrats!"

Sawyer laughed. "Thanks. He looks to be an expensive horse." He unrolled the papers, reading over them. "His sire was a racehorse worth a shit-ton. This horse is probably worth a lot too."

"Well, Billy knew you'd take great care of him and you'd know his worth and appreciate him. He was a smart guy." Jake leaned backward against the gate with a foot up on it.

"Yeah, I guess you're right. Look at that shiny black coat. He's purdy."

"Sure is," Trev agreed.

"Did you know Billy used to barrel race?" Jake mentioned.

"No shit?" Sawyer looked concerned, staring at Harley as Chris laughed.

"He didn't race Harley though. I remember him talking about Harley being fast back in the day but he's been a trail-riding horse for quite a while. He sold all of his horses a couple of years ago except this one. He was his pride and joy, besides his actual Harley of course."

"Good to know. He'll fit in perfectly around here. I'll bring Willow over here so he has a friend in the stables."

That evening when Sawyer got home, he told Marina, "Let's go for a ride. I gotta show ya somethin'." He hadn't even taken his boots off yet.

"Where we goin'?"

"To the property." They went out to the fence and let Dixie out before he helped Marina up onto her back and got on behind her.

"She's gotten so big, I'm nervous to ride her anymore without reins." Marina got comfortable, Sawyer's legs against hers.

"I'm right here, darlin'. I got you," he said in a low voice as he wrapped his arms around her. Dixie clopped through the field and across the wooded trail to the property.

"I wanna show you the progress we made this week."

"You guys get a lot done?"

"We did. I give kudos to the guys, they worked really hard. When I was trying to sleep off a hangover, they were over here working their asses off."

"Sounds like they took care of you."

"They did."

"They shouldn't have had to though. That's on me."

"Nah, I'd do it for them if they were going through a rough time. They know that."

"But I mean, you wouldn't have needed them if it weren't for me leaving like I did."

"Baby, it's okay. You came back and we learned from it. That's all that matters."

"I love that you have great friends and that you're so forgiving."

"If you weren't forgiving, we wouldn't be riding horseback together right now. I'm glad you have Becka to confide in too."

She turned to look at him and he kissed her. Giving Dixie no direction, they stayed in the moment until she entered the property clearing.

"Oh, wow! You guys did all this in a week?" Marina asked, looking ahead at the beautiful stable building and all the pastures that had been divided with wooden fencing.

"Yeah."

"It looks finished. Is it done?"

"Almost. Just have electrical and plumbing left for the stables. The electrician and plumber will be back Monday to finish up. I gotta paint the inside of the office and put the office furniture in, but as far as everything being built, it's done. The contractors worked hard too."

"It all looks so beautiful. You're amazing and I'm so proud of you. I feel bad I wasn't here helping like I should've been. I didn't help with the horses either."

"I don't care about that, darlin'. The guys helped out."

"I owe them big time."

"Nah, they're happy you're back though." He laughed and jumped down off Dixie once she slowed down to a stop, then he took Marina by the hand to help her down.

"We need to hit up the auction with Dave this week," he said, opening the stable barn doors. Harley let out a huff in greeting.

"We have a new horse?" she asked, meeting Harley at his stable door.

"Ol' Billy left us Harley."

"He's beautiful!"

"He's gonna be one of the therapy horses."

"That's great. That was kind of him to trust you with his horse."

"Yeah, he'll be taken care of, that's for sure. So…I added a little something to the office too." He motioned for her to follow him to the end of the stable building and took her into the office.

"I added these sliding barn doors between desk spaces so we can all be in the office together or, if one of us needs some privacy for phone calls, or you and I wanna get freaky and shut Justin out, we can."

"Oh, my goodness, Sawyer!" Marina laughed, tapping his chest.

"Never know." He nibbled at her neck playfully.

CHAPTER 31

All the Pretty Horses

The barn note read "Giddy up" that morning when Marina did chores at home. Sawyer and Chris met Dave at the livestock auction in the neighboring town that morning. The three of them were standing floor-level, arms up on the rails of the metal pen, pointing out any horses with potential. Marina had errands to run that morning after she did what chores Sawyer hadn't done, but decided to go to the auction when she was finished. She spotted them amongst the growing crowd right away. Sawyer had some sexy jeans on, a white fitted t-shirt, and a plaid button-up tied around his waist. He wore his white cowboy hat, as did Chris, so they were easy to pin-point. She was approaching them, sporting bootcut jeans, a ribbed tank top, and her black cowgirl hat when Sawyer turned and saw her. He cat-called her, making her laugh. She waved at Chris and Dave.

"Woo! Look at her, up in here with her jeans and new hat." Chris elbowed Sawyer.

"Yeah, my baby is smokin'." He took those last few steps to her and grabbed her butt when he kissed her. She loved that he wasn't against showing public affection. He was proud to have her and wasn't afraid to show it.

"So, has it started yet? What did I miss?" she asked.

"You didn't miss a thing, it's about to start. I'm glad you came."

"Yeah? I'm not cramping your style, am I?"

"Hell no. I always want you with me." He stood behind her and wrapped his arms around her, then looked back to make sure he wasn't blocking anyone's view. Dave went to get the number paddles and brought them back.

"You have your eye on any in particular?" she asked Sawyer.

"Yeah, I want that bay."

"He's pretty. I love the lighter brown muzzle."

"He's a Lusitano."

"You can tell just by looking at him?"

"Yep. It's a Portuguese horse breed, they date back quite a ways, known as war horses."

"Interesting. What else is special about this one?"

"You'll see when they bring him out. They'll save him till the end, I bet."

"Wonder why he's up for auction."

"I wanna know that myself. Doc will be here in a bit. I wanna have him do an exam before I load any up."

"Good idea," Chris agreed, chewing on a piece of straw.

"There are seventeen horses here today, so after these here few heads of cattle, they'll bring them out." Dave wiped his forehead with his red hanky then stuffed it back in his shirt pocket.

"Marina, let me know if you see one you like." Sawyer kissed her cheek.

"Okay!" She was excited. Hopefully they were about to fill up the stables so they could get the therapy program running soon. The horses started being brought out one at a time after the cattle were auctioned.

"Sabrina said she wants Willow to be used as a therapy horse since she's already at the stables."

"You moved her over to the property? I wondered where she was," she said.

"I did this morning. Thought Harley should make friends. Ooh, look at this one! Whatcha think, Dave?"

"I say you better bid on this one."

A blue roan trotted out and stood quietly. It looked to be a Quarter Horse. Sawyer raised his paddle. A few others raised theirs as well but Sawyer won the bid.

"Nice work, cowboy. You still got a great deal." Dave patted Sawyer's back.

"Hell yeah, I did. Chris, you biddin' on any today? I don't wanna outbid you on one ya want."

"Nah, I'm just here because I didn't have anything better to do. Figured I'd help load up."

"Thanks, man."

"You bet."

"Hey, Sawyer, you've worked really hard with that paint. You want him?" Dave asked.

"You don't?"

"I got my hands full. I don't know why I even bought him. You take him. It's my donation to the nonprofit."

"Wow, Dave. You sure?"

"Absolutely. He's quite smitten with you anyways."

"Okay, thank you. It took a while but he's gotten to be a good horse." Sawyer shook Dave's hand.

A palomino pinto came out next.

"Ooh, she's pretty!" Marina seemed interested so after watching her calm demeanor, Sawyer raised his paddle and won the bid. Marina was excited. Sawyer was right, the third to last horse was the dark bay. His coat was shiny and he stood still and calm, walked when led, and stopped when stopped. It looked to be well trained. Several paddles went up.

"Oh, no y'all don't..." Sawyer kept bidding and ended up paying a few grand for it but he was happy.

"Looks like I'll be making more stall door name tags." Marina held Sawyer's hand, squeezing it, excited.

"Know of any good ranch hands looking for work?" Sawyer asked the guys.

Chris said, "Could always ask around here. The rodeos too."

"Okay, I'll do that."

"There are usually some young guys, just out of high school, that work here for the auctions and such. College kids trying to make a buck too. They might be lookin' for work." Dave walked along with them to the other side of the arena to get Sawyer's tickets for the three horses.

"Where they at?" Sawyer looked around.

"They're over there." Dave pointed.

"You want to hire them for the stables at the property?" Chris asked.

"Yeah, I need a couple on the payroll, even just part-time. Sabrina wants to help out but not every day and when someone needs time off and such it's nice to have a backup or two. If they're experienced with helping riders mount and dismount that would be helpful. Getting the horses ready with tack and taking care of stuff would be great too, along with daily chores."

"I can go talk to them while you get the horses and pay. I'll be right back." Chris headed over to chat with the young guys.

Doc entered the arena and caught up with Sawyer before checking out the three horses and advising Sawyer to quarantine them, just in case, but they all looked good from what he could tell.

Sawyer, Marina, and Dave started walking the horses out on lead ropes after Sawyer paid.

"Well, we didn't fill up every stall but there'll be more auctions and opportunities. I'll work with these before getting any more."

"Hopefully the non-profit is a success so we have an excuse to buy more." Marina led the pinto into the trailer.

"It will be, darlin'."

Marina hung wooden signs she made with names burnt into them on stall doors: Harley, Willow, Spunky is what Dave had named the paint, Moonshine for the blue roan, Sunny for the pinto, and War is what Sawyer named the bay. Sawyer would work with the new horses to make sure they were ready to ride while quarantined. They'd have to stay quarantined for another three weeks so he could keep an eye on their health, having Doc over several times, the ferrier as well. The guys came over one morning to watch Sawyer in the round pen with Spunky. Besides jittering muscle twitches and the occasional hoof stomp to avoid flies, Spunky stood still and calm when Sawyer signaled him to.

"That horse has come a long way," Chris said, leaning on the gate.

"I heard it was a crazy train wreck when Dave bought it." Trev laughed, balancing his butt on top of the wooden fence.

"Marina got a taste of the action on video." Sawyer dismounted.

"You're still talking about the horse, right?" Jake chuckled, adjusting his baseball cap.

"Oh, Jake, wouldn't you like to know?" Sawyer shook his head laughing.

"Oh, snap!" Trev laughed as he jumped down and opened the gate for Sawyer to bring Spunky out. Chris took him from Sawyer with the lead to take him back into the stables.

"Which one ya want in next?" Chris hollered from the stable doorway.

"Actually, hold that thought. I'm gonna go to the quarantine pen in a minute." He walked to the driveway where Marina had just pulled in with passengers.

"Hey, babe. I have a surprise for you." She got out and opened the back door for Luke, who rushed out and ran to give Sawyer a big hug. Whiskey jumped out right behind him.

"That gravel just flung out from under that boy's feet," Luke's mom said as she got out of the passenger side.

"Hey, kiddo! Wow, it's great to see you. How ya been?"

"I'm doing great, Mr. Sawyer! I'm in complete remission now."

"Wow, that's amazing news! Oh, Luke, I'm so proud of you. You're a fighter, you know that?"

"Yes, sir. You helped me be brave and I realized I wanna be a cowboy too."

"Nah, you were already brave when I met ya. Being a cowboy is hard work but I know you can do it."

"You still have short hair?" Luke asked while petting Whiskey, wanting Sawyer to remove his black hat.

"I sure do." Sawyer took his hat off for a few seconds, offering the kid a wink. "In fact, I should be thanking you for the haircut inspiration."

"Why's that?"

"Well, it's too damn hot out here playing cowboy to have long hair. It feels so much better."

Luke laughed, making everyone smile.

"This is a nice place you have," Luke said, looking around.

"Thank you. Come along, I'll introduce you to my buddies. These guys are my bandmates and best friends."

"You play in a band?" Luke gleamed with excitement as Sawyer tipped his hat to the ladies and walked toward the guys with Luke.

"You have yourself one hell of a man, Marina." Luke's mom stood with Marina near the barn.

"Thank you. I sure think so too." Marina nodded for her to follow as they joined the guys for testosterone-clouded cowboy talk.

Chris brought Harley out, already saddled up. "Wanna ride?" Chris asked Luke.

Luke looked at Sawyer with big eyes, then over at his mom. "Can I?"

"Hell yeah!" Sawyer got a nod from Luke's mom then helped Luke mount up.

"Have you ridden a horse before?" Trev asked.

"Once. A pony at the fair a few years ago."

"You want someone to ride with ya or you got this?" Sawyer asked, looking up at Luke.

"I got this. As long as you're nearby."

"You got it." Sawyer led alongside Harley's shoulder and Chris on the other side.

"This horse a safe one?" Luke's mom asked.

"Oh, yeah. He's been a trail horse for years. Sawyer wouldn't put Luke on one he wasn't sure of though." Marina stuck her hands in her back pockets.

"I trust he knows what he's doing."

Sawyer led Harley around the pen for a bit then back around by the gate. His mom had taken probably a thousand pictures of him by the time he dismounted.

"I'll tell ya what. I've been thinking of having a big charity event. Like a fundraiser celebration for our non-profit starting up. You wanna come?" Sawyer asked as the guys took the horse to the stables and got a cold drink.

"Heck yeah! Will I get to ride a horse again? I really like this shiny black one."

"You sure can. You can ride Harley whenever you want to. I'd like for y'all to be the first to sign up for the program."

"That's kind, but after all of his treatments, we can't really afford—"

Sawyer interrupted. "No ma'am. We aren't gonna charge anybody anything. Our programs will be run entirely by the kindness of our donors, so Luke should come often. I'm sure some horses we get here will need the emotional support too, relating to the folks riding them. You'll bring him?"

"You're a kind man, Sawyer. I'm sure he would love that."

"Good. So would we." Sawyer gave a nod to Luke.

"We should start putting together an advertisement so we can get the word out. Social media, the newspaper, local news, and radio stations, I'm thinking we need a spokesman though to help us non-profit presidents advertise. It's a big job but I think Luke could handle it," Marina pondered aloud. He looked up at his mom with a smile.

"Mom?" Luke gave her puppy dog eyes.

"Well, will this picture that I just took of him on the horse do?" She showed Marina her phone.

"It sure will." Marina smiled and gave Luke a high five.

"But I don't have a cowboy hat," Luke sounded bummed.

"We'll just have to fix that, won't we?" Sawyer winked at him. "For now, you're welcome to borrow one of mine. How does a big blowup water slide sound? Maybe a snow cone truck or taco truck would be awesome too," Sawyer thought out loud.

"Seriously?" Luke was jumping up and down.

"Absolutely. Horseback rides too."

"That sounds like so much fun!" Luke's smile was beaming.

"It's gonna be a blast, dude." Sawyer fist-bumped him.

CHAPTER 32

Cleansing Her Soul

The day had proved long for both of them. It was hot, Sawyer had been training horses all day and Marina set up the office inside the stables. She swept the wood floor and put an area rug down, painted the walls, and arranged the desks that had just been taken in and placed randomly around the room the day prior. Once she finished that, she started on paperwork for the non-profit and entered info into the laptop. Sawyer peeked in the doorway, adoring her as she typed away, wearing her eyeglasses that he thought she looked so adorable in. She noticed him in her peripheral view and took her eyes off the screen to look over at him. He leaned against the door frame with his arms crossed, smiling.

"Hey, babe." She sat back in her cushioned swiveling office chair.

He walked over to her and bent over for a kiss. "Darlin, why don't you call it a day? I think I am." He stepped back, not wanting to dust her with the dirt he was carrying on his clothes. He took his work gloves off, then his chaps as she finished up what she was doing. She had never seen him in chaps before and he looked so hot in them.

"I still need to make a few calls for setting up the event."

"It can wait til tomorrow." He reached his hand out for her to take hold of. She clicked save on the computer and shut the lid before taking his hand. His arm hugged her tightly and hers around him as they walked together out to the truck.

"You might have to wear those chaps sometime in the bedroom." She bit her bottom lip and looked away.

He laughed. "Deal."

"No offense, but you look tired." She observed.

"Oh, I am." His brows rose as he shut her truck door.

When he got in and started the truck, he let out a rugged sigh and wiped his dirty forehead with the back of his hand.

"Did you roll in the dirt with the horses?" she joked.

He laughed. "Might as well have. Today was the one afternoon we didn't get a short rainstorm. Go figure. Could've used it today."

"You got some sun too. Hope you drank enough water out there in this heat."

"I probably didn't. I know I need a shower though." He smelled his armpit through his dirty white t-shirt and wrinkled his nose. "Desperately."

She laughed. "You never smell horrible so it can't be that bad."

He whipped his head around, looking at her with his chin tucked and brows raised.

She laughed. "I'd still cuddle with you, even with you being all dirty and stinky."

"I might make ya gag but I'd still cuddle with you too." He winked.

The sun was going down and clouds were rolling in. When they got home, she took medicine for a headache and he went straight for the shower. When he came out into the living room, she was lying on the couch with an ice pack on her forehead and her eyes closed. He snuck back into the bathroom and closed the door quietly. A few minutes later he hovered over her on the couch as he sat next to her.

"Hey, baby," he whispered.

"Hmmm?" She took the ice pack off her head and opened her eyes.

"Come with me. Come on." He took her by the hand and led her to the bathroom. She entered as he stood behind her. The light was dim, candles flickered from the countertop, and a bubble bath had been drawn. Steam rose from the sudsy water in the large stand-alone tub.

"You drew me a bath?" She was touched by such a gesture.

"Hopefully it'll help your headache. Hop in and relax."

"Thanks, babe." She pecked his cheek and proceeded to take her clothes off. Her cut-off jeans flopped to the floor, then her t-shirt.

He stared for a moment then took hold of the door. "You want this shut to keep the heat in?" He was slowly pulling it shut.

"Sure, but with you on this side of the door." She dropped her panties and bra to the floor and stepped into the tub, sinking down beneath the white bubbly suds. She had that devilish smile upon her sweet face. Her perky breasts barely covered by the suds, she motioned with her finger for him to come to her, suds running down her hand.

"Glad I already showered," he joked as he stripped his sweat joggers off. He stepped into the tub and lowered himself into the opposite end, careful not to sit on her feet. His knees up on either side of hers, they both leaned forward for a passionate kiss. The clip which held her hair up was gently pulled out as he kissed her neck. He dropped the clip over the side of the tub. "You want a shoulder rub?"

"That would be lovely, Sawyer." She turned around and sat between his legs with her back to him. His strong hands put just the right amount of pressure on her neck and shoulders.

"You're pretty tensed up."

"Sitting at the desk staring at the computer after painting and moving the furniture I guess took its toll on me today."

"I could've done all that," he said softly.

"I wanted to do it. You were working really hard and this whole project was my idea. I won't let you do all the work yourself when I'm capable of helping."

"I appreciate that but promise you'll let me know if it's just too much. I don't want you to overdo it."

"I'm good, babe, but thank you."

"I'm sorry you have a headache. Wish I could take the pain away for you."

"Aww thank you. I'm sure the bath will help. I love your massages. You hit all the right spots. Feels so good." Her eyes closed, she exhaled a sigh and leaned her head back onto his solid chest. It was relaxing being against him. It was right where she wanted to be. His sudsy hands softly caressed her body.

"I could fall asleep right here with you." She sounded tired.

"Go right ahead, darlin', I'm not going anywhere."

"But you have something else in mind, don't you?" She turned her head, looking up at him.

He grinned. "Gosh, how could ya tell?"

She turned, her body completely facing him. His chest was all sudsy as she laid a hand upon his face, adding suds to his scruff.

"It's too *hard* for you to hide." She smirked.

He laughed. "Pun intended?"

"Absolutely." She grinned.

"My smartassness *has* rubbed off on you. I like it. Just ignore it and relax. I want your headache to go away."

"Maybe it's exactly what I need." She kissed him gently, now straddling him. His fingers mingled in her hair then he gave it a slow, gentle pull tight at the back of her head as he slipped inside her. She moaned as they fused together. She loved the hair pulling and he knew it. Their lips and tongues tangled as they felt each other's bodies completely. Suds transferred from one body to the other as the water swooshed back and forth, waves of delight taking her over. How romantic and sweet it was of him to draw her a candle-lit bath. He was so thoughtful but she'd rather share the ambiance with him than alone. Her headache dissipated as he soothed every ache within her.

CHAPTER 33

Office Work

"Hey, darlin', I'm gonna go to the office for a bit. I left the laptop there but I need to do chores anyway. I need to finish up this paperwork today." He hung the last feed bag and exited the gate but left it open.

"You need help?" Marina was leading Foxtrot and Legend out to pasture.

"Nah, I can handle it. Thanks though." He kissed her cheek. He was glistening with sweat already, and if the dampness of his t-shirt was anything to go by, it was a humid morning already.

"Is Justin working today?" she asked.

"Nah." He brushed hay off his tight jeans and she couldn't resist leaving the horses and pulling him to her.

"Mmm," he moaned, sliding his hands down into her back pockets and squeezing her rear. She grabbed his belt loops, pulling him against her pelvis.

"Damn, baby, you make me not wanna go to work."

"Maybe I'll bring you lunch in a little bit."

"Sounds good." He slapped her rear. "You can leave Foxtrot right there, I'll just ride him over," he said over his shoulder as he walked to the barn for the stable keys that hung just inside the barn door.

"Okay, I'll grab his saddle."

"Nah, I don't need one. I appreciate it though."

"Okay." She let Legend through the gate then shut it as Sawyer came out and grabbed a fist full of mane and jumped onto Foxtrot.

"I'll see you soon, love."

"Yes, sir." She winked.

"Oh, man I love you callin' me that." He tapped his boot on Foxtrot's side and took off galloping, his butt bouncing. She couldn't help but watch for a moment. She did some housework while he did chores at the stables, but she couldn't stop herself from continuously thinking about how he looked in those jeans and t-shirt and that round butt of his bouncing. He only got about two hours or so of work done at the office before Marina knocked at the door and entered.

"Hey, baby." He stopped typing on the laptop and sat back in his chair. She leaned her shoulder against the doorway.

"Is it lunchtime already?" he asked.

"Do you want it to be?" she asked, appealingly.

"Did you bring lunch?" He grinned, noticing she wasn't carrying in food.

"Sort of." She started unbuttoning her jeans shorts as she slowly walked toward him.

"Oh!" He bit his lip and looked her up and down then turned his swiveling chair toward her as she pulled closed the sliding barn door separating her and Sawyer's desks from Justin's.

She walked around his desk to him, her fingers running across the corner of the light oak, and straddled him in the chair, taking hold of his strong broad shoulders with one hand, the other on his thigh behind her, scraping her nails over the denim of his jeans. It was obvious that he was staring at her chest as she was braless under her tank top; her nipples were noticeable. He began breathing heavier, gripping her hips, as she kissed the side of his neck. He smelled of hair mousse and his citrus and cedarwood deodorant. She sucked his ear lobe before gently biting and sliding her teeth off it. He seemed to love that. He grabbed the bottom of her shirt and pulled it up over her head, exposing her bare breasts. She shook her hair free from it as it fell to the floor. She could feel him through his jeans and it excited her. She pulled his shirt up over his head and dropped it to the floor, kissing him roughly, a mouthful of desperate tongue. He lifted her by her ass, as he stood and sat her on his desk. He swiped the laptop, pen, papers, and everything off to the side. Papers scattered to the floor and the laptop teetered a moment on the edge of the desk before settling. He pulled her shorts down and off as she leaned back; she was bare beneath them, much to his surprise.

He kissed her then groaned, "I wanna kiss you, and not just on these lips." He sat in the chair in front of her, his hands slowly running up her parted thighs with a light touch. She swallowed hard, excited about what was coming next. He began kissing at her knees, working his way up her inner thighs, her fingers raking his spiked up hair as she looked down at his blue eyes staring up at her. His perfectly groomed scruffy face was tickling her skin, making her want to squirm. He inched to her groin, then further. She held her breath and tipped her head back, fingers moving to grasp the edge of the desk behind her. Her legs wrapped around his strong back, toes curling, legs quivering...he was talented. He stood and unzipped his jeans. She yanked them down then he leaned over her. He'd talk dirty in her ear in that sexy low voice that turned her on even more. She'd giggle then he'd nip at her bottom lip, sending a sharp jolt of ecstasy through her. He was making her moan and her eyes roll back. Their sexual spontaneity was exciting. She wrapped one leg around him while her other foot pressed against the chair's back directly behind him. He thrust into her repeatedly, holding her close, her chest against his. She moaned loudly, squeezing her thighs tightly against his sides and her nails grasping his shoulder blades.

"Turn around. I want you bent over this desk." His voice was low, almost a growl, and she could hear a hint of desperation in it. She turned around quickly and he grabbed a fist full of her hair.

He slapped her ass, earning himself a yelp and a playful giggle before her long, low moan told him just how much she appreciated his attention. Her moaning pitch climbed higher when he reached around for a handful of her soft, sensitive breast. The desk scraped loudly across the floor a few inches beneath the force of their bodies, more office supplies clattered to the floor; a photo frame smashed, and the lamp crashed, shattering glass and ceramic everywhere. The room fell silent on a shuddering breath from each as they took a few minutes to gather themselves, sweaty and panting, before he turned her around, pulled up his jeans, and held her face, kissing her.

"See what happens when you come in here teasin'?" He looked down at her with fire still lit in his eyes.

"Oh, I wasn't teasin'." She smiled and winked. Completely nude, she searched for her clothes. He retrieved her shorts from under the desk, shook them out, and handed them back to her. She got dressed and told him she would actually go get them lunch from town but had to love on him a moment more. They laughed at the mess they had made and Sawyer told her he'd clean it up while she went to town. They were kissing still as she slid open the door.

"You should've soundproofed those doors," Justin said, smiling and kicked back in his office chair, hands behind his head and feet up on his desk.

Marina looked horrified, her hands covering her mouth and whispered, "Oh, shit!" She looked to Sawyer, who stood beside her in the doorway trying to catch his breath and with glistening sweat upon his brow. Sawyer looked surprised at first but then laughed.

"Good thing she closed that barn door." Sawyer nodded.

"At least one of you closed a barn door." Justin looked down at Sawyer's pants and pointed, clearing his throat. Sawyer looked down and zipped his jeans.

"How long ya been here?" Sawyer asked, grinning.

"Long enough to know we need a new lamp for your desk."

"Oh, so not that long. Yeah, go ahead and put that on your list. A new photo frame too."

"Did the laptop survive?" Justin smiled.

"Surprisingly, it did," Sawyer said in a sarcastic tone with a shrugged shoulder, rubbing his chin scruff.

"Justin, you want lunch? Actual lunch?" Marina asked as she gave Sawyer a hug and he snickered.

"Sure. Thanks."

"I'll be back soon." She quickly headed for the door.

"Love you, baby." Sawyer winked at her.

"Love you too." She winked back.

Justin sat up, his feet on the floor and his elbows on his desk, staring at Sawyer.

"What?" Sawyer looked around for his shirt.

Justin shook his head and laughed. "Now I know what the deal is with these doors."

"I should've made them soundproof, huh?"

"Yep."

"Hmm. I didn't know you'd be here today." Sawyer tousled his hair then picked his shirt up off the floor.

"Obviously." Justin laughed.

"Sorry." Sawyer put his head and arms through his shirt and pulled it down.

"For what?"

"We wouldn't have done that if you were here beforehand."

"Is that true though?" Justin snickered with a lowered brow, checking out the design of the door slides.

"Actually...I don't know. She came in here asking if I wanted lunch while unbuttoning her shorts and she wasn't wearing a bra, so..."

"Yeah, I don't blame ya."

"Were we really that loud?" Sawyer tilted his head.

"Dude! It sounded like a good time to me." They laughed as Sawyer cleaned up and they started on paperwork before Marina got back with food...and a bra.

CHAPTER 34

The Culprit

Afic visiting the local flower shop together and confirming floral arrangements for the wedding, Sawyer and Marina walked across to the coffee shop for a fancy coffee. Sawyer paid and was waiting for their drinks when Marina spotted an acquaintance waving at her from outside. Holding a potted orchid in her hands, Marina excused herself to go say hello. The woman's back was to the window but she still looked familiar to Sawyer. He recognized that long dark hair.

With a coffee in each hand, he stepped outside and asked, "Marina, baby, who's your friend?" He knew exactly who the woman was and she grinned as she told Marina they'd do lunch that week.

"This is Joselyn. Joselyn, this is Sawyer, my fiancé."

"The hell it is." Sawyer just stared at her as she held out a hand.

"Sawyer, why are you being rude? That's not like you." Marina gritted her teeth and smiled apologetically at Jos.

Sawyer turned to Marina and asked, "Where'd you two meet?" He sipped his coffee, his eyes going back and forth between the women.

"We met here at the coffee shop a few weeks ago."

"I see."

"What's wrong?" Marina asked him.

"Marina, let me *re*introduce you to your new friend. This is Gabby." Sawyer glared at Gabby who was trying to fight her grin.

"What?" Marina was shocked. Tears instantly welled up in her eyes as she looked at Gabby, "Wait...*the* Gabby? As in the ex?" Marina looked down at the cracks in the sidewalk, trying to keep her composure. "So that's why you were so interested in my fiancé, all the questions. Why did you befriend me? Asking me to dinner...lying about your name..." Marina was feeling all kinds of emotions, but mainly angry.

"I needed to know you, to know who Sawyer was involved with and what he sees in you, to know your weaknesses. I think Sawyer and I still have a chance if he would just—"

"Are you crazy?" Sawyer interrupted. "You're out of your damn mind. You almost split Marina and me up. Do you know what kind of chaos you brought upon us? Normally, I'm a gentleman around ladies but you're no lady, Gabby. You're a conniving bitch."

Marina's eyes were huge. She had never heard him talk that way to or about a woman. The hard, cold look on his face showed how angry he was. His brows turned in, lips pursed together, his jaw tight.

"I don't know what kind of sick and twisted game you're playing but we want you to stay out of our lives. You and I breaking up allowed me to find the woman I was meant to be with. You're done trying to ruin our relationship. You tried once before over the phone and failed. Then you tried again and failed again because she and I have trust in each other, more so now after your second attempt. No more of your bullshit, you hear me?"

"Sawyer, I'm moving away." Jos rolled her eyes.

"Good!" he quickly replied.

"I want you to come with me." Gabby seemed so sincere but

Marina was appalled at her audacity. None of what Sawyer just said was sinking in at all.

Sawyer looked as though he was confused. "Are you shittin' me right now?"

"No, I'm serious. Please," Gabby pleaded.

Marina set the orchid on a table and pressed her hair back, preemptively pacing the sidewalk, her arms behind her head. She blew out a sharp breath while shaking her head. "Un-fucking believable!" she shouted. The stress of wedding planning along with the non-profit coordination was building up and she hadn't realized she was stressed until this moment.

Sawyer slammed the coffee down on the patio table next to Marina's orchid and crossed his arms. He stared at Gabby with a blank look on his face.

"If you were a dude, you'd be on the ground right now. I can't forgive you for what you've done and trying to befriend my fiancé...that's the last straw. You should leave." He nodded, looking away.

"I don't plan to come back so—"

"Good. I don't ever want to see you again."

"I can't return, especially if you don't come with me, because I can't stand to see you with someone else."

"Not my problem. You didn't care that I didn't want you with other guys when you and I were together so why should I care now how you feel?"

Gabby tilted her head and threw her arms down to her sides like a toddler not getting her way.

"Marina, you ready to go?" he asked.

"Yep, so ready." She stepped up to Gabby and slapped her hard across the face then snatched her coffee off the table and stuck her finger in Gabby's face.

Gabby's jaw dropped as she held a hand against her cheek.

"Sawyer was so right about you. You should be ashamed of yourself. You're jealous because you can tell he's head over heels for me but you took advantage of his kindness and ruined things for yourself. Don't meddle in our lives again. You can't have him and he doesn't want you anyways, but I'll make you sorry you ever met him if you ever come near either of us again." And there it was; the release of stressful tension that had been unknowingly brewing inside her. She took a deep breath after acting completely out of character.

Sawyer handed Marina the orchid and took Marina's hand after grabbing his coffee. They walked past Gabby who stood stock still, still in shock, a scowl on her face.

"Feel better?" Sawyer asked, unsure whether he dared to ask but did anyway.

"You have no idea. I can't believe she made me believe she was a potential friend."

"I can't believe you just slapped her in the face! That was amazing!" He laughed. "For real though, it's not your fault, she's sly like that. She's like a damn rattlesnake. It pisses me off she did that to you. I'm so sorry, baby."

"It's not anything you should be sorry about. She should be the sorry one, and she will be sorry if she shows up around here again. Becka and I felt a negative vibe the last time we ran into her. I'm surprised you were with her. You're so much better than that."

"Me too. I was an idiot. I learned from it though. It just took a while for the snake to shed its skin and for me to see her true self. I wised up. I wasted time and got my heart broken but it ended up for the best."

"Now you know you deserve better and what to never settle for again." Marina smiled up at him, his arm around her as they walked side-by-side.

"Oh, you're stuck with me." His brows rose.

She laughed. "That's what I wanted to hear."

CHAPTER 35

Flirtatious

The barn note read "Picking up hay load, Sabrina has a friend helping her. Love you."

Marina finished chores at home then went over to the property to make some phone calls at her desk. Marina greeted Sabrina when she arrived on Dixie. She let Dixie out into the round pen with the alpacas and pony then offered to help, but Sabrina said she brought a friend and Sawyer had approved it. Her friend came out of the stables, a fellow high schooler.

"This is Jordana."

Marina shook her hand and welcomed her.

"There's a ton of chores to be done out here each morning so, Sabrina, if you need help, you can bring a friend, but some days, there'll also be another guy here to help. Sawyer hired two when we went to the auction."

"Thanks, Marina."

"I need to make some phone calls then I'll help Sawyer unload hay when he gets here. Y'all need my help first?"

"Oh, no, we're good. Thanks though."

"I'll be in the office if you need me."

"Yes, ma'am."

Marina went into the office as the girls carried on with chores.

She had just finished her last call when Sawyer pulled in, the large flatbed loaded with hay. He backed up that trailer like a pro, which she found so incredibly hot. Marina grabbed a pair of work gloves and met him at the truck. Of course, she received a kiss before they started unloading just outside the big-end barn door. She put her gloves on as he grabbed his gloves from his back pocket. He donned a white Stetson to go with his white t-shirt and blue jeans. She couldn't help but stare at him as he tossed hay bales down. All the muscles he was using, those arms and the veins bulging...he looked amazing. When she would turn to stack the bales just inside the barn doors, he would stare at her in her cut-offs and tank top. They barely covered her rear and when she bent over, they'd sneak higher a little. She caught him staring and smiled a sexy, teasing smile. He bit his lip and moaned. She giggled and told him, "I know what you're thinking because I'm thinking it too, but we have a lot of hay to unload, mister."

"Yes, ma'am." He looked disappointed.

Jordana came over to ask Marina if she could show them where the grooming brushes were, so Marina led the way, apologizing for having moved them. Sabrina asked Sawyer to help her so he showed her how to safely apply fly spray on Willow's face and told her if it didn't work by the afternoon to put the fly mask on her. The Arabian's big eyes attracted gnats like crazy. He went back to the trailer and tossed a few bales down before Marina made it back to help.

"Oh my God! *That* guy is Sawyer? The guy that bought your horse and gave it back then gave you a job?"

"Yeah, that's him. He's a really kind man. Marina is sweet too."

"Yeah, I'm sure, but he's like, super-hot! You didn't mention that!"

"Shhh."

"What? I'm just sayin'. Have you hit on him yet?"

"What? No!"

"Why not?"

"Because I work for him. Plus, he's almost twice my age."

"So?"

"So. I wouldn't do that. He's kind of a friend. My horse stays here. I can't risk losing her, I almost did once."

"Well, if you're not gonna hit on him—"

"No! Don't! Jordana, I'm serious. Please don't." Sabrina pointed her finger at Jordana.

"How serious could they be anyways? Maybe I'll find out." Dust flew off the horses' backs.

"They're getting married this weekend."

"Oh, man! Ugh, not fair."

"Keep brushing and stop thinking about him, okay?" Sabrina instructed.

"Girl, I don't know how you've refrained from flirting with him or grabbing hold of those arms. He's like a Roman God."

"Jordana..." Sabrina shook her head as she brushed Willow's mane.

Marina and Sawyer unloaded almost all of the hay.

"Baby, I can finish these last few bales. Would you mind grabbing us water?" Sawyer wiped the sweat off his brow.

"Sure." She flopped her gloves onto the trailer and went to the office.

Jordana saw Marina entering the barn.

"I'm going to get us water. I'll be right back." Jordana handed Sabrina her brush and walked away.

Sawyer jumped down off the trailer, his shirt wet from sweat and sticking to him. He took his hat off and set it on the trailer, ran his fingers through his drenched hair, and grabbed the bottom of this shirt. He got it pulled up halfway when Jordana came up behind him and slapped his rear, hard.

She shouted, "Ooh yeah, take it off, cowboy!"

His eyes were huge and he jerked his shirt back down before he whipped around and scowled at her, but she was walking away already. He didn't say anything to her but he was not amused. In fact, he was downright pissed. "What the hell?" he mumbled to himself.

Jordana rejoined Sabrina in taking care of brushes and fly spray.

"Where's the water? I'm thirsty," Sabrina asked.

Jordana had a deer-in-headlights look on her face.

"Oh, crap. Jordana, what did you do? You weren't really going to get water, were you?" Sabrina tossed the brushes up on the shelf. "Damn it!"

"His ass is rock solid! My hand bounced right back off it." Jordana laughed. "I bet that guy could crush walnuts between those thighs." She flipped her hair back, proud of her scandalous behavior.

"After I fill this trough, we're done for the day so I'll take you home."

"You're no fun."

"I'm trying to be responsible, Jordana. I need this job. Those two did a generous favor for me without me asking. They were complete strangers yet were kind enough to help me out. I owe them. I don't need you making trouble for me. I don't want to be on bad terms with them."

Marina had brought water out to Sawyer and could tell he was pissed. She unhooked the trailer from the truck and asked, "Babe, you look upset, you okay?" She cracked open her water and took a drink. "The phone rang so I answered it. Sorry, it took a minute."

He chugged more than half the bottle before he answered, "It's okay. I'll be fine. I'll tell you in a minute."

The girls were walking by and Sawyer turned his back to them at first, then hollered at Sabrina. He nodded for her to come to him then he walked toward the barn, telling Marina, "I gotta take care of something first real quick."

"Great," Sabrina said sarcastically to Jordana then handed her the car key and told her to start it.

Marina sat on the edge of the trailer drinking water, curious as to what had happened.

Sabrina entered the barn and Sawyer was leaning against a stall door with his arms crossed.

"Sawyer, I'm sorry. Jordana probably did something she shouldn't have and I tried to stop her."

Sawyer hung his head for a moment then said, "Listen, Sabrina. I don't care if you bring a friend to help you, but please don't bring *her* again."

"Yes, sir." Sabrina hung her head, not able to look him in the eye. He stepped closer to her and tipped her chin up.

"I'm not mad at you."

"You're not?" She seemed relieved but surprised.

"No. You're not the one that slapped my ass and told me to take off my shirt."

"Oh, God." Sabrina's cheeks flushed a brilliant red.

"In a way, it was flattering, but she's too young and it's disrespectful to do that to someone who's in a committed relationship. It's not respectful to me because now I have to tell my fiancé and it's not respectful to Marina for another woman to be touchin' her man."

"I know, I know, I'm so sorry." She looked down. "I told her not to do anything stupid when she kept going on about how hot you are—" She stopped and looked up at him, ashamed she said that out loud.

He smirked. "Thank you for trying to talk her down. She's bold."

"Yeah, she has a mind of her own."

"I'm not going to risk my relationship with Marina over a teenager hitting on me. That girl won't stop there, I know her type. She's bound to be trouble."

"I understand. I won't bring her again."

"Thank you."

"Of course. I'll apologize to Marina too, it's the right thing to do."

"If you care to, that's fine. We can go tell her together then." He patted her shoulder and walked out of the barn; she followed.

Jordana was waiting in Sabrina's car. Marina was sitting on the trailer still, dangling her legs off.

"Hey, guys." She smiled, but that smile dissipated when Sawyer stood in front of her with crossed arms and Sabrina stood next to him looking like a puppy who had just been scolded.

"What's going on, Sawyer?" Marina asked, setting her empty water bottle next to her.

"Sabrina's friend, while you took that call and got water, made a bold move and slapped my ass. Hard. She told me to 'take it off, cowboy' as I was starting to take off my shirt. I didn't know she was behind me. Sabrina had a feeling her friend would try something and tried to talk her down."

Marina just stared at the two of them until Sabrina spoke up and said, "She said she was going to get us water but didn't come back with any. I knew she did something stupid. I'm so sorry for bringing her. I won't bring her again."

Marina was quiet for a moment.

"Darlin', say something," Sawyer said.

Marina looked away then back at him, her head tilted; she shielded her eyes with her forearm and said, "Well, she's got good taste."

Sawyer's brows turned in. "What?"

"She has good taste. Babe, you're hot. Chicks are gonna hit on you. The fact that you came to me right away to tell me tells me you have no interest in her and you've proven I can trust you anyway."

"No, I don't have any interest in anyone but you."

"I know. She had her fun but it was disrespectful of her, knowing you're taken."

Sawyer nodded. "I'm surprised you aren't pissed."

Sabrina told Marina, "Ma'am, I don't want to cause any trouble. I owe both of you a lot and I'm thankful for everything."

Marina hopped off the trailer and gave her a hug. "Honey, I know you didn't mean for that to happen. It's not your fault. You can't really control how someone else acts. Bless her heart. You don't worry about a thing, just take your friend home and don't bring her back because if I see her again...it won't be pretty."

Sawyer snickered.

"Yes, ma'am. Again, I'm so sorry."

"It's okay, Sabrina." Sawyer smiled at her and she quickly walked to her car and left.

"She has good taste? What the hell?" Sawyer was confused.

Marina laughed. "Well, you're hot. She was probably thinking the same thing I was when I came to work for you. That's how we started out. Flirting."

"No..." He pulled her to him. "We started out that very first second I laid my eyes on you. That's when I came up with an excuse to *keep* laying my eyes on you. Leaving you barn notes gave you another reason to want to come back, and *keep* coming back, for me to spend time with you. Marina, I fell hard and fast for you long before that first kiss."

"Well, I'm glad to hear it because when I laid eyes on you that day, I didn't wanna ever look into another man's eyes again; not like I was looking into yours. I wasn't coming back just because of the barn notes, or your music notes, I was coming back for you to sweep me off my feet, which you did over and over again. There was no way I could've resisted you. Sawyer, I still get butterflies every time you kiss me. It's been a year. I think I always will."

"I hope so." He caressed the side of her face and looked into her eyes before kissing her.

"There they go, the butterflies. I think she's right. You should take this off, cowboy." She tugged on the front of his shirt.

He laughed and peeled his sweaty shirt off as she watched.

"Dixie will be fine for a while. She's made new friends. Wanna hit the pool?" he asked, flinging his shirt over his shoulder.

"Absolutely." She handed him his hat and he carried it back to the truck, holding her hand with his other.

"Good. I've been wanting to try out my new Speedos." He got all excited as he opened her door.

She climbed in. "Your what?" she asked as her door shut.

209

He hopped in and started the truck.

"Did you just say you have a pair of Speedos?"

"Yes, ma'am, I did."

She looked at him, confused. "Like, the men's swimming briefs?"

"Yeah, I'm excited to try them out." His white pearly smile made her smile.

"I'm excited to see them on you! Although, I'm sure they won't stay on for long." She was trying to contain her uncontrollable smile.

CHAPTER 36

Road Trip

Marina came out onto the porch in a t-shirt of Sawyer's to find him sitting on the swing, drinking coffee and on the phone with Chris. He tapped the seat next to him for her to come to sit. She sat, careful not to spill his coffee. She hadn't yet poured herself a cup so she took his for a sip and handed it back. He smiled and kissed her then covered the phone speaker against his chest as he said quietly, "Good morning', darlin'."

She whispered back, "Good morning, handsome," and rested her legs up over his. He continued his phone conversation.

"Nah, It's about three hours from here. I'll leave here shortly. Sure, you're welcome to go. Yeah, I'll let you have first pick then I'll take the rest of what he has for the stables if Grant decides he doesn't want them. He said three or four. Nah, he didn't say what condition they're in but he's selling them cheap. He couldn't get down here to this auction. Might be a messy situation, just a fair warning. He said two had been abused before he acquired them. I'm bringing them back either way. Grant asked me to bring them to him. We'll figure it out. Wanna head on over here then? Sounds good."

"Where you goin'?" Marina asked after he hung up as she, once again, shared his coffee.

"I love that you like to share my things." He chuckled and rubbed her smooth leg. "North of here to a ranch. A guy hollered at Dave but Dave can't take any more right now til he gets some sold so he had the guy call me. I figure we can use them at the stables, but at the very least, they'd have a home and be taken care of if Grant doesn't end up wanting them."

"Ok. Will you be back tonight? Who's Grant?"

"Oh yeah, hopefully by dark. Grant's a sanctuary owner who talked to Dave about these horses. Good guy too. You wanna come along?"

"Well, the chores here—"

"I can go do them while I wait for Chris," he interrupted, playing with her hair, which hadn't been combed yet.

"Well if Chris is going, I don't want to intrude on guy time." She squeezed his arm.

"You wouldn't be."

"Maybe Chris would just rather it be you guys."

"He wouldn't mind, baby." He sipped his coffee and offered it to her, knowing she would take it anyway.

"I'll think about it. We should get chores done, though. I'll go get dressed." She sipped his coffee then handed it back, patted his thigh, and stood.

He followed her and slapped her mostly-covered rear on the way in and said, "I'm so glad that ass is mine."

After chores, Sawyer hooked up the large horse trailer and Marina went inside the house. He went in and got his hat and wallet and took it out to the truck. Chris pulled in a few minutes after and parked over by the barn, out of the way. He threw his hat in Sawyer's truck and, as the guys were talking outside the truck, Marina came out of the house with her purse.

"I reckon she changed her mind." Sawyer smiled, watching her walk toward them.

"Looks like I'm ridin' bitch." Chris grabbed his hat from the passenger seat and got in the back. Sawyer laughed. "Maybe she'll let you ride shotgun on the way back."

She was snackin' and singin', her tan feet tapping on the dash, sun on her legs, her jean skirt hiking higher. She looked adorably sexy. He thought to himself that he was the luckiest man on Earth to have her next to him. His knees were wide apart, a foot on the gas, the other bouncing with the beat of the music on the radio. His right shoulder moving with muscle memory from playing guitar to the song playing. His hand ran from her knee to her thigh. He'd look at her, then glance back at the road, then at her, then the road, repeatedly as his hand inched higher. He looked up in his rearview mirror to find Chris still sleeping. Apparently, he hadn't gotten much sleep lately. There weren't any other vehicles near them either.

His hand groped the inside of her athletic thigh then he walked his fingers up under her skirt to her groin. *What is he doing?* She thought to herself. She looked over at him with wide eyes, then looked in the backseat to be assured that Chris was sleeping. Her heart began to race as he held the truck steady on the road as he crossed that line...her panty line, that is.

She gripped the door with one hand, the other gripping his arm. His forearm muscles flexed as she tried to keep her breathing quiet, those sudden, deep, sharp exhales. Her head leaned back, pressing against the headrest, and her knees parted, allowing him better access. Her eyes kept dancing to the rearview mirror to make sure they weren't being watched, then they'd go right back to him. Goddamn, he looked so hot in that tight blue t-shirt and those tight jeans. His shirt was lifted onto the edge of his jeans enough to show a couple of inches of his leather belt. She was trying her best to resist the urge to crawl on top of him. She reached over and grabbed his thick thigh, squeezing it tightly. She was probably leaving bruises with how her fingernails were digging into his leg, but she didn't care. She was concentrating more on what he was making her feel; complete ecstasy. The deeper he played, the more saturated she became. His smirk turned into a grin and when he bit his bottom lip and got more aggressive with those fingers, she bit her fist and closed her eyes. Her pink painted toes gripped the dashboard and her calves quivered. She was almost there...almost.

A semi-truck entering the freeway from an on-ramp came up next to them and the driver pulled that cord and honked that loud horn. The noise woke up Chris and, as he sat up, Sawyer's hand retreated to her thigh at her skirt hem.

"I told you I owed you." Sawyer snickered. She released a deep breath.

"Thanks to the rude semi-driver, you still do," she said with a cheeky smirk.

Sawyer laughed and winked. "Yes, ma'am."

"Why'd they honk?" Chris asked as he rubbed his eyes.

"A car wouldn't get over for him to enter the lane," Sawyer said as he looked at Marina and shrugged at the fib he had made up so quickly. She couldn't contain her smile as she looked out her passenger window.

"Yeah, it had to be embarrassing for the driver he honked at." Marina stared straight ahead, trying hard not to laugh.

"Nah, they'll never see that semi-driver again." Sawyer smirked that smartass grin that she found irresistible.

"I don't know about y'all but I have to piss," Chris said.

"Me too," Marina agreed.

"I'll get off on the next exit." Sawyer turned his blinker on as Marina snickered. He caught on that she took it as a pun and laughed.

"I have no clue what y'all are up there snickering about but I really gotta piss, so punch it, dude."

"I got ya, I got ya. You want me to hit all these potholes then, right?" Sawyer swerved on purpose as he exited the freeway.

"You're a dick," Chris said.

Sawyer found it hilarious. They pulled into a large gas station truck stop. Sawyer dropped Chris off at the door before driving around closer to where the semis park. He stopped and put the truck in park in an open area.

"How bad you gotta go?" he asked her.

"What?"

"How bad?"

"I figured I'd go while we were stopping."

"Not an emergency?" He seemed to be asking these questions in a rush.

"No. Why?"

"Climb in the back." Sawyer got out of the truck and got in the back as she was climbing over the console.

"What are we doing?" Marina asked, fully aware of what Sawyer wanted. She could tell from the bulge still in the front of his jeans.

"What do you think we're doin', baby?" He unfastened his belt and unzipped his jeans then pulled them down just past his rear. She was looking around out the windows as she grabbed his shoulders and straddled him. He slid her wet thong over to the side as she hiked her skirt and lowered herself onto him.

"It's broad daylight, Sawyer." His beard felt soft against the palm of her hand.

"Mmmhmm, I know. I don't care. You look irresistible. I just wanted you. Right now." He sounded almost angry and she liked it, it was almost a demand. They were definitely more exposed than in the car wash. The little black cowboy hat air freshener hanging from the rearview mirror was swinging side-to-side.

"Chris isn't gonna be long." Her fingers raked through his hair then she gave a little tug before biting his bottom lip.

"Neither will I," he said in her ear then kissed her aggressively. He squeezed her rear with both hands then pulled her hair hard enough that her head tilted back for him to suck softly on her neck. She climaxed quickly with him grabbing her hips and the excitement of taking such a risk. Her slick wet heat excited him and he erupted right after. Her forehead gently connected with his as they took a second to calm from the daring, public extracurricular activity. As she was lifting herself off him, a semi pulled in and parked next to them and honked.

"Oh, shit! It's the same semi!" Marina was horrified but Sawyer was laughing as he zipped his jeans. Marina climbed to the front as Sawyer got out of the back and got back in the driver's seat. He pulled the truck around to where the cars parked and he and Marina got out of the truck to go in. The semi-driver was walking a ways behind them when Chris came out of the building with a bunch of snacks in his arms.

"Good timing. Here are the keys." Sawyer passed Chris the key as he and Marina went in to use the restroom. When they came out to get in the truck that Chris had running already, the semi-driver waved at them. Sawyer nodded and waved. Marina was still horrified.

"Oh my God, he totally saw us messing around, Sawyer."

"Yeah, he did." He found it hilarious and seemed almost proud as he opened her door.

"What was that about?" Chris asked as Sawyer got in the truck.

"What snacks did you get?" Marina tried to derail his train of thought.

"Bunch of stuff. I'll share. Y'all needed a minute to make out and that trucker caught ya, I'm guessin'."

Marina looked at Sawyer.

Sawyer nodded. "Yes, sir."

Chris laughed. "Y'all don't be doin' stuff while I'm sleeping back here."

"Nah, we wouldn't do that, would we?" He tapped Marina's knee as he waited for a truck to pull in so he could pull out the drive.

"Nope, that would be rude." She chugged water and cleared her throat. "But it wouldn't be a bad idea for Chris to ride shotgun on the way back."

Sawyer bursted out a laugh as he took a drink of water.

With Sawyer drumming on the steering wheel and sometimes

pulling out the air guitar, Chris drumming on the console, and the three of them singing, they rolled up to the ranch. White fencing lined the property and the bright green maple trees were lined in rows. Dirt settled as they lowered the trailer ramp just outside the big barn. The rancher came out, a tall thin man wearing a buffalo plaid shirt with jeans and sporting a long dark beard. They shook hands and spoke of the horses' backgrounds and demeanor before exchanging paperwork and cash and loading up the horses. They seemed to be in decent shape but two had been previously abused before being taken in by this ranch, so extra care was taken getting them loaded. Sawyer would have Doc come out for an evaluation within a few days; he called him on the drive home. Chris helped them unload when they returned home before heading home himself with one of the four horses, a black and white Tennessee Walker paint. Sawyer kept the two that had been mistreated so he could work with them and one other that was pregnant. The brown Appaloosa seemed healthy but the silver dapple flaxen and the chestnut looked to be a bit under-weight. They were all beautiful, just needed some TLC, and now they were in the right place to receive it. Sawyer and Marina got the horses settled in the separate quarantine area of the stables at the property.

"We don't have any two horses that look similar. You realize that?" Marina asked on their way up to the house.

"I like a variety."

"Thanks for bringing me along today. You knew I'd be excited about new horses, didn't you?"

"Absolutely, darlin'."

"I like road trips with you." She squeezed his hand.

"I knew you would."

CHAPTER 37

Pulling Strings

S awyer had the music speaker on while chopping herbs in the kitchen. He was pretty talented with a chef's knife. One hand was on top of the Santoku knife, pressing down sharply as the other rocked the handle. He had been in there a while; the rack of lamb was almost done in the oven. He opened the oven door and slid the rack forward to add the herbs then shut the door. Marina arrived home and set her purse on the end table and followed the sound of the music to the kitchen. He heard her enter and turned the music down.

"Babe, it smells amazing in here. What's the occasion?" she asked.

"Thanks! I don't need a reason to spoil you," he said as she entered and saw him in a blue apron. *Just* a blue apron.

"Oh, babe!" She dropped her shopping bag.

He had batter on his face.

"Have you been licking the beaters again?" she asked as she licked it off his cheek. It was sweet so he must have made dessert too.

"I like to stay on my game." He fumbled to untie his apron as he snatched her and pressed her against the counter near the sink. He started kissing her neck but, luckily, fought the urge to rip his

218

apron off so soon after she returned home. She was snickering and tapping his arm, trying to get his attention.

His bare rear could be seen by Raquel, who had come into the house with Marina. She had a side view of the two of them. Sawyer looked at Marina, biting his lip like he could bite hers off. Marina's eyes looked over at the doorway. Sawyer's eyes slowly followed.

"Oh shit!" He quickly turned so she couldn't see his backside. Raquel and Marina both giggled.

"Sorry, babe." Marina shrugged.

"Well, I mean she's already seen my ass now. No point in hiding it. Sorry, Raquel."

"Oh, Jesus, don't be. Really. You have *nothing* to be sorry for. Whose strings do I have to pull to get a meal like that made for me?" She laughed.

"Thanks." He grinned and winked. "You staying for dinner?"

"As much as I'd love to, no thank you. I just needed to use the restroom. So, I'm going to go do that real quick and splash cold water on my face." She went through the kitchen and down the hall, hand up next to her face to block her view, but peeked through her fingers at his rear, which he was not covering.

"Think we can get in a quicky before she comes back?" he whispered, pulling Marina to him.

"No!" She slapped him with a dish towel.

"What is it with ladies and dish towels?"

"What is it with men being so horny all the time?"

He slapped his arms down to his sides. "You've never complained before. If you weren't so sexy all the time..."

She laughed. "Oh, I'm not complaining, definitely not. Just making an observation. For the record, you're sexy all the time too. In fact, you're sizzling right now. Maybe it's the timing, again."

"Maybe. But geez that's what you do to me. Besides, you like it risky." He was kissing her when Raquel came out.

"Y'all are like wild animals." Raquel giggled on her way back through the kitchen.

"It's true." Sawyer shrugged with a smirk.

"Life will never be mundane with this man." Marina smiled back at Sawyer as she walked Raquel out.

Raquel whispered to Marina, "Wow! Good for you!" She gave Marina a thumbs up and a hug on the porch before heading to her car.

Marina laughed, waving goodbye. She went back into the kitchen and opened the oven.

Sawyer was getting a glass of water. "It's almost done."

"Rack of lamb? Wow, you got all fancy. I didn't know you could cook like this." She shut the oven door.

"Oh, I can cook, I just don't like spending the time going all out often. I figured it's been a while since I cooked something fancy. My girl deserves it." He smirked.

"Aww, you're sweet." She pulled him in by the front of his apron for a hug then squeezed his butt cheeks with both hands and told him, "You better go put pants on before we decide dessert comes before the meal."

"Hey, we're adults. There's no rule now that says we can't." He nibbled her neck, making her giggle but she pushed him away. "Fine," he pouted. He strutted those tight, round, muscular cheeks to the bedroom, dropping his apron in the dining room on his way.

As they ate dinner, fully clothed, which was delicious, Sawyer told her, "Sabrina called me today."

"Yeah? What's she up to?"

"She said she's attending the bridal party at the bar tomorrow night so I told her I'll put her down on the list but she isn't allowed to drink. She also wanted to know if we had a way for her to earn more money. Something about expensive jeans. I told her I'd talk to you and let her know. I know you don't like giving up yard work."

Marina laughed. "That's very considerate of you. I do like

doing our yard work. What about taking care of the landscaping over at the stables though? Or the bar?"

"I'll let her know. I'm okay with that if you are."

"Sure. Maybe she could help with chores more over there too in the mornings. It's a lot for one person to handle, so even if one of the guys you hired is there she can help. There are evening chores over there too. We have our own to do here, so between those and work, we'll be putting in some long days."

"True. I guess it'll help. I'll pay her from our personal account for landscaping. I don't wanna use donation money for that."

"Oh no, I agree."

"Okay, I'll give her a call back. We have a tax-exempt account at the hardware store now too."

"Okay, good to know...just don't be leaving her barn notes." Marina looked up at him and smiled.

He set down his fork and walked over to her side of the table, sitting next to her, his leg against hers, and looking her in the eyes. "Oh, baby, those were only for you, remember? I told you I had to keep you coming back and give you something to look forward to every day."

"Oh, Sawyer. I would've anyway because I just couldn't wait to see you again. You're irresistible so I couldn't resist watching you in those tight jeans unloading hay...but who knew barn notes would lead to our next chapter?"

"Well, I sure hoped they would. To be fair, you did actually resist me just before dinner tonight."

"I'm not sure how I've held out so long either. I'm ready for dessert *now*." She stood and started walking toward the bedroom, giving a flirty off-the-shoulder glance with those pretty wide eyes. He quickly jumped to his feet, tipping the chair over as he ran after her.

CHAPTER 38

Party up in Backcountry

Thursday morning, the barn note read "You've got me Love Drunk". She loved it but had no idea it meant something special. She carried on with chores while Sawyer was over at the stables working on a few last-minute things. One of those things was hanging a big country-style sign on the front of the stables that read *The Brandton Ranch* at the top and *Taking the Reins* in a smaller font below.

That night was about to be hoppin' at Backcountry. Bob and Gladys arranged for the bar to be open only for a private party for Marina and Sawyer. Everyone attending the wedding had been invited and the guys planned to play music. They had asked that any gifts for the bride and groom be given at the party instead of the ceremony. The brick oven pizzas that the bar had become practically famous for would be served and drinks would be flowing freely.

Sawyer and Marina arrived at the bar shortly before everyone else, except for Bob and Gladys. Gladys asked them to follow her to the back.

"Is this going to be enough alcohol for the reception?"

"Holy shit, Gladys! Yes ma'am, I'd say so!" Sawyer laughed. "There's a problem if we were to need more." He rubbed his chin scruff as he looked through the bottles of liquor on the shelf and boxes and boxes of beer.

"Well, I'd rather have more than enough than not enough. I can always use whatever's left here."

"True." Marina shrugged, agreeing.

"Anything else I need to order? There's champagne for the toasts too."

"No ma'am, looks like you have everything covered. I appreciate it."

"Oh, we appreciate you, Sawyer." Gladys slapped him with her dish towel.

"One of these days, all those damn dish towels are gonna come up missin'." He side-hugged Gladys on their way back out to the front.

"You wish, cowboy."

"I want y'all to have a good time tonight, Gladys. Kick back and relax, dance, drink, just have a good time." Sawyer leaned against the bar.

"Yeah, we can make our own drinks if we need to," Marina assured.

"Okay, I'll just let y'all help yourselves. Besides making the pizzas, we'll hang out with y'all."

"Perfect." Marina nodded then excused herself to take a quick phone call.

"She's got something up her sleeve." Sawyer watched her, curious, until she came back over to him. She didn't say anything about the call so he didn't ask. Some of the guests started to arrive and the band came in and started setting up. Their girlfriends came with them and Marina was thrilled that they did. She didn't see them often but they all got along so well when they did get together. Jake didn't bring his girlfriend, whom only Sawyer and the other guys had met. Jake said she had made prior plans but he wasn't thrilled that she didn't want to come.

The bridesmaids came, even Bailey Rose, Savannah, and Aliza from out of town. They were all excited to hear the guys play.

Aliza and Savannah had a blast when they came months prior and had told the other girls all about it. Justin got there and helped the guys up on stage, putting stools and microphones out. Even Tom, Caroline, and Drew went straight to the bar from the airport. Dave, Doc, Danielle, and Sabrina came too. The photographer was ready to savor memories and brought along a second photographer to help out. Everyone greeted each other warmly and introduced themselves to each other. It was great having all their favorite people in one place.

A couple of strangers came and sat at the bar. Bob served them and Marina waved at them.

"It's a pleasure having all of you here with us tonight to celebrate our marriage coming up in just two short days," Sawyer began, standing on stage at the microphone. "I can't tell y'all how freaking excited I am to be able to call that gorgeous woman my wife." He pointed at Marina and the crowd cheered. Marina wore the biggest smile as her eyes connected with his. She loved that he was so excited to marry her. He looked so good in that tight black t-shirt and tight jeans, making the simplest outfit look absolutely amazing. "It makes me so happy to have all of our favorite people in one room together. We're gonna have a blast tonight. It's the party before the party! What do y'all say?" Sawyer raised his glass then everyone else followed. The crowd cheered, "To Marina and Sawyer!" Sawyer tipped his glass back for a chug then set it down on the stool and strapped his guitar over his shoulder. Guitars started strumming as Jake and Sawyer both stood at the microphones. *Cowgirls* by Morgan Wallen and Ernest was a fun way to start the evening. They had everyone up dancing as they rocked it out singing it together.

"Woo! That was a warm welcome, y'all! We appreciate it. We're just getting started though." The guys got arranged on their stools and Sawyer sang *Tennessee Whiskey* by Chris Stapleton. He knew everyone would enjoy that one, it was popular on the radio. Justin asked Marina to dance during that song and Sawyer pointed at him as a playful warning but then nodded and smiled. Most of the couples stood to dance.

Sawyer called Marina up to the stage and she stood as they remained seated. She had gained a bit more confidence so she passed when offered the third stool. Her white country sundress flowed with her as she stepped up to the microphone. Sawyer couldn't help but smile; she looked beautiful in that dress. It made her tan look tanner and it went perfectly with the white cowgirl boots and hat he bought her to wear that night. She sang *Tennessee Orange* by Megan Moroney since her man was from Tennessee. Since she was already up there, Sawyer stood with her as they sang *Need You Now* by Lady A together. Their parents thought it was adorable. They were two stars shining brightly up there on that stage. Marina sat with her mom when she stepped down.

"Jake is taking this next one, y'all. Tear it up, Jake." Sawyer and Jake both stood but Jake took the lead on *Y'all Life* by Walker Hayes and Sawyer sang background. As a southern crowd, that song was much enjoyed. They took a break, ate pizza, and had a drink while mingling.

"Who's the couple up at the bar?" Sawyer asked Marina in a quiet voice.

"Well, they're kind of your gift."

"What do you mean?"

"They're from Nashville. They own a record-producing company. I asked them to come watch tonight."

"Are you serious?"

She couldn't tell at first if he was happy or not. "Yeah, I hope that's okay. I thought since you guys are so good at playing music and your voice is amazing, maybe you would want to take a shot at recording it professionally."

"We've only written a few of our own songs."

"Which I haven't even heard yet, but I believe in you. If it's something you care to try, go for it. If not, I can ask them to leave. I don't want to overstep."

"No, no, don't ask them to leave. I think it's awesome that you did this."

"Yeah?"

"Yeah, I'm thankful that you think that highly of us. This is an amazing gift! Thank you." He kissed her excitedly, his hands upon her face. "This is an exciting opportunity. What if they don't think we're good enough though? I'm nervous."

"Babe, you don't have to worry about that. I mean, really."

He smiled wide and kissed her again. "You know you'd be featured on the album with us, right?" He nodded and raised a brow.

"Really?"

"Oh, yeah. So, you better get back up there and sing again tonight."

"We all gotta give it our all then."

"Let's do it." He squeezed her hand before heading back to the stage with her.

"I'll feel bad if it doesn't work out. I don't have a backup gift." She stopped mid-way to the stage, holding his hand still.

"Baby, you're gift enough. The fact that you tried to make it happen means the world to me."

The couple gave Marina a thumbs-up and a smile. She nodded back as she placed a nervous hand on the microphone. The guys took a seat on their stools as they started playing *Heart Like A Truck* by Lainey Wilson. Marina sang it with all her heart and soul as her hips swayed. Sawyer was so proud of her. Gladys and Bob shared a sweet slow dance. When the song was over, he told her to go solo with Trev on piano. She insisted the couple was there to see Sawyer and the guys play, not her, but he told her it was important to him and to her friends to see her up on that stage having just as much fun. She sang *Always Remember Us This Way* by Lady Gaga as Trev played the keyboard and the other guys chilled on stage with a beer. She gave Sawyer a sweet kiss before stepping down and telling him, "The rest of the night is about y'all. Tear it up like you always do."

He smiled and nodded as he rested his guitar on his leg, but then Aliza shouted, "Play *I Wrote The Book!*"

"Yeah, that's hot!" Savannah hollered. The guys all laughed. Sawyer shook his head, laughing, then stood, readjusted the microphone with his wrist-banded hand, and said in a deep, sexy tone, "I can't sing that without rolling my abs though."

All the ladies stood, cheering and whistling. The guys were cracking up.

"Okay, okay. Whatever the ladies want is what the ladies get. They're askin' for it so I'm gonna give it to 'em." He took off his black cowboy hat and set it on his stool over his glass. There he stood with his feet apart, thick thighs moving, a good shirt-lifted ab roll toward the end of the song included, and complete with a smoldering look on his face. The bridesmaids loved it. They fanned themselves as if they were cooling a hot flash. Trev went and poured the guys each a drink and took them back to the stage as folks took a bathroom break. Once everyone came back, Sawyer and Jake sang *Dirt* by Florida Georgia Line together.

"We've got a mash-up for y'all tonight. We couldn't decide which of these three Keith Urban songs to play so we're playing bits of all three rolled into one song. Hope y'all enjoy our drunkin' creativity." Sawyer laughed as the band started with *You're My Better Half,* then blended into *Sweet Thing*, then into *Once in A Lifetime*. Chris ended with killer drumming skills.

"Now that was cool!" The Nashville gentleman hollered.

"Thank you, sir! We've just got two more for y'all tonight. This next one is a favorite of mine and Jake's. I play it in the truck often—"

"He plays it in the office a lot too! On the air guitar he pulls out from under his desk!" Justin cupped his hands around his mouth and hollered.

"It hasn't killed ya yet. Another reason for those sliding office doors." Sawyer laughed as Justin shook his head. Sawyer and Jake still stood, Jake adjusting the tuning pegs on his electric guitar. They played *Springsteen* by Eric Church, their heels were clunking, pounding the hollow stage floor, shoulders jerking with the beat, heads bobbing, as they showed their talent with those guitars. Jake sang harmony backup like he always did; sometimes facing each other and sometimes their backs together while jamming.

"Y'all seemed to enjoy that one. That makes me smile." Sawyer took a gulp of liquid courage as soon as they finished that song. "So, this last one, only the guys have heard. I wrote it, we've been rehearsing it, but Marina hasn't even heard it yet. We're taking a stab at writing songs now, so let us know what ya think. Marina, baby, I wrote this for you as your wedding gift from me. I hope you like it. I love you."

She smiled excitedly, her hand upon her heart, then blew him a kiss. The girls were all excited. He stood at the microphone, Jake standing back further, giving Sawyer the floor.

"This song is called *Love Drunk* because it's how you make me feel." He smiled a sexy, sly smile and winked at Marina then began playing. He threw in an ab roll on the *"slide over here, baby"* part and made all the girls go crazy.

Love Drunk
   Verse 1
   Those cut-off jeans drivin' me wild
   I know what you're thinkin' behind that smile
   You've got me swervin' on the road and I'm stone-cold sober
   Gotta get me some of that, I need to pull over

   Verse 2
   Hypnotized by your eyes
   My Southern girl on a summer night
   Throw a blanket in the back and share a 6-pack
   And do the thing we do that we know we're good at

         · · ·

Chorus
> *You got me tipsy*
> *Like on vodka, or on whiskey*
> *Girl, just sippin' you up*
> *Intoxicatin', it's amazin'*
> *The love we're makin'*
> *Here in the bed of my truck*
> *Love drunk*

Verse 3
> *Stumblin' on my words*
> *I'm a mess*
> *Feeling your body*
> *Leaves me breathless*

Verse 4
> *I can't kick it, can't quit it*
> *I'm on a binge*
> *Slide over here, baby*
> *Let's do it again*

Chorus
> *You got me tipsy*
> *Like on vodka, or on whiskey*
> *Girl, just sippin' you up*
> *Intoxicatin', it's amazin'*
> *The love we're makin'*
> *Here in the bed of my truck*
> *Love drunk*

. . .

The whole crowd stood clapping and whistling for minutes. The guys took a bow and thanked them, feeling relieved they all enjoyed it. Sawyer grabbed his hat off the stool and put it back on, taking his glass with him as he jumped off the stage. Marina took Sawyer by the hand and led him over to the Nashville couple.

"I absolutely loved the song! Best gift ever. Thank you," she told him on their way across the room.

"Glad you liked it, darlin'."

"Sawyer, this is Todd and Anna Copelle. Todd and Anna, this is my talented fiancé, Sawyer."

Sawyer gladly shook their hands.

"From what we saw tonight, you're extremely talented," Anna said.

"Thank you. The guys are great."

"They are. You all are. Even the stage presence, everything. The mash-up tonight was done just perfectly. I can't say we've ever had anyone do that before," Todd added.

"Yes, and the song you wrote...well, if you've got more that you've written, we can't wait to hear," Anna encouraged.

"Um, I wrote her one when I proposed but besides some acoustics, we haven't finished the melody. I'll get on that. I started writing a duet for her and me but it isn't finished."

"That's okay. When you get them finished, let us know. Either we'll have you send them digitally or we'll have you two and the band come to Nashville. We want to offer you guys a record deal if you're interested," Todd offered.

"Seriously?" Sawyer was so excited, his eyes lit up.

"We're serious," Todd assured.

"Oh my God! Is this happening right now?" He turned to Marina and she excitedly nodded her head yes. He yelled "Yee-Haw!" and picked Marina up around the waist, spinning her around in a full circle. He barely let her feet touch the floor before kissing her a good one right there in front of the Nashville producers.

"I apologize, I'm just so damn excited."

"No worries, you should be celebrating," Todd said.

"Wait, does this mean we'd have to tour for long periods? We're so busy here."

"Nah, start out with small venues and see where it takes you from there," Anna suggested.

"Okay. We could do that. I gotta tell the guys. Will we go over the details of the contract and such?" he asked.

"Absolutely. We can arrange the contract to fit your terms."

"Perfect. I don't think I care to be famous. Having a record for us though and to have some fun...hell yeah!" Sawyer clapped. "Excuse me." He ran over to the table where the guys were chatting with their ladies.

"Guys. Sidebar." Sawyer nodded sideways. The guys went over to him.

"So that couple over there with Marina...they're from Nashville. They're Marina's wedding gift."

"How so?" Trev's interest was piqued.

"They're record producers. They loved us and offered us a record deal."

"Holy shit! Are you for real?" Chris shouted.

"Yeah, I'm serious."

"Wow! This is insane!" Jake was stoked.

"Dude!" Trev grabbed Sawyer's shoulders.

"I know!" Sawyer's wide eyes stared into Trev's and he gripped his friend's forearms. "Best gift ever!"

Marina came over, wrapping her arms around Sawyer.

"Thank you again, baby." He kissed her forehead.

"I know music means a lot to you."

"Music is the soul's voice. It's expressing yourself and your thoughts through sound. A good song should hit ya right in the heart and take your mind off everything else."

"That's what you do to me. You have a way with words, you know that? Music too."

Guests watched Sawyer kiss her, showing his appreciation the best way he knew how.

After the guys settled down a bit and thanked Marina, others approached to give the gifts they had brought. Everyone gave something meaningful in one form or another. The girls went in together to gift Marina a boudoir photo shoot session, which she loved and was excited for. Sawyer was excited for it too. Raquel couldn't wait any longer to give the gift she brought. She had waited patiently to go next to last. Sawyer told Marina to go ahead and open it as he stood next to her. She pulled a book out of the gift bag. It was Raquel's newest published novel titled *Stable Sweethearts* and it was based on Marina and Sawyer themselves.

"Oh, my goodness! That's why you were so secretive about book details! I love it!" Marina gave her a huge hug.

"That's an amazing gift, Raquel. So special and unique. This means a lot." Sawyer gave her a hug too. "I'm not much of a reader but I'll read this one. I love that you used Justin's photo of her and me dancing under the white lights."

"I hope after reading it, y'all realize how unique and special your love is. You two have that timeless love. It's unstoppable. I'm planning a sequel too, so I'm going to be needing honeymoon details," Raquel teased.

"Maybe a trilogy?" Marina raised her brows and shrugged.

Sawyer laughed when Marina gave Raquel a wink and nod.

"Okay, we're last." Jake ran to the back storage room and came back out with a guitar case. He handed it over to Sawyer.

"What's this?" Sawyer placed it on the table and opened it up.

Chris handed Marina a gift bag.

"So, all four of us guys, including Justin, went in on these for you guys. Y'all are hard to buy for," Jake said.

Sawyer stared at it for a moment then picked up his new electric guitar out of the case. It was teal and white pearl. The guys looked around at each other wondering why Sawyer hadn't said anything.

"This was the one we saw in the music store that day we were uptown trying on wedding attire..." Sawyer checked it out all over.

"Yep. That's the one," Jake said.

"This damn thing was expensive! Aww, I can't believe you guys did this!" He went to each of them for a hug. "Y'all are the best!"

Marina opened the gift bag and pulled out an expensive professional microphone.

"How did you guys know?—" She started to speak but Becka laid a hand on her shoulder and said, "I might have told Jake that you've been eyeing that for a while."

"Aww, thank you!" She hugged Becka then made her rounds to hug the guys. "We have the best friends in the world."

"We sure do, darlin'."

Everyone chatted and mingled for a while longer before cleaning up and heading home. Family from out of town stayed with Sawyer and Marina, including Drew. They were all going to take care of the place while Sawyer and Marina were on their honeymoon. Bailey Rose would stay as well until the day after the reception.

CHAPTER 39

Last Minute Touches

F riday, the girls, including moms, went into town for manicures and pedicures, and to check in on the floral arrangements and the cake. All was going as planned; everything would arrive the next day at the time it was supposed to. Meanwhile, the guys were horsing around with the horses in the round pen. Sawyer showed the guys a few tricks he had tried with Tango so Trev and Chris decided to try those tricks with Athena. It didn't go as smoothly. That palomino wasn't having it. She played bucking bronco and they hit the dirt, one after the other.

"Maybe we should've tried standing on Tango instead," Trev said, brushing dirt off the butt of his jeans.

"Y'all must like a challenge. Ya just gotta bend the knees like you're surfin'." Sawyer chuckled as he acted out a surfing stance.

"I'm tryin' again," Chris said with a cocky attitude as he took Tango by the reins and hopped on. He carefully stood and bent his knees like Sawyer suggested but Tango jolted forward, dumping Chris off the back. He landed on his side with a hard thud and was holding his side when he stood, a dust cloud surrounding him. Sawyer and Jake were standing against the fence and Jake was laughing so hard he could barely catch his breath.

"Why don't you try, Jake?" Trev tried to coax him.

"Nah, I know I'll hit the dirt so there's no need to get all dirty and break ribs."

"Y'all are hilarious." Sawyer shook his head laughing.

After dusting themselves off, the guys moved the temporary bar they had built into the stables for the reception. Bob and Gladys brought the load of alcohol over and dropped it off. Sawyer had bought glasses and told Bob and Gladys they could have them for Backcountry after the wedding reception.

Tom asked as he was carefully stacking glasses, "So how did all you guys meet, anyways?"

"The band?" Sawyer asked.

"Yeah, and Justin too."

"At the rodeo." Sawyer carried a keg behind the bar.

"All of them?"

"Yep. A few days after we got the house built, I took a break from unpacking and hit up a local rodeo for something to do. Chris, Jake, and Trev knew each other from the rodeos and were standing together, leaning on the gate. I walked up to them and asked if they knew who I should buy a good horse from. They told me Dave and I introduced myself to them. We all stood talking for a bit. They asked what I did for a living and I mentioned needing an accountant just as Justin happened to walk by. He stopped and said that he was an accountant and was looking to leave the job he was currently at. We settled on a wage and I hired him right there. He's been a solid dude. The other guys got talking about how they could've played the anthem better so I asked what they played. That's all she wrote."

"Sounds like that rodeo called your name for a reason, son. It was meant to be that you were there that day."

"I think so too, Dad. They've all been my best friends. I don't know what I'd do without them. I seem to have that whole right time right place thing down pat." He smiled, looking at Marina as she entered the stables.

"I checked on everything in town. All is good." She gave him a smooch, her hands in her pockets.

"Good. You ladies have a good time?" He leaned against the bar and motioned for her hand.

"Yeah, we did." She held her hand forward and he took it in his.

"Let's see this manicure. Your nails look beautiful, baby." He pecked the top of her hand with a kiss.

"Aww, thanks. What did you guys do?"

Chris and Jake carried in boxes of beer and Trev followed with a box of liquor bottles.

"This is pretty much it," Sawyer said. "We've kinda been horsin' around. Found out Chris and Trev are not trick riders." Jake busted out laughing as Chris and Trev told him to shut up.

"Okay, a story for dinner I suppose. Well, us girls are starting to cook if y'all wanna take a break in a bit to eat."

"Sounds good, baby, thanks. I like your shirt by the way."

She grinned as she looked down at the shirt she was wearing. It read "Dibs on the Cowboy". She replied, "You're the cowboy, in case you were wondering."

He laughed and said, "I was hopin' so." He watched her leave like it was the first time he had laid eyes on her. The guys just looked at him till she had left and he snapped out of his trance. They just smiled and shook their heads.

"What?" He asked with a lowered brow.

"Nothin'." Jake chuckled.

"So, what is it you boys do besides play in the band?" Tom asked.

"I do rodeo pretty much full time," Trev said, opening a box of beer.

"My wife and I have a hay farm, a few cattle too, and horses of course. We also grow a pretty impressive range of crops so we run a little farmer's market every Wednesday morning." Chris took bottles from Trev to stock them neatly in the fridge behind the bar.

"I organize rodeos sometimes," Jake said, looking through liquor bottles. "And work remotely for a cowboy magazine."

"That's interesting. What do you do for the magazine?" Drew asked as he entered with Justin.

"Pretty much cowboy equipment and style articles, I research stuff they wanna feature and promote. Basically, whatever I'm told to do, based on who's paying the most for ads. I write reviews for the products too."

"Sounds like an easy job." Drew popped open a warm beer.

"It is. It's fun. Pays well too. Deadlines suck but I work pretty quick."

"Maybe when y'all make your album Jake can get y'all featured in the magazine," Tom suggested.

If they were cartoon characters, the guys all would've had lightbulbs above their heads. Many brows raised then they all looked at Jake.

"I'm not the editor-in-chief but I do know her. I could try!"

"That would be awesome!" Sawyer got all excited.

Caroline called Tom's phone, telling them to come to the house to eat.

"I can't wait to tell everyone about you guys falling off the horses into the dirt," Sawyer said before sprinting for his truck ahead of the rest of the guys. They took off after him, racing him back to the house.

After dinner, the crew returned back to the stables to finish decorating. They played music and chatted, having a good time until after the sun had set. The white party lights they had strung began to glow brighter.

At dark, Sawyer came into the doorway and leaned, watching Marina until she noticed him. He held a finger to his lips to signal her to be quiet then motioned with a head nod for her to come to him. She looked around, the girls had their backs to her, finishing the centerpiece layout for tables. She snuck away and took Sawyer's hand. They walked out to the round pen that was closest to the stables. He put his hands on her waist, her arms up around his neck as he began dancing with her.

"We can't hear the music out here." She smiled.

"That's okay. We make our own music together. I'll dance with you for as long as our song lasts."

She laid her head upon his chest as they danced. The white party lights and the moon lit them up like a stage spotlight as fireflies danced in the air surrounding them. Marina and Sawyer were oblivious to the girls all watching from the side of the barn. The guys were headed out so the girls thought they should too. The parents went back to the house so Sawyer and Marina were left alone to dance out their imaginary song amongst the stars.

CHAPTER 40

The Big Day

The Brandton Ranch stables were ready for a wedding, the day both Sawyer and Marina had been looking forward to for months. Sawyer looked in the full-length mirror, straightened his teal tie, and tucked it into his black vest. He slowly exhaled a full breath as he rolled his white dress shirt sleeves up to his mid-forearm. Jake came up behind him, carrying Sawyer's black cowboy hat. He was wearing a white one himself, matching the rest of the groomsmen. They all wore white dress shirts with rolled sleeves and medium-washed—which looked faded on the front of the thighs—bootcut jeans. They fit tight on the thighs and rear, especially Sawyer's. Their brown boots all matched. The groomsmen wore tan vests with a yellow-orange tie to match the roses in the floral arrangements.

"You look great, man." Jake patted Sawyer's shoulder and handed him his black hat.

"Thanks, you guys do too." He took his hat from Jake and fit it onto his head just right.

"You nervous?"

"Nope. I'm excited. I can't wait to see her. I can't wait to call her my wife."

"You found a wonderful woman, Sawyer. You're a lucky man. I'm happy for you."

"Thanks, Jake. I'm the luckiest." Sawyer gave him a manly hug.

"We all know you've been looking forward to this for a long time," Justin said.

"Son, let's pin this boutonniere on ya." Tom placed it on Sawyer's vest, a yellow-orange rose with green hypericum berries. Tom made sure it was pinned on straight and stood with Sawyer in the mirror as the other guys pinned their magnolias on. A photographer took precious moment photos of the guys.

"Son, I'm proud of you for choosing the woman you chose to spend your life with."

"I appreciate that, Dad. More than you know. There's nobody I'd rather spend life with than her."

Tom patted Sawyer on the back then turned and asked the officiant who walked in if the papers were ready to sign. Sawyer signed the marriage license and Tom signed as a witness. The guys went outside and made their ways to the barn for photos.

"My baby is getting married! I'm so happy! You look so hand-some." Caroline hugged Sawyer, careful not to squish his boutonniere.

"Thanks, Mom. I'm so glad you all are here for this."

"Oh, we wouldn't miss it."

"I figured you'd be telling me it's too soon to get married, that we haven't known each other long enough."

"No, not with what you two have. Y'all are different; so much in love. Your dad and I knew that the first time we met her at Thanksgiving."

"I know you gave her the secret cookie recipe, Mom. I found it."

Caroline gasped. "You didn't read it, did you?" She pretended to panic then laughed when he did.

"Marina doesn't know that I know about it, but it means a lot to her and I both."

"Well, you both mean a lot to me too. Y'all are perfect together. You did a good job finding that girl."

"I agree, Mom. Thank you, both you and Dad, for welcoming her so warmly."

"Oh sweetie." Caroline lay a hand upon Sawyer's face for a moment.

Meanwhile, Marina perfected her makeup and changed from her robe to her wedding gown. It was white, spaghetti strapped, low-cut floral lace over chiffon and was mermaid style, ruched down the butt and backless. It fit her every curve perfectly. She slipped into her white strappy heels. The girls helped put curls in her straightened hair. Her fragrant sweet olive blossom and star jasmine perfume spritzed upon her as she stood and walked to face the mirror.

"You're stunning." Raquel smiled fondly.

"You think Sawyer will love it?"

"Oh, honey, he will absolutely love it. You look absolutely gorgeous." Aliza gave her a hug.

"Thanks, Mama."

"He's going to be speechless," Savannah agreed.

"You know he'd still love you, and marry you too, if you wore a garbage bag down that aisle," Becka agreed.

"Luckily, I found the perfect dress instead." Marina laughed.

The officiant came in for Marina and Savannah to sign the license and the photographer was there to capture pictures. Marina reapplied her light pink shimmering lipstick that matched her nails.

"You look nervous suddenly, are you okay?" Andrea asked as she started handing out bouquets.

"A little. I don't know why though. He's the man of my dreams. There's not a doubt in my mind. Maybe it's just the pressure of being everything he expects."

"You always have been that for him. I can't wait to see his reaction when he sees you," Becka said as she took her bouquet from Andrea.

"Me neither." Marina smiled.

"You're the most beautiful bride we've ever seen." Bailey Rose handed Marina a gift bag but before she opened it, Caroline came knocking. She entered slowly and her hands flew up over her mouth, wide-eyed.

"Oh, Marina, darling!" She walked over to her. "Oh, honey, you look breathtaking!" She hugged her gently, careful not to crush her curls.

"Thank you, Caroline." Marina looked her in the eyes. "Thank you for approving my marriage to your son. He's absolutely perfect and I'm so thankful for him."

"Aww you just take care of him like I know he will take care of you and I know you'll both be happy together forever."

"We will. I promise I'll take good care of him."

"I can't wait to officially welcome you to the family."

"I'm excited to officially be a part of it. You ladies...you all look amazing."

The bridesmaids wore teal chiffon sundresses, hemmed just above the knee, spaghetti straps and flowy below the waist. Their bouquets were made of white magnolias, complete with magnolia leaves and a pale-yellow ribbon tying the stems. A single magnolia bloom graced their hair as they all wore their hair down with curls. Marina's bouquet was of orange roses, purple cymbidium orchids, pink boronia heather, green hypericum berries, and yellow with purple dendrobiums. She chose colors that resembled the sunsets that they watched together. Their dresses were chosen to be teal for the blue skies Sawyer and Marina brought to each other's lives and it was Marina's favorite color pallet, as well as... well, he was a knock-out in blues too.

"We have a tradition to carry out, Marina. Open up that gift bag," Savannah told her, barely containing her excitement.

"Yes, ma'am!"

All the gals had pitched in to carry on the tradition of something new, borrowed, old, and blue. A white garter belt with teal ribbon woven through the center was something blue from the bridesmaids. Something old was a set of simple diamond earrings that Aliza gave her as a hand-me-down from her grandmother. Something new was a white mini hanky with her new initials embroidered on it in teal that Caroline made for her. She tucked it down the side of her garter belt, which she had pulled up onto her thigh. Something borrowed was a hairpin with a porcelain magnolia on the end. Savannah had bought it at a boutique a couple of months prior. Lastly, there was a folded note on horse stationary, just like she finds every morning in the barn. It was a barn note from Sawyer that read "We do! Forever & always, my love".

"How did that get in there?" Aliza asked, genuinely confused.

"Oh, Sawyer." She held it to her chest, her smile stretching across her face. It was her favorite barn note yet.

The officiant popped back in the doorway to let the ladies know that the guests were seated and the groomsmen were about to line up. The ladies thanked him and gathered their bouquets before Savannah lifted and turned the back of Marina's dress then fanned it out behind her. It didn't trail far but no snags from wood floors were desired.

"Are you ready?" Aliza asked.

Marina exhaled a deep breath before replying, "Absolutely."

Caroline walked out with the bridesmaids and waited at the back of the line for Sawyer. The bridal party paired up in the hall just outside the dressing rooms. Tom with Savannah as best man and maid of honor, Jake and Becka, Justin and Raquel, Chris and Bailey Rose, Trev and Andrea, and Drew and Olivia. The guys and gals complimented each other on how wonderful they looked. Bright floral arrangements matching Marina's bouquet had been placed up around the outdoor altar. The altar arbor was a small square pergola that the guys built and a blooming wisteria vine crawled up the sides and across the top, purple fragrant blooms hanging down. Magnolias were tied with white ribbon on the chairs along the aisle, just as they were along the front of the bar in the barn. The chair backs were wrapped in white silk, the same as they were set up in the barn for the reception. A white runway led the way to the altar. There were only about two dozen guests, since they wanted to keep the occasion small and intimate, but they were friends who were thrilled to witness their marriage. Soft live acoustic music played as the ceremony began and the bridal party walked in pairs down the aisle and parted at the altar. Sawyer and Caroline walked arm and arm down the aisle and he gave her a sweet kiss on the cheek before she left him under the pergola so she could take her seat in the front row.

"Sawyer, you look amazing!" Andrea complimented quietly. The rest of the girls all nodded and agreed.

"Thank you. You ladies all look lovely yourselves." Sawyer made the girls blush.

Aliza had watched from the back and told Marina, "The handsome groom is ready for his bride."

Marina closed her eyes for a quick moment and exhaled deeply then took her mom's arm in hers. The acoustic music blended into a different melody as Aliza walked out with Marina on her arm. Marina almost stopped when she saw Sawyer; he looked so handsome. Striking. He looked at her, his lips parted but he wasn't inhaling or exhaling, he was breathless. His nostrils flared a bit as he caught his breath and held back tears. The girls were all looking over at Sawyer to see his reaction. He remained standing tall and proud. Marina smiled at him the whole way down the aisle and he couldn't help but flash those pearly whites back at her.

When she reached him, he whispered to her, "You're a Goddess."

"God, you look incredible," Marina whispered back.

The officiant asked who was to give away the bride. Aliza accepted the duty proudly before taking her seat next to Caroline. The two moms were excited, it showed all over their faces. Sawyer took Marina's hands in his right away. Their eyes were locked on each other's as the officiant spoke a few moments about love and marriage before asking if they would each like to say their vows, then told Marina to go first.

"I believe in miracles because I found you. I didn't know what true love was until you came into my life. When I was drowning, you held out your hand and pulled me from the depths. Your perfect soul has added bright colors to my dull canvas, making life itself into art. You shined your light so I could find my way and now I can shine too. Together, we shine brighter than the sun. I want to spend life with you, so many more trips around the sun with my hand in yours. You are my moon, my stars, my other half, and I'd never be whole without you. I want you with me for every season of life. A lifetime with you doesn't seem like enough. You showed me I could trust again, opened my cage, and set me free to fly...but free is right here with you. You're my whole world. Forever and always."

He blinked a few hard blinks and sniffled once before quickly wiping a tear from his cheekbone. "I love you."

"I love you too."

It was his turn but he was suddenly slightly nervous. He was afraid of breaking down in front of everyone. It wasn't the same as being on stage at the bar behind the microphone. He took a deep breath. She anxiously waited, smiling a sweet, loving smile and looking up into those ocean-blue eyes.

"I can't imagine life without you nor would I *want* to live life without you. I truly believe our souls were meant to find each other. We're soulmates and I'm proud to call you mine. Gravity doesn't exist in the place you take my soul to. I'll be your anchor if you'll be my sails when I need a little breeze. I'll be your lighthouse, continuously guiding you home. Every constellation in the night sky will always lead me to you if we're ever lost from each other. We'll never fight battles alone and I'll forever remain within the walls you've built. You've relieved my longing for lust, desire, and unconditional love. Only you can do that for me. I promise to always show you how much I respect and appreciate you. I promise to always protect your heart, be your rock, and never break promises. Forever and always."

Marina wiped tears rolling down her cheek.

"Do we have the rings?" the officiant asked.

Sawyer smiled before whistling. Whiskey was lying in the grass next to Bob and Gladys's chairs and came scampering down the aisle with a white collar on. Sawyer crouched down and untied the teal ribbon that was tied to the collar and slid the rings off into his hand. He petted Whiskey's head and Bob whistled to call him back.

"That was adorable," Savannah said quietly.

Sawyer handed his ring to Marina. They placed rings on each other when instructed. They held hands, anxiously awaiting the best part. She wore a glowing, beaming smile while looking at his smiling face.

"I now pronounce you: husband and wife. You may kiss your bride."

The officiant barely got the words out and Sawyer already had his lips melted to hers, her face in his hands. She wrapped her arms up around his neck; they didn't hold back on that lingering kiss. He dipped her to kiss her again and everyone cheered. They were sincerely happy, smiling at everyone and each other as he took her by the hand and walked side-by-side up the aisle. Everyone stood, clapping and cheering. Dried white flower petal confetti was tossed above the couple as they walked, falling upon them with best wishes from everyone tossing it.

CHAPTER 41

Reception

The wedding party took photos along with the bride and groom and parents after the ceremony. The photographers managed to catch a few great candid shots and fun photos as well. The romantic shots of Sawyer and Marina were the photographer's favorite to take. The sincere passion was obvious and breathtaking to capture. Their hearts were in it one hundred percent.

A rustic chandelier hung from rafters in the large, open event room in the stables. Magnolia centerpieces were centered on the teal table runners atop the tables. White tablecloths hung low and white, wooden folding chairs were dressed in white silk. White party lights were strung from rafters and were the only lighting besides the chandelier and windows. As the sun was about to set, an orange-yellow glow shone through the windows, lighting up the dancefloor as if on cue. Guests were chatting as the hired band played acoustic music. The band announced the wedding party's entrance and then announced the entrance of "Mr. and Mrs. Brandton!" The couple walked in holding hands and all aglow.

Change Your Name by Brett Young was played by the band as the newlyweds' first dance song. He held her close, staring into her eyes like she was the only person in the room; they were the only two people in their world at that moment in time. He twirled her, her hair flowing behind her, her dress twisted below her knees then flowed as they took the floor like a fairytale couple. They were graceful. Their eyes never strayed from each other's. He held her close again, swaying as one. They were a perfect love story. One for the ages. The bridal party joined on the dance floor and paired up for the second song.

The caterer was thereafter ready to serve so everyone took their seats. The bridal party's table was long, the table centerpieces matching Marina's bouquet, adding a dash of bright sunset colors on top of the teal table runner. The best man, Tom, and maid of honor, Savannah, said a few words, which brought tears to the eyes of the bride and groom. His parents welcomed her into the family and Aliza welcomed Sawyer. Sweet, encouraging words were shared as well as advice and best wishes. Marina noticed that there was an empty chair at the front table where their moms sat, and a single red rose had been added to that magnolia centerpiece. She squeezed Sawyer's hand and whispered, "Was the rose your idea?"

He nodded. "Yes, Mrs. Brandton, it was." She kissed him with a tear rolling down her cheek. He gently and discretely wiped it away and told her, "He's here today."

She placed her hand upon her heart and whispered, "Thank you. That was so thoughtful," with a lump in her throat and tears welling in her eyes, before wrapping her arms around his neck. Their moms were brought to tears, knowing it was a surprise to Marina. After everyone enjoyed the delicious food, it was time to cut the cake. It was a three-tier white round cake with a teal ribbon at the base of each tier and two large magnolia blooms placed just so between the tiers. The cake topper was a simple *B* monogram in black and the cake was served on a wooden slab. Together, they cut into the cake and gently fed each other a piece. The bakery did a wonderful job. The vanilla cake with vanilla buttercream icing was perfect, moist but slightly dense, and tasted like angel food. It was Marina's favorite. She loved that he didn't smash the piece into her face out of respect, he was a complete gentleman, as always.

They went on to dance other traditional dances, including the mother-son dance, and the singer would tap on a champagne glass before slow dances. Of course, it called for the newlyweds to kiss as well. It gave them a moment to find one another around the room and signaled to them to take the dance floor. They danced to *Made For You* by Jake Owen and a few fun songs later, glass tinged again. They danced to *My Love* by Little Texas, then *Blessings* by Florida Georgia Line. Everyone was dancing with them and the dance floor was crowded for the upbeat songs.

Dance With You by Brett Young separated a few lively songs when the glass tinged again. Sawyer and his friends knew how to tear up that dance floor, impressing everyone with a few unexpected pop song dances. Marina didn't know they could dance like that. She loved it, all the girls did. He couldn't help but throw in a mildly dirty dance with her. Marina threw a secondary bouquet so she could keep and dry her own. Becka caught it happily. Sawyer had fun with the garter toss, making it the sexiest event of the night. Marina had no idea what she was in store for. He bent over her, hands on her thighs as she sat in a chair in the center of the dance floor. He kissed her lips, down her neck, her chest, then he bit his bottom lip and looked her in the eyes as he slowly lifted her dress and caressed his hands up her leg as her foot rested on his shoulder, kissing all the way up to the garter on her thigh. She tensed up, loving every second. He slid it down and off her foot, handed her the embroidered hanky, then flung the garter like a rubber band into the crowd of guests, who cheered for them and whistled. Jake was the lucky catcher. Bob and Gladys served drinks all evening.

Glass tinged yet again so they danced together to *Can't Have Mine* by Dylan Scott then danced their last dance of the evening to *God Gave Me a Girl* by Russell Dickerson. That was another surprise of Sawyer's which Marina absolutely loved.

The white lights shone brightly along with the stars. It was a beautiful night. Sawyer opened the big barn door so they could all enjoy the moon and stars and the sound of crickets as the party came to an end. The guests lined up just outside the big barn doors and lit sparklers. Sawyer and Marina used the microphone to thank everyone before Sawyer took her hand and walked the path between friends amongst the sparklers, snapping and glowing in the night air. Sabrina led Tango to meet the newlyweds at the end of the path and Sawyer mounted before pulling Marina up. She held onto Sawyer as he spun Tango around. That long black mane flowed elegantly and Marina's dress draped down the horse's side. They waved at their guests as fireworks blasted into the air over the field. They galloped off into the field that led to the trail, Whiskey and a trail of stardust following. Under the dark sky, led by the moon, they rode Tango back to the house.

CHAPTER 42
Flying to Cloud 9

They galloped to the barn at home where Sawyer descended off of Tango then helped Marina down. He put Tango away in his stall and she gathered her dress to keep the bottom from getting dirty as they held hands, rushing up to the house, excited to have a moment alone together as a newlywed couple. Up the steps, he said, "I've waited over a year to carry you over this threshold." He picked her up sideways, her arms around his neck and pushed open the door before carrying her through.

"You're my home sweet home," she said before sharing a sweet kiss and her feet touched the floor.

"As beautiful as you are in this dress, I can't wait for it to hit the floor." He held her face in his gentle hands. Her delicate fingers wrapped around his wrists as their foreheads leaned against each other.

"How does it feel to have my last name?" That sexy bass tone in his voice made her melt every time and that question almost seemed barbaric in a way, which was a turn-on.

"It feels amazing. I feel like it was fate. I've imagined having your last name many times but those fantasies don't compare to reality."

"You've imagined it? For how long?" His smile widened.

"Since that day we met." She was looking up into his blue eyes. He didn't say a word, he just kissed her, gently at first, romantically, as if trying to win her heart from the very beginning. Their lips began to tangle more aggressively but Whiskey was starting to jump up onto them.

"Oh, you're not ripping this dress, little mister." Marina bent over to pet him.

"To think this day may not have happened for us just kills me. Thank you for forgiving me, Marina. You've made me the happiest man alive and I know you always will."

"There was nothing to forgive, Sawyer. You didn't do anything wrong and I panicked thanks to traumatic past relationships. We won't ever have to worry about any of that again. You've made me the happiest woman alive. This day was perfect and absolutely magical. We're newlyweds!"

"I know! This is so exciting!" Sawyer looked at the clock on the wall. "We'd better get changed. Is your stuff all packed?" he asked as he took his vest off.

"Yep, I'm all packed. You've been kind of secretive about honeymoon details. Do we leave first thing in the morning?"

"Nope. We're leavin' right now." He tossed his vest onto the bed then loosened his teal tie, tossing it from the doorway, and dashed to the kitchen.

"Seriously?" she asked excitedly.

"Yes, ma'am." He wrote a note and left it on the kitchen counter for the parents.

"Oh, how fun!" She began to pull one of the straps down off her shoulder but he hurried in and said, "I'm supposed to be doing that for you." He shut Whiskey out of the bedroom as he stood close to her and tucked a finger under the other strap, then slowly slid it down. She loved his gentle touch. Her dress lowered by his hand, down below her breasts, before it hit the floor. She had been looking at him the whole time but his eyes would wander down her body. She unbuttoned his dress shirt and peeled it back. He released it from his arms and tossed it onto the bed.

"As much as I'd love to lay you back on this bed right now, we really do have to go or we'll miss our flight." He kissed the side of her neck, then her lips, ever so gently. Her eyes were closed but she slowly opened them and cupped his face in her hands. "Oh, but it's so hard to be this close to you, undressing, and not have you."

"Oh, trust me, I know it's *hard*." He chuckled with raised brows then turned around to get a t-shirt from his dresser drawer. He left his jeans on and grabbed his packed bag. She pulled a sundress off its hanger in the closet, the hanger left to swing. He rolled their suitcase to the front door before coming back for her carry-on bag as she finished dressing.

"The fireworks were a beautiful surprise," she said while slipping her dress on.

"I know a fireman who felt he owed me a favor."

"It was spectacular."

"I knew you'd enjoy it." That sly smirk of his was so attractive.

"I love that you added surprises to our big day."

"The day isn't over yet."

She changed from her wedding heels to wedge sandals and he traded his boots for his HEYDUDEs. They headed out and loaded up after saying goodbye to whining Whiskey.

CHAPTER 43

Runaway Bride...and Groom - Part 1

T he plane ride to Tahiti was long but, between naps, they kept each other occupied. Movies played during the flight on the overhead screens and they had packed snacks in a carry-on backpack. They leaned on each other, reading the book Raquel gave them. Sawyer wasn't much of a reader by choice but he was curious about this book. She bookmarked at the end of the seventh chapter and removed her glasses. They were beginning to distract him anyway.

"You feel adventurous?" she asked him quietly.

He smirked. "Whatcha thinkin'?"

"I'm thinking I'd like to join the mile-high club," she whispered close to his ear. His brows raised, surprised at her less-than-passive, inappropriate idea. Then there it was, his devious sideways smile. He looked around and found most of the other passengers were sleeping or had earbuds in. He looked back at her, she had that sultry, biting-her-bottom-lip look that made him bite his own. They weren't far from the rear lavatory. He rubbed his face scruff, watching to see if anyone was going in or coming out. She slid her hand up the edge of his t-shirt sleeve and squeezed his bicep.

"These jeans look so hot on you." She dug her nails into his thighs, scraping the denim as she strolled higher.

"I'll go see if it's occupied," he whispered before standing and walking casually to the lavatory. She watched him go in and waited a few seconds, looking around. Nobody seemed to be paying attention so she went back there and joined him, locking the door behind her.

"There's like, no room in here...at all." He snickered.

"It's okay. We don't need much," she said as she unzipped his jeans and pulled them down.

"Is this why you wore a skirt?" he asked, his hands gliding down her hips.

"Yep. I'm not wearing panties either," she whispered in his ear before reaching up and biting his earlobe.

"Oh, dear God." He kissed her aggressively and hoisted her up. She wrapped her legs around him tightly and locked her ankles, his hands holding her bare rear, her arms around his neck and shoulders.

"You'll need to be quieter than you are at home, Mrs. Brandton."

"Oh, but you make me wanna scream, Mr. Brandton." Her head tipped back as he repeatedly bounced her up and down. She braced her hands against the walls and refrained from making noise. She ignored the indentation being made under her butt cheek from his wristband as she kissed him assertively. It was hotter than Hades in that lavatory it seemed. It didn't feel that way going in there but it did by the time they came out. They sat back in their seats just as the captain instructed to ensure seat buckles were fastened.

After their short layover at their connection airport, they were in the air again. They read a couple more chapters together, loving the book so far, before she fell asleep against his shoulder while watching a movie. He held still for her even though his arm had passed the tingling stage and was now completely numb. The captain announced that they were about to let down the landing gear and that the view out the windows was one they'd want to capture in photos.

"Hey, baby, we're landing in a few minutes." He hated to wake her but she wouldn't want to miss the breathtaking view. He reached over her and pulled up the window shade.

"Oh, wow! Marina, you gotta see this!" He tapped her leg, rousing her so they could enjoy the view together. Once they landed in Tahiti, they hopped on a small plane to Bora Bora. They were exhausted but watched out the window as they came in for a landing. The view was spectacular. The shades of turquoise varied around the lush green terrain.

"I can't believe we're really here!" Marina was so excited, squeezing Sawyer's hand as he leaned over her to look out the window.

"Look at that view." He was looking at her at that moment.

She turned to look at him and said, "Aww," then kissed his soft lips. She pointed out reefs as the plane descended. They captured photos on their phones to forever remember it vividly.

"This time change is going to mess with us," he pointed out.

"We'll be on vacation, we can nap whenever we want to." She grabbed his chin and smiled.

"I don't plan on sleeping much at all. I even brought our little sex game. Although, I doubt we'll remember to play it." He winked.

She slapped his knee and giggled. "You're naughty."

"You know it, baby."

"We have an itinerary?" she asked as the landing gear hit the runway.

"Nope. I figured we'd wing it."

"I love that. I'd say we should nap first but I wanna take it all in right away."

"I bet you do." He laughed. He carried their luggage and she rolled the one on wheels as they exited the small passenger plane.

They boarded a boat to get to their accommodation, which was an overwater bungalow.

"Sawyer, this place is perfect. It's straight out of a magazine."

"It's beautiful but still not as beautiful as you." He stopped on the boardwalk to give her a kiss before he opened the door to the bungalow. There was a glass window in the middle of the floor. Sheer white curtains flowed down from tall bed posts, red rose petals lie on the bed, and as they walked out onto their private balcony deck, there was a private plunge infinity pool with a potted palm set near a hammock.

"We can snorkel right from our room." Marina leaned over the rail looking at the aqua water below. He walked up beside her, wrapped an arm around her back, and admired the water with her.

"This really is paradise." He looked out over the lagoon, nothing but blues and green. The infamous Bora Bora view of Mount Otemanu and towering palms along the beach was straight across from their bungalow.

"I could look at his view every day for the rest of my life." She brushed her hair out of her face as the ocean breeze carried it.

"Me too. But I'd miss my horses too much."

"I know you would. The fresh air here is so pure. We'll just have to enjoy these five days the most we can."

"Then another three days in the Maldives. We're gonna have so much fun." He pulled her into his arms.

"I'm not even tired anymore," she said, feeling the curvature of his back, their faces close together.

"Me neither. I've got my second wind and I want to use it wearing you out."

"Mmm, I was thinking the same thing." She looked up at him.

"Good..." He inched his face even closer, his nose next to hers. "Because within these five days we're here, I'm gonna do you on every surface of this place: in that hammock, in that pool, on that bed...I wanna enjoy this hut and you naked in it, all fucking day, every day...starting right now." He kissed her passionately, smashing their lips together. She didn't get a chance to react in any way except raised brows and parted lips. Her heart was racing as if it was the first time he had kissed her like that. She could feel her face blushing and she felt a tingling sensation rush through her whole body. Hands groped each other, clothes went flying as they walked, lips locked, tripping over each other's feet back into the bungalow. This time, her dress did hit the floor, a trail of clothing following them. Stripped naked, he lifted her and laid her on the bed before leaning over her, supporting his weight with his broad shoulders, and slowly kissing her from her lips down to her toes then all the way back up. A fire began to stir within her. The anticipation was barely bearable every time he would do that. Her honey hair sprawled out all around her on the luxurious silk pillow. Her fingers raked through his hair and reached around to his shoulder blades. He could feel her fingernails digging into his skin and he liked it. It made him thrust into her a little harder. She knew he liked it but she couldn't have resisted doing it anyway. He drove her crazy. He felt amazing. His eyes looked at hers provocatively, so she arched her back, inviting him to kiss her chest, which he gladly accepted. His fingers traced over her breasts before he kissed them, allowing his hand to trail down her side and squeeze her rear. He couldn't be in any deeper. She could feel herself become even more saturated. He was exotic. The way he made love to her was dramatically erotic, the steamiest she had ever had. To him, she was extremely seductive; her lip bites when she'd look at him, the way she'd bat her lashes and look up at him with those wide damsel eyes. She aroused him whether she was doing it deliberately or without trying and he had never been with anyone like that. He couldn't easily control himself around her. Her legs wrapped tightly around his waist and her ankles locked. Holding him close, she gripped his hips with her fingers. The blanket had been shoved almost completely onto the floor. She looked straight into those lagoon eyes as he put her arms above her head, interlocking his fingers with hers, but only briefly before slipping from his grip. Desire was heating up the blood running through her veins. He continued gyrating his hips in a consistent rhythm, his six-pack rolling as she felt from his hips to his pecs and shoulders, she couldn't keep her hands in one place. She couldn't get enough of him. His perfectly sculpted body was that of every woman's fantasy. Her chin tilted upwards and her eyes closed as she drifted to cloud nine and his warm breath grew tired upon the bend of her neck. His deep voice rumbled a feral moan as his elbow folded, then he lay next to her. She lifted her head for him to put his arm under her neck. Resting her head on his bicep, she faced him, her leg overtop of his beastly thigh and her hand upon his chest. Besides "I love you" from each of them, no words were needed. He kissed her forehead and held her hand against his chest.

The next morning, after their room service breakfast, they snorkeled just outside of their hut.

"You know your butt floats like a buoy when your face is underwater?" He laughed.

"Does it really?"

"It's cute."

She laughed at how he'd try to talk through his snorkel when pointing out sea life. Later in the day, they took an island tour by boat through the calm cerulean waters then went on an excursion on ATVs, then jet skis, and enjoyed a Polynesian barbecue on a Motu. They snorkeled the lagoon just down the beach from their bungalow, then further into the lagoon, spotting sharks and rays and a wide variety of fish species. On their third day, they went whale watching. A mother and calf humpback whale passed through and were close enough to take photos of. The helicopter ride made for a magnificent aerial view. Their last day was spent in their room and walking the boardwalks and beaches after morning yoga. That was the most relaxing and perfect yoga they had ever experienced. They had a couples' massage on the beach, holding hands as their tables were close together. This environment was perfect for an aquatic resort photo shoot so they took advantage of the opportunity. They went on a short hiking adventure, admiring the landscape. He picked her a tropical bougainvillea bloom, then they took a relaxing catamaran sunset sail while enjoying chilled drinks. The entire experience was once in a lifetime, but the time they spent together in their breathtaking bungalow was the best part.

CHAPTER 44

Runaway Bride...and Groom - Part 2

S awyer and Marina hated to leave Bora Bora; it was Heaven on Earth. They weren't disappointed, however, when they arrived in the Maldives; the grouped atolls amidst the still, aqua water, many of them barely more than a sandbar. Shades of blue for as far as the eye could see met the blue sky. White, wispy clouds trailed in the distance. The sand rippled beneath the glassy aqua water near the shoreline outside their room and they dropped their bags off in their hut and enjoyed a dip in the infinity pool to cool off before heading to the beach. She was quiet, in deep thought.

He lifted his sunglasses and looked at her. "What are you thinking about, daydreamer?"

"That we could've spent the rest of our lives without seeing any of this and what we would've missed out on."

"True. We're extremely lucky to be here. We're lucky to have each other too."

They walked the white sand beach, hand in hand, leaving footprints behind.

"I still can't believe you're mine," she said sweetly. "I'm obsessed with you."

"I'm all yours, baby. And you're all mine. We put our exclusive claim on each other with these rings and our vows. There's nothin' sexier than that." He squeezed her hand.

"This is my ultimate fantasy. In paradise with the man of my dreams."

"I hope Heaven is just like this. I'd be content spending eternity here with the woman of my dreams."

"Oh yeah? Who is she?" Marina smirked. He stopped and picked her up by her waist, spinning her around, and smooched her lips as her feet landed in the sand.

"I'll fall for you a little more each and every day." She pressed her slender index finger against his lips before kissing them again.

"Good, because I'll be forever chasing you."

"To think of how we started out and how far we've come so quickly...it's been a dream come true, Sawyer. I never would've imagined any of this for myself. It's been a fairytale. The perfect life."

"We both deserve this fairytale."

Their attraction to each other turned into something real and undeniable in the blink of an eye. They were a perfect balance of friendship and romance that became stronger every day. They were the perfect love story after all.

The next morning, they were served a tropical floating breakfast in their infinity pool, complete with hibiscus flowers and fresh fruit. He put one of the flowers in her hair. She fed him a strawberry and put her arms up around his neck. He kissed her, the taste of strawberries on his lips. Together, they leaned on the edge of the pool, side by side. The rising sun kissed the apples of her cheeks as she took in the view of the vast ocean.

"What should we do today?" She turned to him and took his hand. He was looking at her already, still admiring her beauty.

"I thought maybe we could go for a horseback ride along the beach. What would you like to do?"

"Ooh, I like that idea. Then later maybe you and I can just chill in the water and on the beach."

"Sounds perfect. I'll go make the arrangements." He let go of her hand and stepped out of the pool. She leaned her back against the pool's edge, watching water dripping down his tan skin. His white swim shorts clung tightly to his skin. He walked a few steps before she said seductively, "Sawyer."

He grabbed a nearby towel before turning around and said, "Yeah, baby?" She motioned with her index finger for him to come to her. He tilted his head to the side, a brow raised in question. She held her bikini up above the surface of the pool as the water barely covered her nipples. Her half-wet hair hung in front of one of her eyes, her lips parted. She was irresistible. He took his swim shorts off and slowly stepped into the pool. Her eyes scanned every inch of his ripped body then she said, "First, I'm going to devour you right here in this pool." He didn't say a word, just swam to her and stood close in front of her, their eyes locked like missiles on a target. He grabbed her waist and she grabbed his face, kissing him aggressively, tongues competing. Their skin glistened in the overhead sun as they indulged in each other, water ripples reflecting on them.

Before eating lunch at the resort restaurant, Sawyer arranged for horseback riding for the afternoon. They enjoyed the breezy open-air atmosphere and each other's company until it was time to ride. A local walked two white horses along the shore, meeting Sawyer and Marina. The horses wore no tack. Sawyer helped Marina up onto one before mounting the other. Her long hair flowed with the long white strapless maxi dress she wore. His white linen beach shorts and open shirt matched her. They walked the horses a ways then galloped along the edge of the water, parallel to the shore. White sand flew in the air behind them as hooves pounded the earth. Water splashed with every beat. The horses waded deeper to cool off, Sawyer and Marina both wet to their knees.

Later on in the early evening, they ate dinner at a beach bar and grill. The food was amazing and served fancy for a tiki bar. It was a barefoot-on-the-beach type place. Sawyer even wore a tropical button-up shirt, which he left unbuttoned, and gray cargo shorts. A few locals were starting a bonfire even though it wasn't yet dark. The sun was sinking behind the palms but it wasn't in a rush. Sawyer spotted a guitar propped up next to a local at a nearby table and walked over to him.

"Excuse me. Do you mind?" He pointed to the guitar.

"Go ahead," the local said.

Sawyer smiled and nodded, "Thanks." He took the guitar over to a lawn chair near the fire and waved Marina to come join him. She occupied the chair next to him, her tropical-print dress fluttering with a breeze. She crossed her leg over the other and leaned in toward him, holding her drink. He placed the guitar on his leg and made sure it was tuned. He started pickin' and a few folks gathered closer, some stood, some sat, some got drinks from the tiki bar and leaned against palm trees listening. Sawyer played *Paradise To Me* by Nikko Moon and *Barefoot Blue Jean Night* by Jake Owen. Folks sang along with that one. He passed the guitar back to its owner, who played a few songs; Sawyer sang with him as harmony on the songs he knew. The sun hadn't stopped to listen, it kept setting. Party lights strung from the bar and restaurant huts grew brighter. It was a fun and kicked-back environment.

"How about we head back toward our hut and take a walk along the water's edge?" He took her by the hand and pulled her up out of the chair.

"Sounds perfect." They wrapped an arm around each other and said goodnight to the nice folks. They walked along the shore, feet in the water. Bright blue shimmers glowed in the water with each step.

"Look! Bioluminescence!" She swirled her painted toes and blue light radiated.

"That's so cool." Sawyer waded in higher than his ankles and splashed around. It looked like swarms of blue fireflies dancing in the water.

"It's beautiful." Marina admired the light produced by chemical reactions as the water rippled. They couldn't see the living organisms but the organisms let them know they were there in the most beautifully displayed light show.

"The moon is bright too." He pointed up at the full moon that shined down on the water, lighting a reflection trail. Sensuality fell upon them as night fell upon the sky. A long sweet kiss under the moon, feet surrounded by glowing blue magic, was the perfect way to end the day and there was nothing more romantic.

The next morning, she woke to him lying on his stomach on the bed, the sun beaming in, lighting up across the skin of his back and shoulders as his chin rested upon his hands in front of him. She took hold of his tight, smooth bicep. So strong he was.

"Good morning, my love," she said softly as he gently swiped her hair from her face.

"Mmm good morning." He smiled. She crawled closer to him as he rolled onto his back and began kissing from his neck to his chest. He wrapped those big arms around her and they lay together, cuddling in blissful harmony until they were both hungry enough to call for their breakfast. They spent the day snorkeling with whale sharks at another atoll. The boat ride out there wasn't long and they were served lunch onboard. They spotted a sea turtle, flapping its flippers over a reef with abundant colorful fish. They spent the afternoon and early evening walking the whole atoll on which they were staying. They swung on an overwater swing, hung from a palm that leaned over the water, and had a fancy dinner for two on the beach. They wore their suits under their clothes and walked a sandy path that led through native flora to a beach that was unoccupied by other resort guests. They sat together on the beach, swam, then sat on the sand again, lost in each other's eyes.

"I'm so thankful that I get to look into your eyes for the rest of my life." She rested her hand upon the side of his perfectly groomed face, her thumb on his chin.

"I plan to look into yours for the rest of mine."

The sky was turning teal and navy ombre as the sun lay to rest for the night. They lay on their backs looking up at the sky, her toes rubbing the top of his foot.

"There's a definition for this." She stared up, the stars reflecting in her pretty eyes.

"For what?"

"The term is Novalunosis. It's how gazing at the stars makes you feel relaxed."

"You're so smart, you know that?"

She smiled, "Nah, I just read about it recently. It could even be a made-up term, who knows? But stargazing is something I cherish doing with you."

"It's important to me too. The little things we do together are really the big things. They're the times we remember most and I'm so glad I've experienced all of it with you. Screw Paris; these places we've been to this week are the most romantic places on Earth."

"I absolutely agree. There's nobody I would've rather come here with. I had a star named after you, by the way, so now we're both in the sky together. Thank you, Sawyer, for a honeymoon we'll never forget."

"I love that we both have a star. We're about to make another unforgettable memory." He didn't even look around first before sitting up and crawling overtop of her. It wouldn't have mattered if anyone was around anyway, he was completely in the moment. He swept her hair away from her face and ran his hand through it. She stared up at him, memorizing his face as the dark blanket of bright white stars poised as a backdrop behind him.

"You make my soul smile." Her hands ran up his back.

"You have my heart and soul." His lips twisted with hers. This time it was a wet, soulful kiss. She felt as though she had sunk further into the sand as his pelvis pressed against hers. His lips and tongue trailed down her neck, a hand still tangled in her hair, he gently and gradually pulled it harder, leaving her almost-dry white sparkly swim bottoms practically soaked. She started sitting up so he sat back to let her. She commanded control without saying a word but she didn't have to instruct, he knew exactly what she wanted. They read each other's body language well. He laid on his back as her wild instinct took over. He couldn't deny that he was perfectly fine with being submissive. Moonlight shone down upon her now-bare breasts as he removed her matching string suit top. She sat upon him, his shorts pulled down just below his rear and her suit bottoms pulled to the side. She made his mouth water something fierce with the way she moved upon him. His chin tilted to the stars as her fingernails raked his hard pecs, abs, then groin and inner thighs. Her hair flowed down her shoulders and back, she moaned loudly then lay on his chest. He grabbed her rear and flipped her over into the sand. Sand fell from his hair onto her chest and his back was covered in grit but she didn't mind. She was embracing everything about this moment. He slid her bottoms off and stripped his shorts off. As he infused himself into her again, he kissed her, then down her cleavage. She felt his scruff against her soft skin. He framed her face with his hands as he moaned in her ear. She held him tightly. She loved having all that muscle overtop of her and the sweat sheen on his forehead was sexy. He caressed her smooth leg, making her feel like the most desirable woman in the world. He appreciated her, all of her, and he knew how to prove it.

CHAPTER 45

Bittersweet – Back to Reality

W hiskey's nails rapidly tapped on the wood floor as he squealed his wheels running into the bedroom. His front paws hit the mattress as he whined. Vacations are always nice but there's no bed like one's own. He scratched at Sawyer, barely able to reach his arm. Sawyer rolled from facing Marina onto his back. Whiskey's tongue managed to reach Sawyer's face.

"Ugh, go away." Sawyer flopped his arm at Whiskey but the pup was relentless. No dogs were allowed on the bed; that was a rule. At this point, Sawyer didn't care if Whiskey pissed on the floor, he just really didn't want to get up. Whiskey let out a bark and Sawyer popped his eyes open and looked at Marina, but she remained sleeping.

"Okay, okay, Jesus. I'm getting up. Don't you wake her," Sawyer whispered hastily to Whiskey as he slowly sat up and sat on the edge of the bed rubbing his eyes. Whiskey stood waiting in the doorway, ears perked. Sawyer got up and walked down the hall in his underwear, stretching, following Whiskey. He left Whiskey outside and returned to the bedroom to find Marina lying awake where he had left her. He smiled and lay down next to her.

"Did we wake you?"

"I'm not sure. I feel like I woke up on my own. Back to reality, we are. Whiskey couldn't wait, huh?" She smiled.

"I guess not. I wasn't ready to be up, I do know that." He stretched an arm around her.

"Maybe we can take a nap together later."

"That sounds like a plan." He inhaled deeply. "The islands were amazing. The scenery was unbeatable. Being there in paradise with you was a dream come true, but I can't deny that I'm glad to be back home, in our own bed, and in the dirt."

"You missed the dirt?" She giggled.

"I did. The horses too. Sand is messier than dirt."

"Hmm, I don't know about that. I miss that water though."

"It's a good thing we have a slice of paradise in our own back-yard then." He leaned in for a kiss.

"I love our slice of paradise."

"Me too. I love it more now that you're a part of it."

"I'd follow you anywhere, Sawyer."

"Good because I'll forever want you with me." He kissed her forehead.

"I always will be."

"If we ever become lost in any way, or begin to drift apart, we'll find our way back to each other. I truly believe that. I want you to always find your way home to me."

"I don't think that will ever happen; not again." she assured.

"Promise, darlin'?"

"I promise."

"Hey, I have an idea!" He seemed excited.

"Can't wait to hear it." She sat up onto her elbow.

"I saw a compass tattoo I'd like to get." He showed her a picture on his phone.

"Ooh, I like that! Where are you gonna put it?"

"I'm thinking my chest. Here on my left peck."

"Where your heart is?" Her head tilted adoringly.

"Yep. But my heart lies with you, darlin'."

"As mine does with you, so mine should go in the same place, I suppose." She smiled.

"Really? You sayin' you want matching tattoos?" He got all excited.

"Sure! Mine would have to be much smaller than yours though. Maybe some watercolor around it."

"You are awesome, you know that?" He wore the biggest smile.

"You really wanna get matching tattoos?" She sat all the way up, holding the sheet to her chest.

"I think it would be awesome. It'll be like we're always with each other no matter what. What do ya say?"

"I'm game, cowboy."

"Hell yeah!" He gave her a high five, making her laugh.

"Since you have musical notes on your arm, maybe I'll get a note or two, small somewhere. You did win me over with your 'notes' after all."

"Music notes or barn notes? And I thought it was my charm that won you over."

"Exactly." She gave him a cheeky wink and smirk. "Both, actually, and so much more."

He chuckled and tackled her with kisses.

He did, indeed, make an appointment for them for that afternoon. He dressed in a deep teal button-up collared short-sleeved shirt and jeans; that way he could just flap it open. She wore a black tube top to make it easier.

They each had a different artist so they could get their tattoos at the same time.

"You need me to hold your hand, babe?" Marina asked with a pouty face and her hand held out.

He laughed. "Nah, you need me to hold yours?"

"Nah, I'm tough. I got this." She turned her nose up playfully.

"I know you're tough." His smirk was sexy as he sat there with his shirt open, waiting to get started. The artists put gloves on and it was game on. Marina got a few little musical notes on the inside of her wrist.

"I love that you're getting music notes." He stared at her with such admiration that even the artists noticed.

CHAPTER 46
Charity Luau

Marina advertised their non-profit organization on every social platform she could get her hands on and even had the local news come out to the stables for a short segment. It was aired the evening before on the news. The charity event was mentioned and the Brandton's invited everyone to come to support the cause while having fun in hopes that folks in need of horse therapy would sign up for the program. They would run it two days a week to start. Later on, if the turnout was big, they could add days to the schedule. If they needed extra horses for sessions Sawyer could bring Legend and Foxtrot over to the stables until he bought more.

"The water slides are filling up pretty quickly. I'm so glad we had sod brought in a few weeks ago. This place would be a muddy mess," Sawyer pointed out.

"Most definitely. My heart isn't broken about the taco truck having been booked already; that Hawaiian barbecue truck smells delicious. Thanks for putting out tiki torches. I love that this turned into a luau. Hey, you're wearing swim shorts today, right?" Marina asked with a smirk.

Sawyer laughed. "Well yeah, baby, they're in the office. Not the white pair either. Luke's gonna be thrilled we were able to get the snow cone truck."

"He sure is. We couldn't let him down. He was so excited about that."

Vehicles rolled in, folks were welcomed by Marina and Sawyer, who handed out leis. Kids, veterans, you name it, they were showing up. Harley, Willow, Foxtrot, and Legend were saddled in a paddock in the shade. Sabrina volunteered to help out along with the other new ranch hands. The alpacas and pony were fun for the little kids who were too little to ride the big horses. Marina and Sawyer's friends came for support and donated as well. Justin sat at a table under a tent taking donations. They didn't expect a large turnout, but that's what they got.

Many kids flocked to the horses where Chris, Trev, and Jake volunteered to help out, some to the snow-cone truck. The aroma from the food truck filled the air as kids began sliding down the water slide. A few were scared because it was twenty-four feet high so Sawyer went into the office and changed into swim shorts. He came running out, climbed the blowup steps, then slid down on his back with his feet in the air. The splash was extreme when he hit the pool at the bottom of the slide.

The kids were yelling and got excited that Sawyer wanted in on the fun too. He stood up in the pool end and yelled "Wooo!" He whipped his head, shaking water everywhere. The kids that were scared began going down. Luke challenged Sawyer to a race. That couldn't be passed up. Challenge accepted! They raced up and back down, then circled again, waiting their turn in line. Marina loved watching him. He was having fun, like a big kid himself. She went to the office to change into her pretty aqua suit, snuck in line where the kids secretly let her in, and came sliding down just behind Sawyer. He was exiting the pool when she flew down. He laughed, loving that she joined in on the fun, and took her by the hand as they stepped out of the pool together. They slid a few more times before letting the kids have all the fun. Everyone enjoyed the food. Sawyer and Marina took plates to their friends who were helping out then tagged in to take their places. Several folks signed up for the therapy program before leaving and took information fliers. She had worked hard to prepare for this day and couldn't have been happier with the turnout. Andrea took some pictures to send to Marina for the website. It was all coming together. Her vision was becoming a reality and she owed it all to Sawyer.

CHAPTER 47
Fun in the Sun

After lunch the following day, Marina laid out on a pool float, catching rays. Her head was tipped back, sunglasses shielding her closed eyes, a hand swirling the water.

Sawyer had been at the office finishing up some paperwork all morning, so the sudden splash jolted Marina into an upright position, holding onto the float as it moved with waves. She looked around, startled. Sawyer swam beside her underwater and popped up a few feet away. He shook water from his hair like a dog would shake after a bath.

"You startled me!"

"I'm sorry. Well, I kinda meant to, honestly."

She dipped her toes into the pool and playfully flung water at him. He flipped the float, dumping her into the water. She popped up and wiped her face.

"You're in trouble, mister."

"Oh, yeah? What are you gonna do? Spank me?" He bit his lip and raised his eyebrows.

"I just might."

"Threatenin' me with a good time?"

"Absolutely." She swam to him. "Are you wearing those Speedos?"

"Yes, ma'am. You like?"

"Oh! Oh, I like all right. I liked the other ones you bought too. You're going to have to wear actual swim shorts for the party though."

"Why? I don't care if the guys laugh."

"Well, I don't care to share your junk."

He laughed hard. "Okay, I'll wear shorts. I was gonna anyway but I wanted to see what you'd say. Those guys would never let me live it down."

"You're right about that. Probably because they'd be jealous."

"Think so? Maybe I should wear 'em then." He winked, making her laugh.

"I wish we had time to...ya know, before we have to get ready for the barbecue." She got out and toweled off.

"Oh, baby, there's always time." He followed her and didn't bother toweling off. He scooped her up sideways and laid her on the lounge chair then crawled on top of her. "You would've laid there on that pool float another fifteen minutes or so if I hadn't interrupted you, so don't tell me we don't have time." He was assertive and kissed her aggressively. She loved it. She grabbed his rear and pulled him down onto her. His huge thighs were on either side of hers and he put his weight on one hand while his other groped her body, everywhere. "Forget those rays, I'm soaking you up now."

She loved it when he talked dirty to her. She reached under him and grabbed his junk. His abs sucked in as his eyes widened.

"These need to come off then." She snapped his Speedos against his rear like a rubber band.

"Yes, ma'am."

His navy Speedos slapped the concrete, followed by her bikini top and bottoms.

Upon entering the house wrapped in towels, Sawyer's phone was ringing on the kitchen counter. He answered it, "Hey, Chris.

You did?" Sawyer looked at his phone and saw several missed calls and texts. She didn't even care that he was dripping water all over the wood floor. She was soaking him up; that tan, smooth body, that towel so snug around his rear, and tucked in extremely low in the front. Water beads shined on his chiseled chest and ran down his muscular creases.

"Sorry, dude. I was just taking care of business." He winked at Marina, who was rewrapping her towel after drying off better while getting a glass of water. She smiled as she flashed him.

"Chris is stopping at the store. Is there anything we need him to pick up?" He tried to not be distracted and couldn't contain a big smile.

"Maybe ice for the cooler if he doesn't mind."

"Grab ice, will ya? Thanks. See ya in a few."

"A few?" Marina panicked as she ran to the bedroom for her clothes.

"I guess we took more than fifteen minutes." Sawyer snickered as he bit into an apple.

"You gonna put clothes on?" she hollered out.

"I'm replenishing my energy," he hollered back.

"Babe, you always have plenty of energy. You can't be naked when friends start showing up."

"I guess that would be rude, huh? You gotta stop flashin' me then when you rewrap that towel."

He put the apple on the counter and joined her in getting dressed. She got her wet hair combed out and straightened Sawyer's t-shirt out in the back since he barely got it thrown on before the doorbell rang. Marina answered the door to Trev and Trina, who handed her a large bowl to take to the kitchen. Sawyer had gone in to get his apple and Trev met him at the doorway. Sawyer fist-bumped him as he took a bite.

"Y'all have been in the pool already?" Trev asked, bummed.

Sawyer looked at him with a straight face and swallowed before answering, "Maybe."

Trev looked out the French doors and pointed out their suits laying on the concrete.

"Now I know why you didn't answer my text." Trev laughed and shoulder bumped Sawyer's shoulder. Sawyer grinned and shrugged.

"I brought a shit-ton of fireworks. Jake is bringing a bunch too." Trev took Sawyer's apple and took a bite then handed it back. Sawyer chuckled and shook his head.

"Happy Fourth!" Stacy and Chris announced as they came in the door. Marina took the bags of ice from him and took them out back but Sawyer told her he'd get them opened and dumped in the cooler. She made Whiskey get down from the furniture, he was excited to have company so he was bouncing around like a ping-pong ball. Sawyer broke up the ice by throwing the bag onto the concrete before dumping it into the cooler. The guys had followed him out. Trev opened the grill and asked, "Want me to wait to crank this up?"

"Yeah, we'll let everybody get here first." Chris noticed the swimsuits. "Already get your big bang in for the Fourth?"

Sawyer laughed as he walked over and gathered their suits. He thought he could walk past them without...nope, they noticed.

"Are those Speedos?" Trev asked with raised brows.

"You wear Speedos?" Chris smirked and let out a little snicker.

"I just bought 'em. For swimming laps. Marina likes 'em."

"I bet she does. They probably do look hot on ya." Chris laughed.

"They really do." Marina smiled as she slapped Sawyer's rear when he walked into the kitchen from the patio.

"Don't worry, I'll wear shorts today."

The girls giggled. He didn't even blush. The man felt no shame.

Jake came, lugging in boxes of fireworks and a huge fruit bowl. Justin came, as well as Becka.

"Wow, there's a ton of food. I sure hope everyone is hungry." Marina took the fruit bowl from Jake and thanked him.

"You and Sawyer prepared enough for an army," Becka said, helping Marina carry items outside. The ladies laid the spread of food onto the picnic table out back. Bob and Gladys came and, of course, provided the booze. Sawyer fired up the grill and got the variety of meats out of the fridge while it heated up. He set the various meat platters on the counter to season and tenderize.

Whiskey hung out with them most of the night.

Jake came into the kitchen to see if Sawyer needed help carrying food out to the grill and said, "Dude, I'm starvin' and you're just in here beatin' your meat."

Sawyer laughed and handed him a tray. "Man, I'm just getting *grilled* tonight with puns."

After grilling and eating all together at the big picnic table, the girls cleaned up and the guys used the remaining daylight to set up fireworks out in the field to shoot off later. Everyone changed into their suits, except Bob and Gladys who weren't big on swimming. Sawyer did, indeed, wear swim shorts, but they only came halfway down his thighs and were on the snug side. He loved the seafoam-colored bikini Marina wore; it made her look even more tan. Beach balls sailed through the air between the squooshy footballs being tossed back and forth.

"Bullshit! We totally won." Trev claimed that he and Trina beat Chris and Stacy in a badminton game in the yard but Chris was shaking his head.

"I've got water guns!" Justin dumped out a bag of them onto the grass. The guys were like giant kids, hollering and going all tactical in their gun war. They hid behind the grill, shrubs, and even underwater and behind the ladies who shouted not to use them as shields but were laughing at the fun the guys were having. There was a volleyball tournament in which everyone played, although they lost track of the score near the end.

"You two gonna join?" Jake hollered at Bob and Gladys, who were steering clear of the water balloon fight but were having fun watching everyone else have a blast.

"Nah, we'll stick to what we know best. Pouring the booze!" Bob returned the holler.

Sawyer tackled Marina right into the deep end of the pool. She came up out of the water sitting on top of his shoulders. Her breasts practically rested on his head, her legs tangled in his arms and her feet pressed against his wet back. Her thighs squeezed his neck and shoulders as she balanced. She smacked the beach ball that Stacy served. The girls got on their man's shoulders and they had a shoulder-sitting volleyball game going in the pool with a beachball.

"Come on, Becka. Hop on." Jake waved her over to him. Once again Jake's girlfriend didn't want to come so Becka sat on Jake's shoulders. There might have been a few shots of alcohol involved by that point.

"I need a girlfriend," Justin admitted. He played ball with everyone anyway, jumping higher for the ball. The white party lights turned on as the sky fell dark. Colored lights beamed underwater in the pool. The lights were bright enough to see beads of water in Sawyer's spiked hair as he exited the pool, his rippling muscles practically a tourist attraction as all the ladies enjoyed the view. Marina's bright eyes and water running down her cleavage caught Sawyer's attention under the lights. He held her close for a moment for a long, sweet kiss.

"I think it's fireworks time!" Sawyer announced, everyone agreeing loudly. Sawyer grabbed a few lighters that he had placed near the grill and he and the guys ran out to the field. They lit the few huge boxes that held now-legal fireworks, the big production kind, the kind that the fire department set off for their wedding. Then they hauled ass back to their ladies to watch with them. Marina stood in front of Sawyer, holding on to his arms that were wrapped around her. Smoke clouded the air as glowing colors lit up the sky.

CHAPTER 48

Taking the Reins

"It's our first rodeo" is what the barn note read Saturday morning as Marina started chores at home. Really, all she had left to do was put hay in feed bags and turn the horses out. Sawyer had gotten up early and done the rest. He was already over to the stables, his truck remained in the driveway but the newer four-wheeler was gone. She drove her SUV over when she finished up. As she entered the office, she noticed a plant sitting on her desk; it was a purple curcuma. Sawyer knew she loved them because they looked exotic and the little green tree frogs liked to hide within the petals after a rain. There was a little note on her desk next to it that read, "I'm so proud of you." She held it to her chest, wearing a smile.

Organization was her goal that morning, as it was the first day of the program. She gathered a notebook and pen, then heard Sawyer talking outside so she set it on the desk and went to greet him. Chris had come and Sawyer was holding a basket, chatting with Chris outside the office near Chris's truck.

"Good morning, handsome." She exited the office and walked over to him.

"Good morning, my love." He bit into a peach from the basket, juice dripping down his chin from his wet lips.

"You're gonna be extra sweet today." She planted a kiss on those juicy lips and the taste of fresh peaches transferred from his lips to hers. He offered her a peach, which she gladly took.

"Chris had a few peach trees with fruit ready so he brought us a basket of them."

"Aww, thanks, Chris. That was sweet of you."

"No problem. I won't be able to eat them all before they rot so after Stacy and I filled up the stand at the farmer's market I figured I'd bring some over here. I appreciate y'all taking them. Hey, good luck today, guys. Hope everything goes smoothly and it doesn't turn into a rodeo."

"I hope not too," Marina agreed. "It'll be a day of trial more than error, I hope."

"I worked with these horses; they'll do just fine. Notice Athena isn't out there," Sawyer said with a mouthful of peach.

"Let me know how it goes later today, and if y'all need anything just holler." Chris got into his truck and started it.

"Will do. Thanks." Sawyer nodded.

"Thank you for the flowers." She wrapped an arm around him as they walked to the office together.

"You're welcome, Peaches. I'm proud of you."

"We're doing this together so I'm proud of you too. You've never called me Peaches before."

"You're my juicy peach, with an ass like a peach." He winked then slapped her butt as she walked ahead of him through the doorway. He set the basket of peaches on his desk and she grabbed his face as he turned around, her juicy lips connecting with his.

"Mmm." He grabbed her butt, holding her close to him as he leaned back against the desk.

"Easy, big guy. I think I just opened a can of peaches, didn't I?" She took a step back.

"Why isn't it a can of worms?" He laughed.

"Because it's not a bad thing, it's delicious, but we have horses to go put tack on."

"You really shouldn't have worn these jean shorts then." He looked away then back at her.

"Let's save it for later, stallion. This cowgirl will gladly saddle up." She threw a sultry smile his way and reached for his hand.

"You have no idea how much I'm looking forward to that." He took her hand and she grabbed the notebook as they headed to the stables.

Saddles on? Check. Bridles on? Check. Lead ropes ready to attach? Check. The few staff members Sawyer had hired were ready to roll as a few cars pulled in the drive. There was a physical therapist, an emotional support coach, the two new ranch hands, and Sabrina, who had previous daycare experience and was an experienced rider. Marina thought they'd see how the first few therapy sessions went before hiring any more staff. They may not even need any more. Several kids, most from a foster home, and Luke came to ride. Two ex-combat veterans also came. For the first Saturday the program was being offered, that was a pretty good start.

Marina and Sabrina led horses around carrying kids. She couldn't help but look over at Sawyer often, his pearly-white smile lighting up the arena as he stood chatting with the veterans. He was the most gorgeous living thing there ever was. It was still unbelievable to her that he, that man right there, hands in his jean pockets, black t-shirt and hat to match, was her husband. All hers. He was alluring, captivating, charming, and absolutely lovable. She led Luke around on Harley, letting him get used to handling the reins. Sawyer would catch her looking at him when he'd look over to admire her from afar and she'd smile and shy her eyes away. Just like she used to when they were first getting to know each other. His grin would get wider, his chin tipped up with confidence, and his pretty eyes would lock on hers from under the brim of his hat as she'd glance back over her shoulder at him.

Sawyer chatted with Luke's mom for a moment then helped Luke down off of Harley. He took Luke and a few other kids over to the alpaca pen. Marina watched him interact with the kids, marveling at how wonderful he was with the children. The foster parents gave a generous donation and told the therapist that they wanted to see this program become a great success. A fellow equine sanctuary organization president stopped by. Sawyer had taken horses to that sanctuary that he brought back from the road trip after they had been quarantined. Grant was his name and he'd had the sanctuary for several years.

"Those horses you brought me are doing great. They're healthy enough to be adopted out now." Grant leaned against a gate with Sawyer.

"That's great, I'm glad to hear it."

"I was hoping you'd take them back as therapy horses."

"Yeah?" Sawyer asked.

"Yeah. This is a sanctuary too. The therapy could be good for them."

"Sure, yeah. That's generous of you. Thank you." Sawyer shook Grant's hand.

"This is a great thing y'all have goin' on here, Sawyer. You're a great guy with a big heart and I hear that you married a heart of the same magnitude."

"Thank you, sir. It was Marina's idea and she does have a big heart."

"So which young lady is Marina? I haven't had the pleasure of meeting her yet."

He looked around at the small crowd in the center of the arena.

"The beautiful blonde in the jean shorts and blue shirt."

"*That's* Marina?"

"Yes, sir. That's my wife."

"Lucky man." He patted Sawyer's back.

"Thank you. I sure think so too." He couldn't help but smile proudly and wave Marina over to them for an introduction.

As she approached, Sawyer said, "Marina this is Grant. He runs the sanctuary I took the horses to right after we got back from that road trip."

She shook Grant's hand. "Pleasure to meet you, sir."

"Oh, the pleasure is all mine. Ya know...I've known Sawyer for some time now. I met him in a drive thru."

Marina had a confused look on her face. Even more so when she looked over at Sawyer, who started laughing.

"A drive thru?" she asked, her interest piqued.

"Yep. He and his buddies rode horses through a fast-food drive thru and I was about to pull out of that parking lot with my trailer hitched up. I believe that horse right there was the one you were on, Sawyer." Grant pointed at Foxtrot.

"Yes, sir." Sawyer laughed.

"Wow, riding horses through a drive thru?" she asked Sawyer in disbelief.

"We had been day drinkin'. Couldn't drive." He shrugged.

She laughed, "Well, I guess that was better than drunk driving but I thought horses in a drive thru was illegal too." She pondered that thought.

"They served us so that's all that mattered."

"I can actually picture it. I'm not sure why I was surprised." She laughed at the proud grin he wore.

"So, your organization is called *Taking the Reins*. How was that name inspired?" Grant asked.

"Well, I feel it represents taking control of emotions and direction in one's life. Gaining strength and confidence is important. I know riding horseback with this guy and being around the horses has always brought me peace." She scooped Sawyer's arm up in hers.

Sawyer smiled a sweet smile, one that could melt the sun.

CHAPTER 49

Planting Seeds

The horses were turned loose before chores were done and low rumbling could be heard off in the distance. The horses were running, kicking up dirt and grass behind them like they always did just before a good storm. Whiskey was right on their heels, letting out a loud bark every now and then. The humidity felt to be rising so she knew they would receive rain soon.

Marina went to the store and, upon her return, was surprised Sawyer didn't come out to help her carry in groceries. He always did if he was home. She made a second trip out to the car and back in, still no Sawyer.

"Where is he?" she asked herself aloud as she looked in the bedroom then out to the patio. It took her a moment but she found him. He was laying in the hammock, one leg dangling off the side, barefoot, wearing only jeans and his black cowboy hat laid over his face. Whiskey was half on Sawyer's chest. She rushed to take care of the cold food items so she could join him, then quietly snuck out, approaching with her phone in hand. She couldn't resist snapping a picture. He looked...well, boy, was he a sight to be seen...she wanted to cherish this view forever. Whiskey's ears perked as he raised his head and yawned with a whimper, which woke Sawyer up. Marina took his hat off his face and smiled at him as she leaned down for a kiss.

"I wasn't gone very long. What happened, cowboy?"

"I know, I guess I was just tired."

"Sorry to have woken you."

"Aww it's okay. Come lay with me." He scooched over to make room for her. She sat, careful not to flip the hammock, and laid back onto his arm, his bicep as her pillow.

"This is the life, ya know it?" He seemed very content.

"I couldn't be happier, Sawyer."

"Me neither. Life is perfect." He kissed the side of her head as he petted Whiskey.

"It sure is."

"I don't think that storm will hit for a while yet. What do ya say we go for ice cream?" The thought suddenly popped into his head.

"Yeah? An impromptu trip to the little parlor up town?"

"Yeah. They have the best."

"Sounds good to me." She sat up and let Sawyer's foot touch the ground before getting out of the hammock. "Although, I probably could've fallen asleep right here with you."

"Wanna?" He stopped before getting off the hammock.

She contemplated, "Well, I kinda want ice cream too..." As she stood waiting for him, Whiskey jumped off.

Sawyer chuckled and got up. "I'll grab my shirt." He grabbed it from a nearby crepe myrtle branch and put it on as they walked to the house for his shoes and keys.

Whiskey rode along in the Jeep, excited as they arrived at the small-town ice cream parlor. It looked like a miniature barn and you ordered up at a window.

"Can I get an espresso java chip in a cone please?" Marina ordered.

"I thought you wanted a nap later." Sawyer snickered.

She bumped his elbow with hers.

"I'll take a maple nut in a cone and a vanilla in a cup for the pooch." Whiskey sat panting, slack in his leash as Marina held it. They took their ice cream to a picnic table in the shade and enjoyed it together. A cool breeze blew through, instantly lowering the humidity, and the sky was growing darker. The thunder began rolling louder as they finished and headed home. Sprinkles of rain drops dotted the Jeep windshield on the drive. They got inside just as the rain really started coming down.

"I reckon we had good-timing." He kicked his shoes off and sat on the couch.

"I reckon we did," she agreed, kicking hers off and grabbing his acoustic guitar on her way to the couch. It was propped up at the end of the couch by the end table. She set it up on her lap and strummed random strings, having not a clue as to what she was doing. It made him smile and he moved closer to her.

"Want me to teach you?"

"Sure." She smiled, really not caring too much about actually learning but loving that he was willing to teach her. It was adorable.

He had her place her hands just so and explained what parts of the guitar were called, how to tighten the strings to change the sound and such. He always showed her such patience.

She told him, "I rather you play. Sing me something." She handed his guitar over. He loved playing for her and she loved that he did, his voice was soothing and she knew that he played for her with sincerity and wholeheartedness. She told him to sing something that he was feeling, so he sang *In Case You Didn't Know* by Brett Young. She soaked it all in, snuggled up to him. He set the guitar down and she laid across his lap.

"Do you really think I could keep you happy for the rest of your life?" She rolled onto her back and looked up at him, wondering aloud, his chiseled scruffy jaw right above her.

"Darlin', there's not a doubt in my mind." He played with her hair while looking into her bright eyes.

Thunder clapped and rain pelted the metal roof. It poured like a waterfall from the eves. He stared at her, as though memorizing her face. When she asked what he was looking at, he playfully said, "We'd make some damn pretty babies. You know that?"

After they both chuckled, she realized he was serious when he raised a brow.

She said, "We've never really talked about the subject before. You planting an idea to think about?"

He assumed he screwed up the whole moment by starting the conversation about that specific topic but she assured him he didn't. She was just surprised he brought it up.

"Do you want kids, Sawyer?"

"Yeah, but only if you do. You come first. You're my first priority so if it's not something you want, I'll be fine without."

"I do want kids, especially with you. You're great with them; a natural. Nobody on Earth treats me better and I know you'd be a great influence in every way. We still have time though."

He wore the biggest smile. Just when he thought he couldn't be any happier, she had gone and agreed to plant an even more rooted future with him. She wanted to give him the world. He had her sit up so he could stand.

He took her by the hand and pulled her to her bare feet and said, "Good things come to us with stormy skies. This country boy is ready to plant some seeds. How 'bout we start tryin' now?" He tossed her up over his shoulder and slapped her rear. She screeched and giggled then slapped his in return with both hands on both of his cheeks. He carried her to the bedroom and kicked the door shut, Whiskey sat on the other side with his little speckled ears perked. Sawyer let her down at the foot of the bed. With her endearing face in his hands and his forehead against hers, looking into each other's eyes, he asked softly, "You ready to name more stars in the sky?"

She held him tight and whispered, "Let's create our own little galaxy."

Love Drunk

Are you ready to get Love Drunk?

Check out the actual Love Drunk song on Spotify!

https://spoti.fi/3s3Mt1r

Or on Amazon!

http://bit.ly/Lovedrunksong

Acknowledgments

No matter what stress and chaos gets thrown at my life, I know I have writing and reading to bring me hope and joy. Once the inspiration is sparked, the rest of the writing flows. I wish to share my way of thinking and creativity with readers so they can find hope from the fictitious reality they may become lost in. Thank you, readers!

I would like to thank my closest friends for being an inspiration for the supporting characters in this series. I'd also like to once again thank one of my closest friends and fellow author for our coffee shop writing days. I cherish them.

Here's a shout-out to the musical artists that are mentioned in this series, you're much appreciated. Thank you to Brady Seals for co-writing Love Drunk. That was a blast! The song titles mentioned are personal favorites as well. The lyrics carry volume to the storyline. I encourage readers to listen to the songs mentioned within the book to gain a better feel for the need to mention them as well as to envision the characters performing them.

Thank you to photographer Andrei Vishnyakov for providing exclusive photos of Konstantin. Our chats are always fun. On that note, thank you to Russian model Konstantin Kamynin for being the perfect vision of "Sawyer". Hugs!

Much Love, Marina Skye

About the Author

Marina Skye is from the country in a small southern town. She's a beach girl at heart but loves being around horses and volunteers with a local equine rescue center. As a romantic, this is where her inspiration for the book series bloomed. When she isn't writing, she's working one of several jobs and raising her two boys. She hopes her sons will grow to be respectful gentlemen just like the character in this series.

 facebook.com/MarinaSkyeNovels

 instagram.com/Marina_Skye23

www.ingramcontent.com/pod-product-compliance
Lightning Source LLC
Chambersburg PA
CBHW020004140726
47904CB00018B/1767